LISA SUZANNE

SNAP DECISION
THE BRADLEY LEGACY BOOK 3
© 2026 LISA SUZANNE

All rights reserved. In accordance with the US Copyright Act of 1976, the scanning, uploading, and sharing of any part of this book without the permission of the publisher or author constitute unlawful piracy and theft of the author's intellectual property. No part of this book may be reproduced or transmitted in any form or by any means, electronic or mechanical, including photocopying, recording, or by any information storage and retrieval system without the written permission of the author, except where permitted by law and except for excerpts used in reviews. If you would like to use any words from this book other than for review purposes, prior written permission must be obtained from the publisher.

Published in the United States of America by Books by LS, LLC.

This book is a work of fiction. Any similarities to real people, living or dead, is purely coincidental. All characters and events in this work are figments of the author's imagination.

Cover Design by Qamber Designs.

Also by Lisa Suzanne

Grayson & Ava

Spencer & Grace

Asher & Desi

Tanner & Cassie

Miller & Sophie

FIND MORE AT
AUTHORLISASUZANNE.COM/BOOKS

Dedication

For MMM. ♡

CHAPTER 1

FORD BRADLEY

Pick Up a Regret

I stare at the text message that just came through as my chest tightens.
Tatum: *Archer and I are over. For good this time.*

I feel like I've heard that one before—we're over. But it never had the finality of the for good.

It started out innocently enough. She and my brother were in the same class in high school. She was over all the time, so we became friends, too. We'd have video game tournaments. She'd stay for dinner. We kissed once…long story.

It almost felt like she was the glue that bonded me to my brother.

He played baseball. I played football. We were both very focused on our own sport, and that left little time for brotherly bonding beyond those video game tournaments on the rare nights we were both home.

They got together in college. He drifted further from the family. She forgot about that kiss, I guess. I didn't.

Snap DECISION

She called me the first time they broke up—a few months after they started dating. I was there for her. I was there the next time, too, and the next. She always called when they were fighting.

And then it shifted from her telling me about my brother to her telling me about her own life. She'd tell me of her dreams of creating a destination wedding brand. I'd tell her about practice. At first, it was once every couple of weeks. Then it was once a week.

Then it became daily check-ins with longer chats when we had the chance.

I was a good friend to her.

She was starting to become everything to me.

She belongs to my brother. They've been together for a decade—give or take, on and off—despite that one kiss that probably was never meant to happen.

She can never be mine now, even if it felt like we had a chance for her to be mine first.

I'm not sure how to reply to her text. My first instinct is to call, but logic seems to force its way through. What would I say?

I continue staring at the words as I wait for the answer to come to me, and then my phone starts to ring, the shrill tone cutting into the quiet of the locker room after practice.

It's her.

She's my opposite in so many ways. Where I'm strategic and pragmatic, she's impulsive and whimsical, bordering on chaotic. And yet I find such beauty in the chaos that my chest physically aches when I see her name appear on my screen.

I drop my phone onto the bench in my locker where I'm sitting. It lands with a clatter, and Cole Andrews in the locker next to mine whips his head over to me.

"You okay, man?" he asks.

I shake my head as I lean forward, my elbows on my knees.

He glances around the wall dividing our lockers, and he peeks at my phone. "Who's Tatum Barker?"

"My brother's girlfriend," I answer automatically.

The question leaves an echo in my head, though, and the answer is quite a bit more complicated.

She's someone I've known since I was in high school. She and I have gotten closer in the last few years. She's a friend.

I'm hopelessly in love with her.

And I'm forever fucked because of it.

"Why's she calling you?" he asks.

"We're close."

He narrows his eyes at me. "How close?"

"Not that close."

He chuckles. "Well, either pick up your phone or come out with us and pick up a regret. You know what I'm saying?" He wiggles his eyebrows, and in truth, picking up a regret doesn't sound so bad right now.

In the end, I choose both.

I pick up my phone from the bench and glance at Cole. "I'll go out with you. After I take this call." I slide the button to answer, calling her by her last name in my greeting. "Hey, Barker."

"Can I come stay with you for a little while?" she says with no greeting in return.

I groan. I already know how messy this could get as I fight my feelings for her, just like it has every time I've gotten this same call from her. But none of that is reflected in the words that fall from my mouth. "Yes, of course."

"I have a few things to tie up here, but I'll text you my info once I have it," she says.

"Are you doing okay?" I ask gently.

"Yes and no. You know?"

"Yeah," I mutter.

"Like…I knew it was coming. There were signs."

"So, what makes this time different?" I ask, referring to the *for good* part of her text message.

"He did it this time." She says it simply. "Before it was always me."

"What do you think happened?" I ask.

"We've been stuck in the same place for a long time. I love him, and he loves me, but we've been floating in the friend zone, the roommate region, for quite some time."

"Why didn't you say anything?"

"I don't know." I can picture her shrug as she says it, her delicate shoulder raising up a bit as she tries fruitlessly to put into words why she kept something from me when we talk about most everything else.

Relationships, though, I suppose that's the one field we kept at bay. I don't tell her about mine, and I don't want to hear about hers.

I don't have any to talk about.

The one she had…now it's over.

That doesn't mean this is my chance.

Frankly, I'm not quite sure what it *does* mean other than the fact that it's ripping me up inside, and I think I need to follow Cole's advice to pick up a regret tonight.

My phone beeps with another incoming call, and I see it's my brother Liam calling. With my father being chased by the FBI and my mother knocking on death's door, it feels like I should answer it.

"Liam's calling," I say softly, and she knows me well enough to understand why I'm telling her.

"I'll let you go. But you should know that Archer signed something that could incriminate him in your dad's stuff in Vegas."

My chest tightens. "Shit. Is he okay? Are you?"

"Will be, I guess. I'll let you go. Love ya. Can't wait to do breakfast with you in Tampa." She hangs up before I can tell her that Liam can wait. She hangs up before I can even reply, but I say it in my head.

Only it sounds a lot different when I say *I love you, too* in my head than her friendly *love ya* between two old pals.

"Fuck," I mutter, and I flip over to Liam's call. "Hey."

"Hey. I'm not calling with good news."

I grip my phone a little more tightly. "Is Mom okay?"

"She took a turn. Her vertebrae were too weak and collapsed."

"What does that mean?" I ask.

"She broke her back, and they have this cement to try to keep her comfortable, but they can't do much to fix it. She's wearing a back brace but hates the fuck out of it and knows she's going to have to be honest with everyone pretty soon since she can barely breathe without pain." His voice breaks a little at the end, and I know this is hard for him.

He's the only one still in Chicago aside from Ivy, who's finishing her senior year in college, so a lot of the care falls on him even though he's in season.

"And that's not all. Dad's assets were frozen after the raid, and what he has access to is running short. I don't think it'll last long with Mom's care."

"Okay, so we'll all pitch in," I say. It's the logical answer.

"There's more."

Fuck. "What?"

"Dad got word there's a grand jury convening to bring charges against him. He could be arrested at any time, and there won't be any money left for his bail."

I blow out a breath. "Then he sits in jail. You saw what he's done to this family."

"With Mom in the hospital? You really think that's the best course of action?"

"Fuck," I mutter, knowing he's right. "We could sell the house."

Snap DECISION

"Sell the house?" he repeats.

"Dad asked me if he could put it in my name about a year ago. He must've seen this coming. Madden said he had everyone sign different shit, and somehow he picked me for the house. Probably because he knew I wouldn't be tied emotionally to it like the rest of you simps."

I throw in the jab because it feels like I need to lighten the mood on this call. This is some heavy shit we're dealing with, and I'm used to just playing football, pretending like I'm not in love with my brother's girlfriend, and finding a regret to pick up at a bar when I go out with my buddies.

I'm the only one in Tampa, so I'm pretty far removed from the rest of the Bradley clan. I can't honestly say I don't like it that way. The occasional group text is enough to keep me in touch while I can live my own life away from this drama.

"You can't sell the house, dude."

"Why the fuck not?"

"You always do this. You're focused on the money. The rest of us have a connection to that place. Despite everything Dad has done, it's where the seven of us grew up. It's part of our legacy. Don't you want to take your kids there someday and show them the spot on the wall where we learned how to spackle because Dex plowed right through the wall when he was twelve? Or have a drink in the backyard while we watch our kids run around together?"

"I didn't know you wanted kids so badly," I mutter.

"In the extremely distant future, dickwad. Listen, I'm just saying that it's our history. It's not just Mom and Dad's place. It belongs to all of us."

"Look, Liam," I say, doing my best to be gentle when I'm used to just giving straight facts. "There's a shitload of money tied up in that mansion. If he's not denied bail, it would be plenty to pay that, Mom's bills, and still have some left over to divvy up between the rest of us."

"Where will they go?" Liam asks, and it feels nearly rhetorical.

I'm back to fighting with myself for how gentle to be with my younger brother here. Mom took a turn for the worse. We don't know how much more time she has. She's in the hospital for now. Dad's possibly about to be arrested, and he won't need the mansion if he's in prison.

I blow out a breath, and I take the route of joking because it feels easier than spelling out the truth. He'll get there eventually anyway. "They can stay with you."

He barks out a laugh. "Fuck that, man."

"We'll figure it out," I say. "But this might just be our best option."

"Yeah," he echoes.

Cole peeks his head around the wall. "Ready?" he mouths to me.

I nod at him. To my brother, I say, "I gotta go. We'll talk soon." It's better not to tell too many people what Tatum just told me. She and Archer are notoriously off and on, and I feel like I should talk to my sister Everleigh before starting the rumor mill with my entire family.

I cut the call, and then I head to the bar with my teammates where I plan to get all the way fucked up tonight to try to dull the ache of this total mess I suddenly find myself in.

CHAPTER 2

Tatum Barker

Three Cups

I stare at my screen, lost in thought about what a goddamn walking cliché I am.

I am the wedding planner who can't seem to get her own life together. Paperwork and cups litter my desk, and honestly, organized chaos is my fatal flaw. Or maybe my superpower.

I have three drinks on my desk at any given time. Sometimes more. Sometimes I leave them there for a few days. Water in my hot pink Stanley, of course. I do live in the desert, after all. Coffee because it's fuel. Sometimes a second coffee for later—one iced, one hot—and sometimes a lemonade or tea instead. Either way…three cups.

Archer loved to tease me about the mess even though I do most of my work at the small office space I rent now. It's a place to meet with clients somewhere other than Archer Bradley's house, but it also managed to get the mess out of the house and onto a desk somewhere else where I wouldn't be judged for my chaos.

Snap DECISION

I'm sad it's over, and at the same time, I'm ready to move on. Part of my heart moved on a long time ago while the rest of me felt too comfortable. I think we both clung to that comfort for far longer than we should have.

I started feeling less and less supported where I was. All I did was support his dream career, but it didn't feel reciprocated, I guess.

And now instead of going through the paperwork and finalizing details for a wedding taking place next month, I'm looking at listings for rental homes nearby. It's all wrong, and while it all feels like a big, flopping failure, at the same time, it feels like a fresh start.

Maybe I need to get out of Vegas altogether. I could go back to Chicago where I grew up. My parents retired to Florida, but I still have family back home. My brother and his family. Aunts, uncles, cousins.

I followed Archer to Vegas because we were together when he signed with the Vegas Heat. I attended almost every game but missed a few when weddings I planned fell on game days—though I tried my best to avoid that.

I listened when he spoke. He's a man of few words, and it takes a lot to get him to open up. But I did. I was one of the rare, lucky few...until I wasn't. Until he shut down on me, too.

It's because of him that I decided not to work for someone else when I moved here. I had our future in mind, the need to pick up at a moment's notice always in my periphery because playing professional baseball doesn't guarantee placement stability.

My career started by happy accident, really. A friend wanted to fly to Vegas to get married. I was local. I planned it all for her. I got to know the local vendors and the ins and outs of Vegas weddings.

Sometimes I'm a walking contradiction—having to plan something as big and important as someone's wedding while I tend to fall on the whimsical and disorganized side—but somehow planning a wedding is different. It's what I know. I've planned hundreds now, my business growing by word of mouth mostly, and even though I don't have personal experience planning my own wedding, I'm damn good at what I do.

It's why I want to expand into a destination brand, but now I have to put it on the back burner while I figure out where to live and what to do with my life without Archer in it.

So yeah, I'm sad. Of course I am. It hurts. It's the end of an era. Any way I slice it, my life is about to change.

But part of living in that organized chaos means I'll land on my feet wherever I wind up, and maybe being forced to fly on my own will grant me the opportunities I thought were dead and buried.

"Tater Tater, see ya later!" Kenzie, my assistant who works in the office next to mine, says. I rent two offices in a larger complex that houses a large kitchen, dining area, and all-purpose space, so we eat lunch together nearly daily, and we've gotten close over the two years she's been working for me.

"Bye, Kenz."

She doubles back to my doorway. "What's wrong?"

"How could you tell?"

"You didn't meet me for lunch today," she begins, clearly ticking off my offenses. "And you *never* give me that sort of unenthusiastic *bye, Kenz*. You sound like you're down in the dumps. What's up?" She slides into the chair on the opposite side of my messy desk.

"Archer and I broke up," I admit.

"Oh, babe. Again?" she asks.

Snap DECISION

I twist my lips and nod. "Yeah. Again. But this time feels final."

She wrinkles her nose and tightens her ponytail. "What happened?"

I debate how much to get into it. I know *some* things, but I think those things are meant to be held tightly to the chest. It may be over, but it's not like we're enemies, and I'm not really the type to burn bridges.

"We grew apart. I didn't feel like he supported my dreams anymore while I continued to give things up to support his." I shrug. "You know, that sort of thing." The answer sounds rote even to me, but it's sort of what I *have* to say, isn't it?

I can't exactly go around telling people that I asked my long-term boyfriend if I could talk to his brother, who heads the family's real estate development company, about my plans of creating a destination wedding brand and his answer was a clear, resounding, nearly angry *no*.

It was final. Decisive. Like us. It's what spelled the end, anyway.

I wasn't asking because I wanted to use him for his connections. I was just thinking of who I respect and trust in the industry—someone I'd *want* to give my business to.

I guess it won't be the Bradleys.

"I want you to stay far away from my family." Those were his words. He stayed far away, too, until he didn't. Until he signed some papers for his father, and now he's under investigation.

He didn't share much about the paperwork, but it doesn't take a genius to put two and two together. His father opened a lounge here in Vegas that was a front for something illegal.

I get it. But his father's name is off the Bradley Group now, so I don't see why I can't work with Madden, his oldest brother, on developing venues. I want to start with Vegas, obviously. I'm also considering Chicago, San Diego, and

Hawaii. Vegas and Chicago because they're home, San Diego since Madden is there and it's where he's operating his business, and it's also a gorgeous backdrop for weddings. Hawaii because—*duh*—nearly everyone who has thought about a destination considers it.

Eventually I want to take it to the Caribbean for the same reason. Maybe Florida for a more affordable wedding. Depending on how it goes, maybe someday there will be a Tatum Barker venue in every state and in countries across the world.

If it's not clear yet, I'm a dreamer, and I dream big. What's the sense in dreaming if it isn't big? And I work my ass off to see those big dreams come true.

"Anyway, now I'm looking at places to rent and debating if I even want to stay in Vegas," I finish.

"Stop it," she says. "Listen to me, you're staying in Vegas, and you're staying with me until you figure it out."

I tilt my head. "That's really sweet, Kenz. I couldn't possibly—"

She holds up a hand. "You didn't ask, I'm offering, and I mean it."

"I wasn't going to say that I couldn't possibly ask you that. I was going to say I couldn't possibly stay with you when you have two kids whose combined ages total five."

She laughs. "You know our guest room is the casita, right?"

I've been to their house, and they have a little pseudo-apartment attached at the front of their house that has a completely separate entrance from the main house.

"Then you have yourself a deal. I need to wrap up some details on the Brown-Mayfair wedding and then I'm heading out of town for a few days. Is it okay if I start hauling stuff over this evening and stay until I leave for my trip?"

"Absolutely." She nods resolutely.

"Don't you need to check in with Cody?" I ask, referring to her husband.

She shakes her head. "He once invited his brother to stay with us for a couple months without running it by me. Said brother listened to death metal on full blast at three in the morning when I had a newborn. It may be soundproof, but it's not idiot-proof."

I giggle. "I promise to keep my death metal at a reasonable volume after eight PM."

"Seven," she says, pursing her lips.

"Deal. And can you handle things here while I'm out of town?"

"Of course. Whatever you need, you know I'm on it."

I know she is. She's the best, and she could run Barker Weddings on her own at this point.

"Thanks," I murmur.

She nods. "I need to go get dinner started, but just text me when you're on your way, and we can talk more tonight, okay?"

I nod. "You're the best assistant and friend I could ever ask for."

She grins. "Back at you."

She heads out, and I flip from looking for somewhere to live to somewhere to store my stuff while I'm in my *starting over* era.

CHAPTER 3

FORD BRADLEY
A Little Cliché

I sip from my glass of whiskey as I glance around the bar. I turn thirty in a couple months, and the last time I had this much whiskey, it took me a couple days to recover.

I don't have a couple days this time. In thirty-six hours, I need to be at the stadium warming up for a game.

It'll be fine. I'll sweat it out tomorrow. It might be a little painful, but life's fucking painful, so I'll get over it.

I should call Everleigh. I'm closest to her out of my six siblings, and I will. I'll let her know about Tatum and Archer, and depending on how the conversation goes, I might even tell her what Tate slipped about Archer's involvement with Dad. I'll get to the bottom of it all eventually.

If the FBI doesn't beat me to it.

I'll do it tomorrow. It's late, and I don't need to ruin her Friday night with something I'm not super clear on as it is. Maybe I'll talk to Tatum again before then so I can clarify a few things.

But tonight, as Cole said, is about regrets.

Snap DECISION

I spot a perky blonde walking toward me, but let's be honest. This part of Florida is filled with perky blondes. I could likely have my pick, but it's not my style the way it is for my brother Dex—you know, before he went and fell in love. He was always the player of the Bradley boys. Liam might be a close second. Nobody knows where Archer falls on that list since he was with Tatum for so long, but I'd probably come next, and Madden last.

I wouldn't characterize myself as a player, necessarily. More of a man who's searching for something he hasn't been able to find, but not for lack of trying. Not for lack of sampling. It's the only way to find out if I'm compatible with someone, after all.

I guess it comes down to two things. One, I have this horrific fear that I'll find someone and fall in love only to find out they're just using me for my money, connections, or place on the field, that it was all a lie the whole time.

And two…none of them are Tatum.

That's all I'm looking for tonight. A sample for me. A regret for her. How can it be anything else when my heart is stuck on a woman I can't have?

"You're Ford Bradley," the woman says matter-of-factly when she slides into the small bit of space separating me from Cole, who's on the barstool beside me.

"I am," I agree. "You look familiar."

She sticks out her hand. "Elena. I cheer for the Beasts."

"Ah," I say. It's a little cliché, isn't it? The football player and the cheerleader. I tend to avoid those sorts of entanglements, mainly because getting involved with a cheerleader is bad for the team. It leads to gossip and media attention—something I have enough of given that I hail from the Bradley clan. "It's nice to meet you."

"It's amazing to meet you," she says. "I come here every week on Thursday and Friday." She leans in a little conspiratorially as she says it, like she's letting me in on a secret. Only I don't know exactly what she's getting at.

Maybe she just drinks a lot.

"Why's that?" I ask, taking the bait.

"I've heard this is where players hang out after practice."

"And you were waiting for players to show up?" I guess.

She raises her brows. "Not players. Just one."

"Me?" I guess, and she nods.

She doesn't look away or seem at all embarrassed by that fact.

"Why?"

She lifts a shoulder. "You always just seemed so…I don't know. Balanced. Smart. Not like the other guys, you know? And you're hot as hell." She bites her bottom lip.

I may not be like the other guys, but she's just like the other girls. Laying compliments on me to get me into bed, pulling the bite the lip move…all of it. It's predictable.

And it works.

Maybe it works because of its predictability.

I can't have the one girl I want, but perhaps this one can take my mind off that fact for a little bit.

We head out to her car. As it turns out, she hasn't had a drop of alcohol to drink. She navigates to her apartment, under a ten-minute drive from this very bar, and before we get out of the car, I say, "Are you sure you want to do this?"

She glances over at me. "It's all I've wanted for the two years I've been cheering for the team."

"You won't wake up tomorrow with regrets?"

She lifts a shoulder, and she's really very pretty. She deserves someone so much better than an emotionally unavailable football player whose mind is occupied with another woman. "Only if you're not up to the task."

She's sassy, and I like that about her.

Snap DECISION

And maybe in some alternate universe, it would make sense for me to give this a try with her.

But it's not an alternate universe, and I know exactly where my head is at. "I don't think this is a good idea."

She folds her arms over her chest, as if that'll help keep her from getting vulnerable.

I stare out the windshield as she stares at me. "I've been in love with the same woman for the last ten years, Elena. I can't have her, but a night with you isn't going to change that."

She reaches over to run a fingertip down my arm. "You won't know that if you don't try."

She's just like the rest of them. She thinks she can be the one to change me.

Nothing can change me except figuring out some way to stop doing this to myself. I ruin every potential good relationship over someone I can never have.

It's toxic. It's awful.

It's not like I'm celibate.

I just had sex last weekend.

But tonight feels different. It's the first time I'd be having sex when Tatum is single. She's apart from my brother with no plans to get back together with him after a week or two passes. She said it's final.

And the logical side of me knows it's not fair to do that to some poor, unsuspecting—but horny—young woman.

I shake my head. "No, you're right about that. The problem is that I don't want to try."

She presses her lips together. "Then why'd you come home with me?"

"I thought I could set my feelings aside and just have a fun time with you. But you deserve better than that."

She leans her head back on her seat with a groan. "Why do you have to be so *nice* on top of being so hot?"

I chuckle. "Sorry. For what it's worth, the right guy is out there for you. You're gorgeous, and you seem like a hell of a good time. I'm sorry I'm not what you wanted."

"You're still what I want," she says softly.

I press my lips together, and then I lean across the console and press a soft kiss to her cheek.

Then I exit the car, walk up toward the front of the apartment complex, and call an Uber to come pick me up and take me home.

The only regret I managed to pick up tonight is walking away. Again.

CHAPTER 4

FORD BRADLEY

She'd Be Perfect for You

I'm wearing a hat pulled down low when I spot her across the space separating us. I'm waiting by baggage claim, trying my best to be incognito, when I see her stepping onto the escalator, and I'm transported back twelve years to when I had already turned seventeen and she was about to turn fifteen.

I was a junior—about to be a senior. She was a freshman. It was the last day of school, and my parents were out at some soiree as they always were, so Dex threw a party at the house. He was twenty-one, old enough to purchase liquor for all of us underage kids, already home for the summer from college.

I had a couple drinks, but I was far from drunk when I saw her. She was there because Archer invited her—or maybe because she tagged along. She was always over at our house, and the more I saw her, the more I flirted with her. The more I flirted with her, the more I wanted to kiss her.

Snap DECISION

She was too young for me, and she was always there with Archer, not there for me. None of that stopped me from being attracted to her anyway.

I was filling up my cup at the keg in the kitchen when she marched up to me and asked me for a beer.

"Liquor before beer, you're in the clear. Beer before liquor will make you sicker," I told her.

She laughed, clearly having no clue what I meant.

"I saw you take that shot of rum before. If you drink beer now and then go back to rum, you won't make it through the night without puking," I said.

She wrinkled her nose, and it wasn't the first time that I noticed the smattering of freckles dusting her nose and cheeks.

Her eyes were mesmerizing as they met mine. "I'll risk it."

It felt like she was challenging me to something, but I wasn't exactly sure what.

"You don't strike me as a risk-taker," I said.

She glanced around, saw that we were alone for the moment, and we sort of leaned forward at the same time. Our mouths collided, and fucking fireworks exploded overhead.

I hooked my palm around her neck to pull her a little closer to me as I opened my mouth to hers.

She tasted like raspberries and honey.

It was pure heaven. It was a feeling I have yet to recreate.

I sank into her, wanting this to last forever even though I knew deep down it had to be fleeting. I was reaching to set my cup down on the counter so I could wrap my other arm around her waist to pull her flush against me when I heard my sister's voice calling me.

"Ford?"

My sister wasn't in the kitchen…yet. She was in the next room. She didn't catch us kissing.

I didn't want to let her go, but I knew Everleigh was on her way. I added up the situation. Archer had decided to play baseball, much to my father's dismay, and it seemed like he was drifting from the rest of us. I couldn't be caught kissing his girl here in the kitchen even if they weren't officially together.

I forced myself to pull away. I had to.

"There you are!" Everleigh said as she pushed through the swinging door into the kitchen. "I've been looking everywhere for you."

She was completely oblivious to the fact that she'd just interrupted my kiss with Tatum.

A kiss I've never told a soul about.

We never talked about it. I chalked it up to her being drunk and forgetting about it.

But it was always there for me, always simmering in the background, a memory I will never let go of even though *I have to*. She was with my brother for years. It's not like she can just hop into a life with me now.

I pull myself from that memory and try to push it back to the past where it belongs as I watch her ride the escalator.

She's chatting with a woman who looks to be around her age, as if she and the woman are the best of friends. She pulls out her phone, and I watch as the woman she's with says something and Tatum taps on her phone. She glances up at her friend, who pulled out her phone, too, and flashes it at Tatum. From the looks of it, she just exchanged numbers with this person.

That's Tatum. She can meet someone on a flight and end up with dinner plans next week. Or maybe she'll be this woman's wedding planner.

A little girl on the escalator behind her says something to Tatum, and she turns around and starts chatting up the little girl.

Snap DECISION

She hasn't even seen me yet, and she's surrounded in this airport by people who already regard her as a friend. She has this electric vibe surrounding her, this light that draws people in, this inexplicable *thing* that people want to be a part of.

And she looks like a goddamn fairy princess as the escalator carries her down closer to me. Curled blonde locks fall to the middle of her back. She's wearing a summery, flowery dress with heels. She's almost always in heels. I practically see wings sprouting behind her and a halo over her head, her magic wand glowing in her palm. Or her cell phone. Either way, she's glowing, and everyone in the vicinity can see it.

When the ride ends, she glances up, and our eyes connect across the space. A little smile plays at her lips, and she points me out to her new friend before she rushes across the small space separating us.

I heave in a deep breath, and when she reaches me, first I spot the smattering of freckles that lie across her nose and cheeks before she falls into my open arms as we hug hello, her honey perfume wrapping around me and giving me a sense of comfort that she's really here.

It's the same honey perfume she's worn since high school, back when we spent a lot more time in geographical proximity to one another. A lot has changed. I see her when I visit Vegas, which isn't as often as I'd like. I see her when she's in town for a Vegas Heat baseball game.

That's about it.

Her parents live in Florida, but they're in Boca Raton, nearly four hours away from me. It may as well be Vegas for how far it is.

We study each other for a few seconds, smiles on both our faces that we're together again.

Smiles for two different reasons, though. Her because she's with her friend again. Me because...well, I should probably stop thinking that way.

"Ford, my God, it's been way too long!" she says as she hugs me tightly. She pulls out of my arms to introduce me to her friend, but I can't seem to tear my brown eyes from her gorgeous, light blue ones. "This is Morgan. We met on the plane and became instant besties. Ford, Morgan. Morgan, Ford."

I force myself to look at Morgan. She's beautiful, too, and I'm certain this pair of blondes turned plenty of heads as they walked off the jetway and into the terminal.

I hold out a hand to shake hers. "Pleasure."

"She's a middle school math teacher. Can you believe it? She was in Vegas for her friend's bachelorette party but lives here in Tampa. And she's a totally *huge* Beasts fan."

"My parents have season tickets, and I still bum a few off my dad every season," she says.

"We're doing our best to make you proud," I say with a smile. I wouldn't be making the kind of money I'm making if we didn't have a sea of fans just like Morgan, so I play the nice guy card even though I'm ready to get the hell out of here. This is all nice and great, but the longer we hang around, the better the chance others will recognize me. That's why I want to get out of here.

Not because I want to get Tatum alone. Of course not. That would be ridiculous. She's my brother's ex. Recent ex.

I glance at Tatum. "We're at baggage carousel two," I say.

"Let's head that way," Tatum says, and she links her arm through my elbow.

"Excuse me, I'm going to head to the restroom," Morgan says, and she heads in that direction while Tatum leans in a little closer to me.

"She'd be perfect for you, Ford," she says, her tone full of excitement as she plays matchmaker.

My heart drops as I feel myself physically deflating at those five little words. *She'd be perfect for you.*

Excitement is not quite the emotion I'm feeling.

There's only one woman who'd be perfect for me, but she's not an option. Clearly.

I don't want her to play matchmaker for me and some other woman. It always felt like she was off the table, but this pulls it even further from the table than I ever imagined.

Her suitcase arrives, her friend returns, and we bid her goodbye as we head toward my car. Once we're buckled and on the highway headed toward the high-rise I live in that overlooks Tampa Bay, she says, "How's your mom doing?"

"Liam called me a couple days ago to let me know she broke her back. She's in the hospital."

"Oh, God. I'm so sorry." She reaches over to the hand resting on the console between us and gives it a squeeze, her touch sending a shock of need straight down to my balls. "Does Archer know?"

A cold dose of reality seems to shudder through me at the mention of my brother. "I'm not sure. I haven't spoken with him."

"I can tell him. I stayed with a friend the last few nights, so I haven't seen him," she says.

"How are your parents doing?" I ask, changing the subject.

"Fine." She shrugs. "My dad wears too many flowers on his shirts, and my mom forces him to go out dancing a few times a week with her. They're living it up in their Boca retirement era."

I chuckle, imagining her father in his flowery shirts and her mother dressed in something to match as they dance the night away.

Is it too much to ask for in my own future?

"Depending how long I stay in town, I may pop down to visit them. Or meet halfway or something. How about your dad? What's the latest there?" she asks.

"I don't really know," I murmur. "Liam said Dad heard that there's a grand jury, so we'll see what happens next."

"What does that mean?" she asks.

"A grand jury meets—usually in secret, but not always—reviews the evidence, and they decide if there's enough evidence to issue an indictment," I explain.

"And what's an indictment? I don't really watch those lawyer-y shows. I stick to dating shows, so these fancy terms mean zilch to me."

I chuckle. "A formal charge typically followed by an arrest."

"Oh, shit. What would be the charges?" she asks.

"Federal law prohibits illegal gambling operations, so there's that. But I'd imagine they'd also get him for tax evasion, making false statements to federal agents. Maybe money laundering, possibly racketeering. Depends on what they've found and the extent of what he's done."

"What about Arch?" she asks, her voice softer this time.

"What about him?"

"He's being investigated, you know. He refused to let me get involved with Bradley Group, but the hypocrite signed off on paperwork for your father, and now he's being investigated." She shakes her head as she stares out the window.

"I think we're *all* being investigated." For the first time, it strikes me that maybe the whole reason Archer ended things with her was to protect her from our family. Maybe that's where the finality came from. But she's still here—just around a different brother now. Maybe it would do her well to remove herself entirely from the Bradley family. "What did you want to use Bradley Group for?"

"I don't know," she mutters. "I just had this crazy thought that my destination wedding brand was something I could partner with Bradley Group on. I've been around your family for half my life, and it felt like the right sort of partnership, you know? Keep it in the family even though I've never technically been family."

"I don't think it's a crazy idea," I say softly. Truthfully, it's a beautiful dream, a wonderful goal. It's something I really believe she could pull off, and I love that she wants to keep it in the family. "You know Bradley Group merged with Van Buren, right? It's VanBrad now."

"I heard that. But I think I'll always think of it as Bradley Group."

"I could help you with that," I offer, and I'm not sure why I say it. It's clearly something Archer didn't want, but, well…I'm not Archer, and if he was trying to protect her from our father, he's a separate entity from VanBrad now that Madden extracted him from the company he founded.

"You'd do that?" she asks, an air of appreciation and incredulity in her tone.

She has no idea that I'd do *anything* for her.

I pull into the parking deck. The building I live in is a hotel, but above the hotel, from levels fifteen to thirty-eight, are residences. And residents get a shitload of amenities, including a rooftop pool and sundeck as well as hospitality services. I've ordered meals from the four restaurants located in the hotel more times than I'm proud to admit.

We take the private residence elevators up to the thirty-fifth floor, and I unlock the door to my three-bed, three-bath luxury condo.

She's been here before, and as is her custom when we walk into my place, she rushes to the windows. "God, I always forget how gorgeous this place is."

"It's been a while since you've been here," I say, and I drag her suitcase down the hall to one of the guest rooms.

The last time she was here, she and Archer came to visit and only stayed for a few hours. She dragged Archer. He was quiet the whole time while she filled the space with her light.

Every time I walk by the windows, I picture her standing at them, her fingertips lightly resting on the glass in awe of my view, just as she is now when I return from the guest room.

I draw in a breath.

"Two years," she says.

I guess I hadn't realized it had been that long. More time to grow further from my brother. More time to push away the feelings I can't seem to let go of. And having her here in this space? It's certainly not going to get any easier.

CHAPTER 5

Tatum Barker

Waiting in the Wings

Ford orders dinner from one of the restaurants in this building, and someone knocks on the door half an hour later with our meals.

"Can we eat on the terrace?" I beg.

It's so pretty out there, and it's such a nice night. I hate to let it go to waste sitting here inside.

"I don't have a table to sit at," he points out.

"So we eat out of our to-go containers with our drinks on the floor beside us. C'mon," I say, angling my head toward the private terrace.

I ditch my phone and leave it on the counter, and I ask about how this season has been going for him. We make small talk. He eats the breakfast for dinner he ordered—steak and eggs with a side of bacon, his favorite. I munch on the spaghetti and meatballs, my favorite meal that I deny myself too often in favor of leaving carbs at the door.

Snap DECISION

Archer and I broke up. I can indulge in a little pasta to make myself feel better. And maybe waffles with a side of sausage in the morning.

He fills me in on the latest here in Tampa, and I tell him about the best wedding stories I have since the last time we chatted.

"Have I told you my most recent personal favorite story?"

He shrugs.

I laugh at the memory. "Oh my God, this couple *insisted* on bringing their dogs to the wedding. They were the ring bearers. Well, the reception was outdoors, and these freaking dogs spotted a bird. They proceeded to chase said bird and plowed into the cake table, which toppled down to the ground. It was a total and complete disaster and was absolutely something out of a movie."

"Oh, shit," Ford says, laughing. "What did you do?"

"Super wedding planner to the rescue," I say, holding my arm straight with my hand balled into a fist like a superhero, and then I lean in a little closer. "I drove to Costco and bought the biggest cake I could find. It was chocolate with white buttercream, and it honestly tasted better than the Earl Grey and lavender shit they ordered from some fancy schmancy bakery."

He laughs at that. "What flavor would you get?"

"Mm," I moan. "Something indulgent. Chocolate hazelnut or salted caramel chocolate." As if I haven't planned every single detail of my own wedding that's apparently never going to happen. "What about you?"

"Chocolate hazelnut—like Nutella?" he asks. When I nod, he says, "That. Or, you know, whatever the bride desires."

"You got any lassies waiting in the wings?"

He makes a *pfft* sound as he shakes his head. "Too focused on the game and family drama to invite someone into that mess."

"Maybe Morgan? She seems tough enough to handle the drama."

He laughs. "I literally met her for thirty seconds at the airport. Trust me when I say I wasn't picturing our future wedding."

"Well, maybe we should change that." I raise my brows pointedly.

"How?"

I nod inside toward my phone. "I'll grab my phone after dinner and see when she's free to meet you. What day works best?"

"Never," he mutters—I think. His voice is too low to be sure. He clears his throat. "I'm actually pretty busy."

I raise a brow. "Not too busy to pick me up from the airport and entertain me all evening."

He looks caught for a second. "You know Tuesdays are my only real free day."

"And Mondays. And most evenings except game day and the day before game day. Except if you're traveling." I repeat his schedule with boredom in my tone, and he laughs.

"Exactly. And I'm tired after practice and just want to come home and relax, not go out on a date."

"Then invite her here. Get her on your turf and you can relax together, like we're doing now," I suggest.

"I like relaxing with you," he says quietly.

Something twitches in my belly. I'm not sure what. Maybe it's the pasta I'm currently chowing down on, but it feels like something else entirely.

"I like relaxing with you, too."

If that isn't the understatement of the century. I'm already starting to realize how much I *love* it here. It's slower paced. Ford actually *listens* when I talk. He's kind and understanding. He's a good friend.

Snap DECISION

"But don't you want to find someone to share your life with? Isn't it lonely living in this gorgeous place with this romantic view and not having anyone to come home to?" I ask quietly.

I want him to be happy.

I could make him happy.

I push away that intrusive thought immediately. It's off the table. It's not something I ever considered. Sure, he's hot as hell, and he's kind and sweet and, in general, a really, really good guy who loves bacon and breakfast for dinner.

But he's also Archer's brother. He's *always* been off the table, and just because Archer and I broke up—again—doesn't mean jack shit.

I'll text Morgan after dinner. That will help drive that intrusive thought right off the edge of a cliff, just where it belongs.

Me: *What does your schedule look like this week? I'm arranging a date for you and Ford. It's Tatum, the girl from the plane, by the way.* *[grinning squinting face emoji]*

Her answer comes quick.

Morgan: *I'll clear whatever I have going on for a date with Ford Bradley. [hot face emoji]*

Me: *[rolling on the floor laughing emoji three times]*

Morgan: *I have a parent meeting on Friday I'm happy to move if needed.*

Me: *He has a game Sunday, so can you do tomorrow night? He might be tired after practice, but I can figure out a place to meet that's close to the training center.*

Morgan: *Yes! OMG YES! Are you serious RN?*

Me: *Yep, consider it done. I'll text you the details later.*

Morgan: *Thank you, new bestie! You can be MOH at our wedding!*

I stare at the words, not sure why I feel a stab through my ribs at that. I want him to be happy. It has to be because

Archer and I broke up, and I've never been further from the dream of getting to be the bride for once.

"She's free tomorrow if you are," I say as he finishes cleaning up from our dinner. I'm sitting at the kitchen counter across from where he's rinsing the silverware and cups we used.

He lets out a long, heavy sigh. "I can do dinner tomorrow. Let's plan on seven, and I'll meet her at Gillian's. It's a steakhouse near practice."

"You got it." I text her the details before he can change his mind, and I also text him her number.

Mission one: Score Ford a girl—complete. Maybe. If they hit it off. I guess time will tell.

* * *

When I wake up, the house is empty, but there's a note on the counter in Ford's neat penmanship.

T-
If you need anything and can't reach me, call the hotel concierge. They can get you a car, groceries, whatever you need. You're welcome to anything in the fridge. Have fun.
-F

It was sweet he left me a note. He's thoughtful that way—he didn't text because he didn't want to wake me, and I appreciate that. I wander around the place and realize I'm going to be alone for most of the day. Maybe it was dumb to arrange a date for him right after practice on my first full day in town. I have no real idea what to do with myself.

And so I grab some yogurt out of the fridge for breakfast and locate the coffeemaker to get that going. I grab the big Stanley cup I brought with me from the guest room that's

Snap DECISION

now my room and fill it with icy cold water before I settle in to get some work done. I sip from my first cup of coffee as I reply to several emails from clients and vendors, update timelines and checklists, and book some appointments for various clients. I start a second cup of coffee as I batch create some social media posts—something I always *try* to do but often *forget* to do.

I order lunch from the same restaurant we had dinner from last night. I busy myself with more work.

The later in the day it gets, the more I notice my eyes inching toward the clock.

It's simple curiosity, that's all. I'm excited for Ford and my new friend. I'm excited to be the matchmaker. Maybe someday I'll plan their wedding.

The thought leaves me with an inexplicably hollow feeling.

I bury myself in more work, and I take a stretch break to stare out the window at his view. I let myself out onto the terrace, and I breathe in the salty air.

What would it be like to work here? Maybe I should add Tampa to my shortlist of dream places to own a venue.

Seven o'clock hits, and I know I should order dinner, but I'm not hungry.

Their date is starting.

Those two thoughts are unrelated.

I think.

I'm nervous for them, maybe. I can't stop wondering how it's going. Because I'm curious. Nothing more.

I can't focus on work. I can't eat. So I sit on the terrace and stare out over the water until I hear the door inside click.

I stand and turn to see Ford walking in. He's carrying a container of his leftovers, and I casually open the door and walk in.

"How was the date?" I ask.

"Did you eat?" he asks rather than answering.

I shake my head.

"I somehow knew you didn't, so I brought you dinner." He holds up the container. "It's the same thing I ordered. You'll love it."

"Oh. Thanks. That was really nice of you. How'd it go?"

He sets the container on the counter and grabs a fork for me, and he pushes both across the counter. I settle onto a stool and wait for him to answer before I start eating.

"It was nice. Fine. Fun." He shrugs.

Well...that's not exactly a rousing review, and I'm not quite sure why a small measure of comfort darts through me. "Are you going out with her again?"

He shrugs. "She was nice enough."

"Did you kiss her?" I'm not sure where the question comes from. It's not my business, and even I can hear a slightly dark edge to my tone.

"No." His eyes move to mine. "I didn't feel a spark."

Relief? Is that what I'm feeling?

Why would *relief* pulse through me at his words?

Maybe deep down I knew that she wasn't right for him.

Or maybe, just maybe, I tried to pawn him off on some other woman in some wild and futile attempt to protect myself.

CHAPTER 6

FORD BRADLEY

Gather the Funds

I'm on my way to practice when I see Liam calling. "Hello?" I answer.

I probably should pull over based on the words that come out of his mouth.

"Dad was indicted."

We knew it was coming, but it still makes my heart drop into my stomach. "So what happens next?" I ask.

"He was already arrested, and the arraignment is set for first thing Monday. They searched the house, too."

"Shit," I mutter. "So they're holding him through the weekend. What about Archer?"

"They left him alone—for now. They could still be working on things behind closed doors but wanted to cut off the head of the snake first, so to speak."

I let out a grunt. "Keep me posted. Sorry you're dealing with this on your own."

"Me too. It fucking sucks. I'll let you know what they set bail at when I hear."

"Thanks. How's Mom?" I ask.

"Not well. You should probably call her. I haven't told her Dad was arrested yet."

"I won't be the one to take that away from you," I say. "I'm just pulling into practice."

"Oh, I forgot you're an hour later than me. I'll let the others know."

"Thanks." I cut the call and head into practice as I think about my siblings. I'm in the latest time zone in the family. Moving west, there's Liam and Ivy in Chicago; Dex, Everleigh, and Archer in Vegas; and Madden in San Diego. Based on that, I'm wondering if Vegas should be our family's new home base instead of Chicago.

Not because it'll put me closer to Tatum once she goes back home. Just because it makes sense for the family since more of us live there than anywhere else.

Before I even get out on the field, my head coach, Jonathan Wilder, calls me into his office. He nods to the chair across from him when I knock on his doorframe, and I take a seat.

"You need to talk about it?" he asks.

He's a good coach—no, a *great* coach—and he can sense when his players are going through something. Well, that paired with the fact that since I come from a celebrity family, my father's arrest is already likely all over the news.

"I just found out on my way here," I admit. "I haven't processed it yet."

"Let me know what I can do. If you need a minute today, you say the word."

I nod. "Thanks. I won't need a minute." I can separate emotion from this.

Maybe.

"Are you escaping this unscathed?"

"I wasn't involved in it. My name isn't on any of the documents. I'm not worried."

He nods once, a bit of pride in his eyes that he chose one of the Bradley siblings who's on the right side of this as a player on his team. I wish we *all* were on the right side of it. I have no idea what's going to happen with Archer. I still have no idea how his name ended up on some of the incriminating documents, but the grand jury must have found enough evidence against my father to push out those charges first.

The head of the snake, as Liam called it.

I work my hardest at practice, my mind not in it as it settles on my father, just as predicted by Coach. Before I head out for the day, he pulls me aside.

"I need you in it on Sunday, Bradley," he says, his voice gentle despite the tough words.

"I will be."

He studies me for a beat, and then he nods, seemingly satisfied.

I think about heading to Chicago to see my father behind bars, to talk to him and get a sense of how bad this might get. But I told Coach I'd be in it on Sunday, so I need to stay here. I need to be ready to go at practice tomorrow and Saturday. Ready to play on Sunday. And then my father will be arraigned, and we'll know what we're dealing with when it comes to bailing him out.

As it turns out, he knows my schedule well enough to know when I'm free to answer his call. I'm on my way home from practice when I receive an incoming call from a number I don't recognize.

"Hello?" I answer over the car's Bluetooth system.

"Collect Call from Thomas Bradley, inmate at Chicago's Metropolitan Correctional Center. Press one to accept the call."

I sigh as I click the button.

"This call will be monitored and recorded."

"Hello?" I say into the line.

"Ford," my father says, and it feels…weird. We rarely talk on the phone. We rarely talk at all. "My lawyer's educated guess is that bail will be set between two and three million. I need you to gather the funds."

"From where?" I ask, as if he's going to give up all his hidden accounts over the phone.

"You'll figure it out." He ends the call.

I slam a hand on my steering wheel.

I immediately dial Madden.

"I assume you heard the news," he answers.

I sigh. "He just called me and told me to gather the funds for his bail."

"How much?"

"He said his lawyers are guessing two to three million."

"Fuck," he mutters. "What are you going to do?"

"Why do you think I called you?" I ask.

He chuckles. "Don't look at me."

"You're the CEO of a multi-million-dollar company," I argue.

"Co-CEO," he reminds me. "He put me through hell, and it almost cost me Kennedy. I wouldn't say I'm eager to jump into helping him, and just because he hasn't done that to you yet, don't think he won't. Don't give him your money, Ford."

"What am I supposed to do then?"

"Let him rot. He's not innocent."

"That's it?" I ask.

"That's it from me. I would venture to guess that Dex, Everleigh, and Archer would agree with me. You may have better luck with Liam and Ivy," he says.

"Ivy can't access her trust fund until she's twenty-five," I point out. "Have you talked to Arch?"

"No."

"Did you know he and Tatum broke up and she's staying with me right now?"

"I hadn't heard that," he says. "Did you get anything out of her?"

"Not really. I still don't know how Archer got tangled up in Dad's bullshit."

"It's what our father does," he says. "He manipulates and twists and gets what he wants every goddamn time. And that's why he doesn't deserve your money."

He's right. I know he is.

But he's also our father, and family loyalty means something to me.

It means a *lot* to me.

I try Dex and Everleigh next, and both tell me not to fund Dad's bail.

I call Archer. He doesn't answer. I don't bother leaving a voicemail. He won't call back, and he won't pitch in.

I call Liam next.

"I talked to Dad," I say.

"And?"

I decide to try a different tack with this one. "He told me to gather funds for his bail. If you and I chip in from our trust funds, I can pay us back when we sell the mansion."

"Just us?" he asks.

"Madden, Dex, and Everleigh were in agreement that he should sit in prison and pay for his crimes."

"I figured. But they're not here. They wrote him off because of the things he's done, but I can't let him sit in prison when he could be with Mom in her last days. You know?"

"I know," I say. "It's complicated."

"I'm having dinner with Ivy tonight. I'll check with her."

"She can't access her funds yet," I remind him.

"Oh. Right. Well, just us then."

"Yeah, bro," I say quietly.

"You're really selling the house?" he asks.

"What choice do I have? We'll be out a million bucks each if not more until the end of his trial, which could take years. Are you okay with that?"

"No," he grunts. "But I'm also not okay with you selling the mansion."

"I'm sorry. I promise you, Liam, we're in this together."

"Yeah."

We end the call, and I stare at my phone for a minute as I think things through. Maybe Liam's right in that I'm too practical when it comes to these things, but I'm protecting our finances over this goddamn legacy my father is so adamant about.

And because of that, I'll need to get to Chicago to assess what sort of shape the mansion is in so I can get a crew in to clean it up and get the place listed.

I stick that in the *need to do later* column and head inside to finally get a little reprieve from this God-awful day by seeing Tatum.

CHAPTER 7

Tatum Barker

Brilliance at Work

"Honey, I'm home," Ford calls from the doorway, and I let out a little giggle.

"Welcome home, dear," I call back from the desk in the guest room where I've set up shop.

There are a few stacks of paper scattered on the desk along with my signature three drinks—coffee, water, and iced tea today—and I've made some progress on the mountain of work I left behind when I picked up to stay with my ex-boyfriend's brother in Florida.

The distance feels good. Being in Vegas felt suffocating, but being here with Ford feels...freeing.

The odd thought comes to mind that it's because Ford has always been home. How can that be true when I've spent nearly a decade building a home with his brother?

I push off the thought. I'd cleared enough of my schedule that it was possible, and it's not like this is open-ended. I have events to get back to Vegas for. Weddings. A charity event I've already planned for Archer's foundation. Life.

Snap DECISION

I can't hide out in Florida forever, but the window above the desk in the guest room looks out over the city, and I'm already falling in love with the view.

I could get used to it here.

I can't pretend like I didn't flip through a website featuring the wedding venues here. It's a gorgeous place for a wedding, but that could be the landlocked desert lizard who lives inside me poking its little head out of its hiding place.

I've always had a preference for the water.

Even growing up, my favorite place to escape reality for a few hours was North Avenue Beach. It was a nice enough place to look out over the water in Lincoln Park near home, but it doesn't hold a candle to the gorgeous marinas here in Tampa or the beautiful sandy beaches just a half hour away.

I tug on the scrunchie holding my hair on top of my head, and my hair falls around my shoulders. I toss the scrunchie between my three cups just as Ford appears in my doorway.

"Creativity in motion," he says, surveying my desk.

I glance at the mess. "I'm sorry. This must really grate on your nerves." I scrunch my nose up like that scrunchie sitting on my desk.

He folds his arms over his chest as he shakes his head. "Honestly? It looks like brilliance at work."

I tilt my head, and my eyes soften as I hear the genuine sentiment of his tone.

"Being good at what you do doesn't mean having a clean desk. It means creating a system that works for you, and clearly this works since you excel at planning weddings."

I narrow my eyes. "Okay, Bradley. Now you're just laying it on thick." It's like he heard Archer tease me about my mess and took the exact opposite route.

He lifts a shoulder. "I'm not. I had a rough day, and it's refreshing to see you in your element." His words are sweet, and a feeling of warmth spreads through my chest.

I raise my arms over my head and clasp my hands to stretch, and then I ask, "Why did you have a rough day?"

"My dad was arrested."

"Oh, shit." I jump up from where I'm sitting, not sure if he needs a hug or just some sympathy or some other thing I haven't thought of. "Are you okay?"

His gaze moves to the floor, and he nods. "I tried calling Archer to let him know, but he didn't answer."

Naming my ex has the effect of throwing a bucket of cold water over my head. I sit back down. "I'm sure he knows." I blow out a breath. His relationship with his family has always been complicated. He chose to distance himself from the family when he found he preferred to pick up a baseball instead of a football, and he felt he made the right choice when nobody chased him to come back.

There's other stuff, too—reasons he's always felt like the black sheep, but before I can even form the thought, Ford cuts in.

"My dad called me when I was on my way home."

"He called you? From jail?"

He nods. "He told me to gather the funds for his bail. His arraignment is Monday, but his lawyers gave him an estimate."

"How much?" I breathe.

"Two to three million."

I gasp. The Bradleys are loaded, but putting up two million bucks to get their dad out of jail when he's going to end up right back there again anyway feels…well, a little outside my level of comprehension.

I do pretty well in my business. I'm a freelancer, so it's not like I have a boss taking half my wages—other than the government. I make enough that I'm ready to invest in some properties for myself, anyway.

Snap DECISION

But I can't imagine giving away two million dollars and having it tied up in the courts for however long this trial might take with the hope and prayer you'll get it back when you're betting on someone who's clearly guilty and would likely take any opportunity to flee.

Then again, if he was a flight risk, they wouldn't even grant him bail.

"What are you going to do?"

"Liam and I are going to chip in. It could be up to a year before we see that money back, so I'm going to put the mansion up for sale to pay us back in the short-term. And on that note, I need to head to Chicago after the weekend to survey what the place looks like after the feds searched it. You know, get it into tiptop shape to get it on the market ASAP."

I think of the Bradley Mansion with a feeling of nostalgia. It's a twenty-five thousand square foot monstrosity, one of the largest mansions in the city limits, and it was a place I hung out at often during my childhood. Mr. Bradley custom built the place before he and his wife filled it with a family, and the outside is all limestone with balconies on an enormous plot of land that overlooks the Chicago skyline. The inside is gorgeous. It had the kind of marble entryway that was fancier for prom pictures than the actual venue where prom was held.

Every time I pulled up to the gated mansion, my heart would race—and not just because I had a crush on Archer, who was nothing more than a close friend back in high school before we shifted to something more in college. It was because that mansion meant something.

Archer and I would sit out in the yard at night. We couldn't see the stars so close to the city, but we'd stare at the Chicago skyline as we dreamed together about what would come next. He always knew he was going pro. Some people are just *that good*, and he is. I was the only person he ever opened up to, though.

It's not just nostalgic because of Archer, though. I became friends with Ford then, too, and even though we've gotten closer in more recent years, I remember laughing until I cried about the stupidest things when we were supposed to be working on homework.

But they weren't stupid when they meant so much—when I'd go home to my smaller house several miles away with an aching stomach from laughing so hard and wishing I could just stay just a little longer at the Bradleys' house.

And the kiss.

The kiss we never spoke about again.

The kiss that was probably never meant to happen. The one he never mentioned and probably was too drunk to remember.

I push that thought away.

We were just friends back then, but that didn't mean my parents would allow me to sleep over there like they did at my girlfriends' houses.

I did once—after senior prom when all of the couples in our group returned to the mansion to spend the night. It was pretty much the entire baseball team, and it was against Archer's wishes, but he had the biggest house and therefore the most space to accommodate the twenty kids on the team plus their dates.

"I'd love to help. Can I come with you?" I ask. "The mansion means a lot to me."

"I'd love for you to come," he says quietly, and the way he says it shows me how much he cares for me. Just a few simple words have that power coming from him. "And it means a lot to all of us, but it's also worth a shitload of money. It's just a house. It'll still stand there, and we've got the pictures to remember it."

Snap DECISION

I press my lips together. It feels like a cold response. "You're not sentimental," I say, and it's not an accusation so much as stating a fact.

He shakes his head. "No, I'm not. But even if I was, it doesn't make sense to keep that much money tied up in a house that no longer serves its purpose. You know? My father is in trouble, and he needs the money. We grew up there, but people move all the time. My parents don't need a mansion with nine bedrooms anymore. We don't know how much time my mom has left. We don't know how long my dad will be in prison if he's found guilty. Ivy still lives at home, but it'd be easy enough for her to find somewhere to settle in that isn't a twenty-five thousand square foot mansion for one person."

He looks nearly vulnerable as he says the words, and it's an interesting contrast—the big, bad starting tight end for the Tampa Bay Beasts versus the intellectual strategist trying to imagine solutions for his baby sister as his family falls apart. Maybe he's more sentimental than he realizes.

"Anyway, I'll let you get back to work. I'm going to order dinner from downstairs. You want anything?" he asks.

I nod. "I'm in the mood for spaghetti and meatballs. Again."

"You got it," he says, and he ducks off to let me return to my work.

I stare at the papers in front of me as our conversation plays over in my mind. He'd love for me to come with him. He thinks I'm brilliant.

Why does he have to be so kind, so cute, and also so off-limits?

I'm certain the contrast is only fresh in my mind because of my recent breakup. As I focus on Archer and what brought me here to escape for a few days, I realize that maybe love just isn't for me. It's not for everyone.

So I'll continue to craft dream weddings for others but maybe never for myself.

CHAPTER 8

FORD BRADLEY

A Kickass Wedding Venue

We win on Sunday, and Monday morning finds me sitting on an airplane with Tatum Barker occupying the seat beside me.

She's wearing a black dress and black heels, while I'm in jeans and a Beasts shirt. She looks gorgeous and far too good to be seated beside me. I mean, considering she's not mine, yeah…she is too good to be seated beside me.

I'm reviewing film on my tablet—which I'm currently holding since she asked if I could put my tray table down so she could have a little extra space. Currently on my tray table are a water bottle, a cup of coffee, and five file folders with papers hanging out of them. A handful of glitter highlighters sit on top of the folder, and I've already had to pick up several off the floor because they keep rolling off the tray table. She picks up one color to use it, and when she sets it back, I have to grab it before it falls.

And despite all that, it's somehow endearing.

Snap DECISION

She has a color for everything, and my eyes edge over to her as I try to make sense of it. Pink is for the bride. Blue is for the groom. Green is for anything to do with payments. Yellow is for vendors. She also has a red Sharpie that's for urgent matters. All glitter, except for the Sharpie.

I glance over at her, and she's blowing a breath upward to get her hair out of her face. She tucks a strand behind her ear, which immediately comes untucked, and she glances at her wrist to find it empty before she starts rearranging everything on her tray table to get to her purse under the seat in front of her. She fishes out a scrunchie and ties her hair on top of her head.

It's adorably distracting, and I don't get much of the film analyzed before we land.

I'm too spellbound by her.

I arranged for a driver while we're in town, and he greets us at the bottom of the escalator near baggage claim. We didn't bring luggage since this is a same-day-turnaround kind of trip. Our driver leads us to the car waiting on the curb outside.

It's nearly an hour before we're pulling up in front of the mansion, and I do manage to analyze a few plays on the way there. I hear a gasp beside me, and that's when I see her leaning around me to get a better view of the mansion.

"God, I forgot how gorgeous this place is," she murmurs, and I physically see a transformation take place in her eyes. She seems suddenly...excited.

I stare at the house, too, as I try to figure out what she's thinking.

This mansion holds a lot of memories for us. A lot of history. It's not just a part of my family, but she was a part of it, too.

The place where we shared that kiss I've never forgotten about.

I wish she remembered it, too. I wish she felt what I did when it happened. I wonder how that would have changed our lives if she had.

We get out of the car, and I walk up to the front gate. I tap in a code, and after it opens, I walk up the long sidewalk leading to the front door, ready to go in and assess the damage left behind.

But I find myself alone.

I turn around, and I see Tatum staring up at the front of the house. Her head is tilted as she studies it, and it's my voice that seems to snap her out of her trance.

"You ready to go in?" I ask.

"Oh!" she says, and she rushes to my side. "Sorry. It's just so iconic. Such a vibe, you know?"

I lift a shoulder. "Sure."

She laughs as she smacks my bicep playfully, and we head inside as I brace myself.

The foyer looks...well, just like it always has. The entry to our home is huge, over six hundred square feet of wasted space, including a rotunda and white marble floors inlaid with gold veins.

"Hello?" I call out, curious if anyone's here—sometimes a chef or a repair worker, oftentimes a housekeeper or other staff member.

No one answers.

I glance over at Tatum, whose eyes are wide.

"It's like a fallen kingdom," she murmurs.

I glance around as I try to see what she sees.

It looks the same to me. I walk through the entry and across the house. Everything looks like business as usual. Maybe Dad already sent someone in to clean up.

It's not until I get to my father's office that I sort of see what she's talking about.

Drawers look like they've been upended.

Snap DECISION

Paperwork spills onto the floor, covering every surface, including the leather couch that lines one wall. Like he'd really be stupid enough to keep records of his illegal dealings here in the house. Maybe he was.

Maybe they found something, but the knocked-over lamp and broken artwork that once hung on the wall to the left of the desk tell a different story. They came, they searched, they couldn't find what they were looking for, and they destroyed in frustration.

Another painting hangs crooked, and the perfectionist inside has me walking over to it. I straighten it, and that's when I hear her soft gasp at the doorway.

"They made a mess," Tatum murmurs.

I turn and nod. "Fallen kingdom," I repeat. I walk over to the desk and gather some of the paperwork. It looks like files for the Bradley Group. It appears to be contracts for construction work, not anything to do with an illegal gambling ring.

Tatum helps, gathering papers off the couch. I can't help but wonder what my father is doing right now. Has the arraignment happened yet? Is he still in jail? Should I go visit him?

I'll hear from Liam. He's going to the arraignment. He'll let me know what bail is set at, and we'll make the call to our financial advisors to move forward with dividing it by two and putting the money to cover it into a new account.

It takes a while to straighten the office, and we work in silence. We walk through the dining room toward the kitchen, and she seems to be sizing the place up as I look in every corner to assess whether there's any more damage or if his office took the brunt of it. It could take a while to go through this entire place, and maybe it's a job for someone else to handle.

I look around for anything and everything that might need to be fixed, painted, or otherwise dealt with before we list it. I'll send a professional in to do the same to get the listing up as quickly as we can, but I'm glad I came to assess what needs to be done.

When we get to the kitchen, I glance at the space where the keg was all those years ago, when our lips met and then our tongues danced for the briefest of moments before we were forced apart.

Tatum nearly immediately lifts herself up onto the huge kitchen island countertop. She swings her legs for a beat as she sits there, and then she moves to a stand.

In her heels.

I move over and wrap my arms around her legs by her knees to steady her. It's an automatic move on my part with no other intentions meant, but my hands are on her gorgeous, smooth legs, and my dick vibrantly and willfully jumps to attention.

She sets her hand on my shoulder. "I'm fine," she assures me, but I don't move.

"You're in heels. I saw the way you couldn't keep your highlighters on the tray table. I'm not taking any risks."

She giggles.

"What the hell are you doing up there, anyway?"

She holds her hands out to indicate the space. "Picture this, Ford. We could knock down a few walls, separate the kitchen from the rest of the space, and fix it up a little, and this would be a freaking *kickass* wedding venue."

"I'm sure it would be, Tate. But you know I'm here to list it. Do you have fifteen million lying around to stop me?" I ask.

She pushes my hands away and hops down as if she's not wearing high heels. "Come here," she says, walking out of the kitchen. She taps the wall of the dining room that separates it from the entry. "We take down this wall." She walks out of that room and toward the study on the other side of the entry. "We take down this wall. We unify the flooring, of course, and we have this grand ballroom." She nods to the other walls in the entry. "We open those up, too."

"What about the staircase?" I ask, not because I'm on board with this plan but more out of genuine curiosity.

"A gorgeous backdrop for dreamy wedding photos or beautiful ceremonies. There's, what, twelve or so thousand square feet of space on this floor, minus the kitchen? That's enough for three hundred guests or even more, depending how we set it up. Upstairs could be bridal suites for the wedding party to get ready. Maybe an office."

I can almost see her vision as I listen to the excitement in her tone.

"I see fairy lights and floral arches over here," she says, pointing out the spaces. "And the backyard is a perfect backdrop for a spring wedding or for a photo backdrop any time of the year. It's literally the perfect venue. We could do outdoor or indoor depending on the weather. Big or small."

Jesus, she's gorgeous when she's impassioned and excited.

It doesn't matter, though. Liam is depending on me to get our money back so we can continue to grow it with interest for ourselves rather than tying it up in the legal system. Neither of us wants to be out a million dollars or more.

"I've looked at other venues in the area, Ford," she says. "I want a place here in Chicago. It's home. And this mansion? *This* is home. Literally for you, but also for me. Nothing compares to this. Not even close."

"I get it, but I'm sorry. I need to sell it."

"Can we just talk to Madden? To get an estimate and see if it would even work? I'd want him on the project. No one would give this wonderful space the sort of care it deserves more than someone who grew up here, and I already have the vision. I just need to know what it would cost to execute it."

"Fifteen million plus your construction fees," I say flatly.

She presses her lips together and nods, disappointment written all over her expression. "I get it. I don't have that kind of money, and I know you need to unload it quickly. I have some money in my trust fund, but it wouldn't be enough. I just...there has to be some solution. I feel more attached to it than I was expecting. Don't you?"

I glance toward the kitchen again.

The kiss. The memories. The history.

Maybe I'm a *little* more attached than I was expecting to be.

It's an incredible place, but home is wherever you make it, and that's Tampa now—far away from the father committing crimes, the mother who saw her seven children as more of a burden than a blessing, and the six siblings who send the occasional group message to each other and everyone replies except for Archer.

"Even if I did feel attached, it wouldn't matter," I say. "My dad put it in my name because he knew I'd know what to do with it when the time came. The time has come."

Her chin tilts down as she frowns a little. "Can you just make me a promise?"

My eyes meet hers, and she's got me. Of course I can make her a promise.

"Don't sell it without helping me explore all the options first. Okay? I just think you'll regret it if you pawn it off the second you have the chance to. I want to preserve this place in a way that could give hope and joy instead of this fallen kingdom we see now."

I press my lips together and nod. "We'll explore the options."

Snap DECISION

I say the words because she asked me to. But then I continue working my way through the house to figure out what needs to be done so I can get this house on the market.

CHAPTER 9

Tatum Barker

Garden Party Fundraiser

It's a whirlwind trip to Chicago, and we're back on the last flight out of Midway, heading back to Tampa before midnight.

I get that Ford is choosing his sense of obligation here, but there has to be *some* solution.

My trust fund isn't anywhere near the size of the ones with the last name *Bradley* on the account. But it would be enough for a down payment. The problem is that I don't have enough liquid assets to finance the monthly payments, and it would obliterate my plans to have several venues in different places since all my money would be tied up in one place.

I should let the idea go. But I just can't stop picturing the fairy lights and the floral archways and the white marble…or that damn kiss in that damn kitchen twelve years ago. The nights of laughter. The time Ford made popcorn in the kitchen, and I went down to get a bowl for Archer and me to share, and a popcorn-tossing contest erupted where we each threw a kernel in the air to see how high we could get it and still catch it. He won. I laughed.

I meant what I said to him. I don't want him to rush into this sale. I know he loves his family. He pretends he isn't loyal to them since he's so far removed geographically from everyone else, but I know his heart, and I truly think he'd feel regret if he sold it off to the first bidder when we can work together to find ways to keep it in the family.

The family I'm no longer a part of…or never really was, I suppose. It *felt* like I was, though, and not just because I was with Archer so long. Ford feels like family, too.

On top of all of that, I can't stop seeing myself in white as I stand on that gorgeous staircase lost in thoughtful ruminations as I create the perfect wedding day photos with my husband.

His face is blurry in my daydream. Still, I can't stop seeing it.

It's so vivid and so real in my thoughts that I'm too distracted to work on the plane ride home. Ford's quiet, too, but he's watching football stuff on his tablet, so I close my eyes and first try to come up with a solution, but when that feels totally futile, I allow myself to dream of just exactly how grand it could be.

Dream big or go home, right?

Well, I'm doing both, apparently. Except I don't really have a *home* at the moment. I'm mooching off two different friends because I needed to run away from Vegas for a while, and now I'm getting these big ideas that are probably too big to accomplish.

Ford doesn't have practice on Tuesdays, but he's in meetings all day in his home office. He talks to his lawyer, his agent, his financial advisor, and who knows who else.

My phone starts to ring just after lunch, and I'm shocked when I see it's Archer calling.

"Hi," I answer quietly. I head out to the terrace to take the call.

"Hey."

"Are you okay?" I ask.

"I'm holding up."

"I assume you heard about your parents," I say. Ford got a call shortly before we had to leave for the airport while we were still at the mansion about how much the judge set bail at, and from the way he choked on the phone call, I don't assume it was a small amount.

"Yes."

"Is the FBI still looking into you?"

"I actually called to talk about the fundraiser," he says, dodging my question.

He asked me to plan a fundraiser for his foundation ages ago, and I created this cute little evening garden party fundraiser with a live band. The entire thing has been booked and planned for months, but I'll need to get back to town a few days prior to the event to hammer out the last-minute details.

"What about it?" I ask.

"Is everything still on?"

"You think because you dumped me that I'd be so unprofessional as to fuck over your event?" I ask, more than a little bruised that he'd think so little of me after we were together for so long.

"Of course not, Tate. And you know I didn't *dump* you. That's not what happened."

"Felt like it," I mutter petulantly.

"I'm sorry," he says, his voice all low and raspy in that way he does when he really means something. "I just need everything to go off without a hitch since I'm still being watched."

Snap DECISION

It feels like code. Like he can't talk about it—maybe his phone is tapped, or someone's watching. He can't be too careful.

In any event, I miss what we once had. We weren't destined to make it to forever, and I've come to terms with that.

It still sucks *big time* to have your entire world flipped upside down. We were friends first, and I miss our friendship.

I blow out a breath. "Everything is set in place. I'll check in a week before the event to let you know if we need anything."

"Okay. Thanks."

"Mm-hmm." I very nearly let it slip. *K, love you, bye!*

It was the way I always ended our calls.

Not anymore.

"Well, talk to you then," I say instead. I cut the call before he can say anything else, and then I promptly burst into tears.

And wouldn't you know it? That's how Ford finds me after he finishes up his calls.

"What's wrong?" he asks gently as he settles into place on the chair beside the one I'm occupying.

"Nothing," I lie.

"You can tell me."

I draw in a deep breath and sniffle, and then I wipe my eyes as I square my shoulders. "Archer called. He wouldn't talk to me about the big stuff, and then he presumed to suggest that I'd be immature enough to drop the ball on a charity event I'd been planning for him because of what happened between us. Between that and you selling the mansion, I don't know. It's just been a disappointing twenty-four hours, you know?"

"I know." He reaches over and squeezes my forearm. "I'm really sorry. And I wanted to let you know the mansion is listed."

All the air deflates out of me at his words. It felt like there was still a chance when it wasn't listed, but whoever took that listing, of course, would work quickly because of the sheer scale of how much he or she could make off the deal.

"But I also have good news," he says before I can beg him to help me figure out how we can save the mansion.

"What?"

"You know Devon Pratt?" he asks.

My brows push together as I shake my head a little. "Who?"

He chuckles. "I thought you said you watched every single one of my games."

I hold a hand to my chest. "No, I said I put every single one of your games on. I didn't say I paid attention."

He barks out a laugh at that. "Fine. He's the safety."

"Safety?" I ask, wrinkling my nose in confusion. "Like a security guard?"

He laughs. "No. He's on defense. Anyway, he proposed to his girlfriend."

"Good for him," I say, throwing out a sarcastic thumbs-up. I'm out here crying about how I'm decidedly *not* getting married and especially not at my dream location, and he's all excited about some dude I don't even know who *is* getting married? I'm not sure what the hell he's going on about, but I don't need him rubbing everyone else's happiness in my face when I'm back to square one where my own happiness is concerned.

"Tate." He says my name like a command, and I glance over at him. "He's getting *married*. Here in Tampa. He's planning a wedding."

"Yes, as people tend to do when they propose and the other person says yes."

Snap DECISION

"Oh my God, you're hardheaded. He's going to need someone to plan that wedding. You plan weddings. Are you getting it yet?"

It hits me all at once, and I feel the tension start to dissipate from my chest. I leap up from my chair as it finally hits me. "Oh! Oh my God, I need to score that wedding! If you don't mind me staying here with you a little longer, of course."

"You're welcome here as long as you need," he says quietly as he stands, too. "And I'll gladly hook you and Lindsay up. That's Devon's fiancée."

I glance over at him, and I swear for the tiniest second his eyes flick to my lips. I can't help but lick them a little self-consciously, as if maybe some of the yogurt I ate for lunch has gathered in a crevice and I hadn't felt it. There doesn't seem to be anything there.

"You're the best, Ford. Thank you." I move to give him a hug, and his arms wrap around me, warm and strong and tight.

It feels good here.

It feels great here, actually. Tampa, this condo overlooking the city, the arms of this kind and gorgeous man who so effortlessly seems to want to support me and my career despite the whole thing with the mansion.

I try my hardest to let that go.

He's trying to make up for it, and it's not mine to have no matter how much of a dream it might be. That's all it can be—a dream.

Sort of like whatever it is I'm starting to feel for Ford Bradley.

CHAPTER 10

FORD BRADLEY

Winston Manor

Lindsay and Devon hired Tatum immediately when they checked out her Instagram page dedicated to the work she's done, and she spends the week learning the atmosphere here in Tampa while I work hard at practice. When I get home each night, she's curled up on the couch watching some show about weddings. She pauses it, sits up, and fills me in on her day, and she listens and asks questions as I talk about my day.

It feels like everything I want out of life—you know, except the sex part. Or the no-sex part, as the case may be.

What we have is intimate and close, but there's a clear line in the sand separating what we have from romance.

Still, the base is there. The bones. The foundation. It's strong, and maybe that's why it hurts so much that we can't go any further than where we are.

It's Monday afternoon, and I just got off the phone with my lawyer when I walk into the kitchen, rubbing my forehead. She's there, too, refilling her giant water bottle, a purse slung across her body and sunglasses perched on her head, holding her hair back from her face.

She glances up at me when I walk in. "I'm off to view a couple venues. I don't have appointments or anything. This is more of a vibe check, a pre-appointment visit if you will. Want to join me?" she asks.

It wasn't really on the list of things I want to accomplish today, but I also don't want to pass up the chance to spend a little extra time with her.

With that in mind, I nod. "Sure, I'd love to."

I drive and she navigates, and every passing moment I spend with her shows me just what a powerful team we are. We arrive at the first venue, take a quick tour, and meet back in the car. She shakes her head. "It's a no from me."

I tilt my head and, out of curiosity, ask, "Why?"

"The carpeting."

I chuckle. "The carpeting?"

"People want these grand photographs of their wedding. Every moment captured. I can't have Lindsay and Devon walking into their reception on that hideous carpet."

"So put down a red carpet or something," I suggest.

She shakes her head. "We're not going for a cheesy vibe, Ford."

I hold up both hands. "What's cheesy about a red carpet? Devon's a celebrity."

"Devon's an athlete, and it seems to me that red would be the competition's color. Right?"

"I suppose so," I say, thinking of the *other* team in Tampa Bay.

"It's not the vibe we're looking for. Next up is the Lowell House."

"Lowell House?" I repeat as she punches the address into her phone to pull up a map to get us there.

"Lindsay wants simple and elegant. This is near downtown, very elegant, coastal and cosmopolitan at the same time."

"Let's do it." We head to Lowell House, which is actually a gorgeous venue that Tatum puts directly at the top of her list.

We view a few others, and it's really kind of amazing to watch her at work. She knows as soon as we pull into the parking lot at one place that it won't work because, according to her, "This parking lot can't accommodate the number of guests they want."

We navigate next to a place right on the water, Winston Manor. It's a gorgeous mansion, very Florida with its stucco exterior that could use a fresh coat of paint but otherwise looks pristine.

When she tries the handles on the large double doors, they're locked.

She glances at me, and I try them, too—and I find the same, as if she didn't just try it to find it locked.

"Maybe try the doorbell?" she suggests.

I push the button, and it's one of those ones with a camera. A voice comes through a speaker I hadn't seen.

"Be right there!"

A woman who looks to be in her eighties opens the door. "Can I help you?"

"I'm Tatum Barker, and this is Ford Bradley. How are you today?" Tatum asks, clearly nudging the woman to share her name, but she doesn't.

"I'm fine, dear."

Tatum clears her throat. "We are interested in viewing the manor for an upcoming wedding."

"Oh, dear. You're a lovely couple, but I'm afraid I have some terrible news," the woman says.

Snap DECISION

Tatum and I glance at each other, not bothering to correct her assumption that we're the couple who wants to get married here as we wait for her to spill it.

"Unfortunately, we've had to close our doors to future weddings. We're in the process of trying to find a buyer, but everyone we've talked to wants to gut it and turn it into a mansion. Winston Manor has been in the Winston family for four generations. It's hard enough to sell it. To imagine someone gutting it simply guts *me*. I won't do it." She shakes her head adamantly.

"Oh, that is terrible," Tatum says, peeking past the woman into the space. "You wouldn't consider allowing me to host a wedding here? One final dream day for a beautiful couple before you sell it?"

She sighs heavily. "I'm too old to host another wedding, I'm afraid." She clearly missed the part about Tatum being the host. "I'm the last Winston generation. I never had any children, and I have nobody to leave the manor to. I want it in good hands, so I'm working quickly to find the right buyer. That's taking up all my time right now."

"What are you looking to sell it for?" Tatum asks quietly. She keeps her gaze focused on the woman rather than glancing at me.

"Five million dollars, contingent on a clause that this plot of land cannot be rezoned to residential."

Holy fuck. That's a bargain for this place.

She must not be trying very hard to sell it.

Tatum clears her throat. "I'm a wedding planner, Ms. Winston. I have a vision to buy wedding venues and create dream weddings for my clients. It feels like fate that I came here last today after viewing disappointing venue after disappointing venue only to fall immediately in love with this one before even stepping foot inside. Would you allow us to come in and take a look around?"

She looks surprised by the question, but she opens the door.

We step inside and walk around the first floor, which is basically a huge, open space with a gorgeous view out the back, perfect for a wedding ceremony, a reception, or both. And no red carpet—it's all hardwood floors in here.

The wall along the right side of the room has a set of double doors on it, and the side by the entryway has a beautiful staircase all the way on the left.

"Right here is where the last wedding had the aisle, with the ceremony taking place in front of the windows," she says, and Tatum walks the path the last bride walked.

Jesus Christ.

For just a second, I imagine her in a white dress, and I picture myself standing there in a tuxedo by the windows waiting for her.

I shake the vision out, but it's strange how vivid it is even if it was just for a fleeting moment in time.

Ms. Winston shares the history of the place as we tour the first floor with her, ending up outside in the kind of backyard even I can visualize as the perfect place to hold an elegant wedding reception.

"Winston Manor was built originally in the eighteen hundreds as the home for Martha and Gene Winston, my great-grandparents. When a great gale came through in the late eighteen hundreds, it was one of the few structures that was untouched. They passed the manor to their only son, Gunther. Then the hurricane of nineteen twenty-one blew through, and the home was badly damaged. He rebuilt it, keeping the majority of the framework, but he didn't want it to be his primary residence any longer, so he created Winston Manor, a place where people could begin their happily ever afters. He was a romantic who would do anything to please my grandmother, and there was nothing she loved more than a good wedding. The two of them passed the manor to their only son, Arthur, my father, who passed it to me. We've gone through many renovations over the years, both structural and aesthetic, but the heart of the manor has always been meant for love stories, perhaps like yours." She smiles as she nods toward the two of us, and then she heads back inside and through the double doors we hadn't entered into yet.

We're taken into a vast and expansive commercial kitchen, already supplied with everything anyone would need to cook up the perfect first meal for the bride and groom.

The entire time the woman talks to us, that same vision keeps popping into my head. Tatum walking down the aisle. Me waiting at the end.

I can't shake it out no matter how hard I try.

"This is our back-of-house kitchen, and the stairs over there lead up to the office, which is where I was when you rang. Upstairs are the office, restrooms, an owner's suite, a bridal suite, and a groom's room. I also recently had an elevator installed behind the grand staircase because it's harder and harder for me to get up and down the stairs. The six-car garage has been converted to a storage space where we keep chairs, tables, that sort of thing. Would you like to see upstairs?" she asks.

Tatum nods. "Please."

She nods to the corner. "You're welcome to take those stairs. Give me a few minutes to meet you there."

"It's not necessary. We'll be quick," Tatum says.

"Okay, my dears. I'll be here, then." She pulls out a chair at a small table in the corner that is probably meant for tastings, and we head upstairs together.

"Oh my God," she whisper-screams at me once we reach the top of the stairs. A sprawling office stretches in front of us with a couple of desks, but the back wall is all windows, offering unparalleled views of Old Tampa Bay, the northwestern arm of the Tampa Bay estuary.

I had a feeling that's what she was going to say.

"Ford, this place is *perfect*. Don't you think?" She wanders through the large office and toward another hallway, where we find the elevator at the end of a long hallway that has the suites. Two on the left look out the front of the manor, and the one on the right is the owner's suite that looks over the water.

The owner's suite is huge. She's right. Everything about this place is perfect.

Especially that vision that is nothing more than my imagination working overtime.

"It's incredible, right?" she asks.

"It's more than incredible," I say carefully.

"It would blow my entire budget for my future plans, but I could put down half with my trust fund and finance the rest. This place would easily pay for itself in a few years. I had a couple of reno ideas for downstairs, and God, this view. Could you imagine the kinds of celebrity weddings I could hold here? It's not like I can purchase more than one venue at a time. It's a great dream to have, a beautiful goal, but I'm in love with *this* one."

"You were in love with the Bradley mansion yesterday," I remind her.

"I still am," she says quietly, her eyes flicking to mine. "But this one's a third of the price of that one and doesn't need much work. I could have it ready to hold a wedding in as little as a month or two pending staff hires, and I could turn it around and start making money immediately to fund my next venue—maybe even the mansion. Ugh, this place is just *so* perfect." She grabs my arm and links hers through mine. "Tell me I'm not crazy." She gasps. "Oh my God, Ford, do this *with* me. Reno this place with me while I'm here in town, help me oversee it when I have to get back to Vegas. Or even better, make this investment with me. We could each put up half, and we can figure out logistics to benefit you. Tax breaks, a great investment, a share in the profits, and all that, but we could also use it for team events. We could host charity events, luncheons, even team retreats or sponsorship events. Whatever we can dream up together. You and me, Ford Bradley."

Her arm is still linked through mine, and it's ridiculous. It's wild. I make *smart* investments. I'm careful and strategic with my money—barring the money I had to put up last week for my father's bail.

But this is Tatum Barker.

The woman I've been in love with for as long as I can remember. The *only* woman I've ever been in love with despite the fact that I'm knocking on thirty's door.

This gives me roots in Tampa, where my goal is to play for my entire career, and it gives me a potential project in the offseason and a potential direction once my playing days are over.

I never dreamed of planning weddings after my playing days.

But what I *did* think about was investing in real estate. I never defined what type of real estate, but event venues could be smart.

Still, none of that matters a single bit when the only thing I can think about is that it also gives me a connection to Tatum. It gives us something to work on together. It allows me to continue being with her, and it's something that we're setting up that's just for *us*, with no Archer on the periphery.

And that's why I'm not surprised when the words drop from my lips. "I'm in."

CHAPTER 11

Tatum Barker

Investment

My breath catches somewhere in my throat, and I freeze. "You're in?"

I was waiting for him to tell me what a wild, foolish idea this is. To be the voice of reason the way he often is.

Not to tell me that *he's in*.

But holy shit.

"Are you for real right now?" I ask, letting go of his arm and turning toward him.

A slow grin spreads across his face as he nods. "Totally for real."

I toss my arms around his neck, and he grunts a little at the sudden impact.

"You're not going to tell me this is a ridiculous idea?"

"I don't think it is ridiculous. I mean, obviously I've been surrounded by real estate investments like this my entire life, but learning my father made his money illegally makes me want to double down on finding ways to profit the *legal* way.

Snap DECISION

And owning a property like this at the sort of bargain price Ms. Winston mentioned here in Tampa seems like a no-brainer."

"How will we split it? How will you profit from it?" I ask, trying to quickly work out logistics before my excitement carries me away.

"Logistics my lawyer can work out for us." He glances out at the view again, and then he says, "I'm guessing he'll suggest I buy the place outright and you lease from me, but I know you want a stake. So maybe we do some sort of joint business entity where I get equity in the property and a share in revenue, and you get full creative control." He shrugs. "However you want to set it up. You've got the dream and the vision, and I've got the means to help you make it a reality."

"So you're here to make my dreams come true?" I ask, my tone light and teasing.

He nods. "That's exactly why I'm here." His voice is low and raspy, and there's some sort of promise in it that throws me for a loop.

It feels suddenly like we're talking about way more than just this property.

A sob breaks out of me. A full-on, ugly sob, because after everything felt like it was falling apart, somehow Ford Bradley is here to put it all back together.

He grabs me into a hug.

"Are you sure about this?" I wail into him.

"Positive," he says quietly.

After I pull myself together, we head back down to the kitchen, where Ms. Winston sits at the table in the corner. We walk together to the table, and I pull out a chair and sit across from her.

"Ms. Winston, this is the loveliest property I've ever come across in all my years as a wedding planner. It would be my honor to make you an offer," I say.

She reaches across the table, and I set my hands in hers. Hers are cold as she squeezes mine. "I felt it when you walked in, my dear. The two of you create a light this old manor needs. But I must warn you, I have a list of conditions that have driven every other buyer away."

"Hit me with them," I say.

"The inside may be renovated but not gutted, and the manor must continue to be used for love stories," she begins.

I nod. "Weddings, engagement parties, anniversary events. I can picture them all here. I can also see team building or charity events here, which is just a different sort of love."

She tilts her head a little and squints at me, and then she nods. "Yes, I agree with you. Any celebratory event. I also must ask that the manor never be rezoned."

"Agreed," I say.

"I also demand that the original architectural features remain intact in the way my great-grandparents intended."

"Of course. It's a natural beauty, and I wouldn't dream of changing it."

"I'd like to honor my family's legacy by keeping the name Winston Manor even once it sells," she says quietly.

"It's already a known wedding venue in this town, and I don't see any reason to change it. In fact, I'd love to honor the Winston legacy with a plaque on one of the walls near the entry."

She looks nearly emotional at my words. "That would be lovely, sweetheart."

"Is there anything else?" I ask.

"I'd like to attend the weddings you hold here for as long as I can." There's a twinkle in her eye when she adds, "Maybe even one between the two of you."

𝒮𝓃𝒶𝓅 DECISION

I squeeze her hands, which are still in mine, not bothering to correct an old woman who's excited to sell this place to me. "I'd be honored to have you as a guest and would love to consult with you on the things you've done here."

"I would love to help in any way I can." She sighs and sniffles a little as she presses her wrinkly lips together. "This is harder than I thought. My last question is whether you have the five million dollars. This must be an all-cash closing with no contingencies."

I smile, and I glance up at Ford, who's standing behind me as we talk. He nods almost imperceptibly, and I look back at Ms. Winston.

"We do."

She doesn't smile, but her eyes look deeply into mine when she says, "Then it sounds like we have a deal."

A ripple of excitement races through me.

Holy shit. We're actually doing this.

She pulls out her phone and dials a number, and then she puts the call on speaker.

"Ms. Winston," a man answers. "Always a pleasure to hear from you."

"And you, Mr. Graham. I have here with me today a young couple interested in purchasing the manor. They have the cash and have agreed to the terms," she says.

"How wonderful that you've found your buyer. Let's set an appointment for next Tuesday at my office to sign the paperwork and transfer the funds. Is that enough time?" he asks.

She looks at the two of us.

I glance up at Ford, and then I nod at Ms. Winston. "That's plenty of time for us."

"And you are…?" Mr. Graham asks.

"Tatum Barker, and I have with me Ford Bradley. We'll be purchasing the manor."

"Ford Bradley...as in *the* Ford Bradley?" he asks, his emphasis on the *e* in *the*. "The Beasts' tight end?"

"Yes, sir," Ford says.

"Well, I guess that means you've got the capital for this deal," he says with a laugh.

Ford laughs, too. "The organization was very generous with my paycheck."

"They only do that when a player's performing, you know," Mr. Graham says.

"Thank you," Ford says. "I'm just out there doing what I love."

"And apparently investing in real estate," Mr. Graham adds.

"Yes. My family is in real estate, and I know a great investment when I see one." I glance up at him, and he's looking down at me.

His words say one thing, but his eyes are telling me another.

He's not investing in this property. He's investing in me. He believes in me and in my wild dreams.

And I can't wait to make him proud.

CHAPTER 12

FORD BRADLEY
Honey and Fig

It's back to practice on Wednesday, and it feels good to be back on the field with my teammates. A lot has happened in the last seventy-two hours since my cleats last hit the turf when we won on Sunday, and getting back on the field is the best way to clear my mind. Sometimes it's the *only* way.

And by the time I've finished blocking drills, I feel confident I'm doing the right thing.

It's an investment, plain and simple. In real estate.

Does it help that it's with someone I've known for years? Sure. Of course.

But my feelings for her aren't part of the equation.

I say that over a few times to try to believe it, but it's pretty useless.

Of course my feelings play into it. It's a thread holding us together. It's just for us. My brother has nothing to do with it. It gives her a reason to come back to town, a reason for her to trust me. It's setting us up to continue our friendship beyond whatever happened with her and my brother.

How could I say no to that?

I couldn't.

Just like I can't say no when she invites me to an after-hours cake tasting on Wednesday.

"It's one of the busiest, best bakeries in the area, and I *had* to try them. So I told them you might be coming with me to the tasting, and they offered a private slot after closing so you wouldn't be mobbed by your loyal fan base. Don't be mad," she says, and she folds her hands and holds them up under her chin.

It's a pose that's so goddamn adorable that I can't find it in me to say no.

Tatum plus free cake? Count me in.

"I could never be mad at you," I say softly.

"I'm sure I'll find a way," she teases, and then we head to the parking deck so I can drive us to the bakery.

"I forgot to tell you, I have a wedding in Vegas the Saturday after Thanksgiving, and then my garden party for Archer is the next weekend, so I'll need to head back there soon," she says.

"I was hoping you'd stay for Thanksgiving," I murmur. "It's fine if you can't. It's just—the team offers a meal for players who don't have anyone local. It inevitably ends with someone crying into their turkey about how much they miss their families."

"That's sad," she says.

"For the record, it's almost never me that's crying," I say dryly.

She giggles. "Almost never?"

"I'm joking. It's never once been me. I sort of prefer living out here on my own, you know? But it's been nice having a familiar face hanging around, so if you can stay for turkey…"

She tilts her head and thinks for a minute. "You sure you don't mind having me here?"

"I enjoy having you here. All this space to myself gets lonely." I'm worried I might start crossing lines with these confessions.

"Would it be okay if I invited my parents and my brother here, too? I've always wanted to attempt a big Thanksgiving meal, but my mom always made the turkey, and Arch and I always went there. Might be nice to pay her back and let her relax for once."

I chuckle as I picture Tatum in an apron, flour dusting her cheeks as she prepares a huge meal for her parents, her brother and his family, and me as we host her family for the holiday.

It sounds...

Well, it sounds too good to be true, for one thing. But it also sounds like a lot of fun. Her brother was in my class in high school, and we played football together back in the day. He didn't go on to play in college, and we lost touch, but we were good friends in high school.

"Absolutely," I say. "Invite everyone. I'm happy to help with the cooking. You know, by ordering food prepared in someone else's kitchen."

"God," she mutters, and I'm afraid I've offended her for a beat until she adds more. "You're just so *easy* to get along with. If I ever asked Archer if I could invite my whole family over, he'd eventually give in, but he'd gripe and moan about it."

I don't picture Archer as a griper or a moaner, but I've also never invited Tatum's entire family to my home before. If they're anything like Tatum, multiplying them could get interesting, I suppose.

"I aim to please," I say.

We arrive at Calla's Crumbs, the bakery Tatum is so excited about, to find the door locked, but we can see workers milling about behind the counter. A moment later, a woman who looks to be in her thirties appears at the door and opens it. "Welcome in," she says. "I'm Calla."

"Tatum," she says, sticking her hand out. "And this is Ford."

"Mr. Bradley," Calla says, clearly sizing me up. "We're big fans here at Calla's Crumbs."

"I appreciate it," I say. "And I'm a big fan of cake."

She laughs a little too heartily at a weak segue into why we're here. "Come on back to our tasting room and we'll get started."

She leads us through the quaint front of her shop and into a room on the side where a small table and chairs are set up. "Would either of you like champagne or some water to begin?" she asks.

"Champagne would be perfection," Tatum says, and I nod. I'm just along for the ride.

She snaps her fingers, and a moment later, someone appears with a tray and some glasses on it. Calla hands us the glasses, and we each hold them up.

"To cake," Tatum says, and I chuckle as I repeat her toast, tap my glass to hers, and take a sip.

We set our glasses down, and Calla begins her spiel.

"Typically our planner tasting tours are much busier, but as you are VIP clients, we've curated our most popular flavors for you to try today. I understand you're planning another football player's wedding, is that correct?" Calla asks, directing the question at Tatum.

She nods. "I'm in the process of purchasing a local venue for weddings, and I'm compiling a small list of the vendors my clients will be able to choose from. My first client here in the area is a teammate of Ford's."

"Which is why you're here today? Or you're a couple and she dragged you along?" Calla asks, clearly investigating whether Tatum and I are an item or not.

I offer a curt nod. "She asked, and I came."

"How lovely."

A moment later another woman appears with a tray, and she sets it on the table in front of us.

"We have our orange blossom with vanilla bean, lemon with lavender, raspberry with almond cream, and honey with fig for you to sample today," Calla says, pointing at each piece of cake that's also labeled on the tray. Two small tasting forks sit in each sample, so we don't mix the flavors on our forks.

I really want to ask where the normal flavors are. You know, yellow cake with chocolate frosting or chocolate cake with buttercream.

I don't think the question would go over well in this atmosphere.

"Let's start with the orange blossom," Tatum suggests, moving from left to right across the tray. We each take the fork and try it, and it's fine. A little flowery for me, to be honest. We try the lemon and lavender next, and then the raspberry with almond cream. They're all fine, but nothing as good as a nice slice of chocolate cake with a layer of that raspberry jelly shit in between. Or that Nutella cake Tatum mentioned once before.

"Finally, we have the honey and fig, two flavors often considered aphrodisiacs," Calla says.

I catch Tatum's eyes with mine, and I swear that a heated moment passes between us as we each pick up the fork with a bit of the cake on it. Rather than lifting the fork to her own mouth, though, Tatum's fork moves toward *my* mouth.

I'm not sure why she's feeding me the aphrodisiac-inspired cake, but as the sweet honey and caramelized fig touch my tongue, the way it melts in my mouth is unexpected and absolutely delicious.

I bring the other fork up to her lips, and her eyes are on mine as she opens her mouth, takes the fork, and closes her mouth over it. I pull it out, and it's clean. My dick wakes all the way up at the sensual way she did that. I watch as she closes her eyes and leans her head back with a moan at how fucking delicious the cake tastes, and I nearly come in my pants.

Fuck.

I need to pull myself together.

"It feels like it just got about a million degrees hotter in here," Calla says, interrupting the moment as she fans herself. "See? It's why it's labeled as an aphrodisiac and also why it's one of our top-selling flavors." Tatum's eyes haven't left mine despite Calla's interruption. "I'll give you two a moment to discuss."

She leaves the room—I think. I'm guessing. I hear a door click shut, but I haven't ripped my eyes away from Tatum's.

There's something here between us, and it's not just me.

What I do next is stupid, probably. Emotionally suicidal, maybe.

But I do it anyway.

As her eyes hold mine, I lean in toward her. I drop the fork, and my hand comes up to cup her jawline. She leans into my touch a little, and I brush a crumb of cake away that escaped to her lip. Her eyes flick down to my lips, too, and I get the sense that she wants me to kiss her.

God, do I want to kiss her.

And so I do.

I lean closer and closer until I can smell her, the sweet honey the pervading scent, but then, she always smells like honey, and maybe that's what is doing this to me. Smelling her, tasting her. Needing her.

Our lips connect, and it's the sweetest, softest brush of a kiss.

I want to dive in deeper, but I don't want to scare her off, either.

It's everything I've dreamed of since the day I realized I'm in love with her. Since the day I realized she deserved better than my brother. Since the day I met her, maybe, and definitely since the day I last kissed her.

She leans in, too, moving so one of her hands is gripping my bicep, the other sliding along my jawline. I let her take the lead, and she opens her mouth first, her tongue moving tentatively at first until she finds mine, and we dance.

The dance turns urgent, desperate, as I push everything I have into this kiss, as if I can make her fall in love with me through one single kiss filled with delusions.

I fucking love her, and kissing her like this is only going to ruin me.

Well, fucking ruin me, then. It'll be well worth it just to have lived in these seconds that are far too short.

The door opens again, and Calla's voice says, "Oh! So sorry."

The door closes, but it's too late.

Tatum realizes what we were doing, and she pulls back.

"I'm sorry," she says quietly. "We shouldn't—I shouldn't have. Um, you know. We can't."

Can't we? I want to ask her why, even though I already know why. We can't ruin this friendship with feelings.

Especially not now that we agreed to become business partners by co-purchasing a wedding venue.

It's too messy. Too hard. Too wrong.

But that one single kiss told me everything I needed to know—or confirmed everything I already knew.

I'm hopelessly in love with Tatum Barker, and I'm pretty damn sure there won't ever be anyone else who could possibly measure up to her.

CHAPTER 13

Tatum Barker

Out of the Question

It's not as fun to preview various vendors by myself, but it's necessary today. Ford's at practice, for one thing, but for another…

We kissed.

He kissed me.

I kissed back.

This is Ford. Ford Bradley! He's my friend. He's the one I turn to when I can't turn to Archer.

Do I have *feelings* for him?

Only…

The kiss.

The *kiss*.

I think back to our first kiss again, back when I'd just finished my freshman year of high school, and I had a little crush on both Archer and his older brother, Ford.

Archer and I had classes together, so we spent more time together.

Snap DECISION

But if I was being really honest with myself, back then...it was Ford who I had the biggest crush on.

I swept that crush away when he seemed to sweep me away.

We kissed, and he pulled away. We never talked about it, and I assumed it was because he'd been drinking and didn't even remember it happened.

Regardless, I was in his friend zone. He saw me as belonging to his brother, and I was probably too young for him anyway. We were only two years apart, but in high school, that mattered. He was a senior, and then he went off to college, and he got busy with football.

Archer and I grew up together during those years, and we grew closer when Ford wasn't around as much. I pushed aside my feelings for Ford since they weren't reciprocated, and I got together with the other boy I had a crush on...the one who happened to be Ford's younger brother, the one who seemed to be the right pick for me.

But those old feelings are simmering at the surface again, and I can't just set aside this newer kiss like it didn't happen. It *did* happen, and it was magical. Thigh-clenching, belly-flipping, butterfly-flapping magic.

It was the first time I've kissed a man other than Archer since...well, since the last time we broke up, and I went out to a club with some friends, got a little tipsy, and let some guy kiss me on the dance floor. That had to be five years ago, and it was fairly forgettable.

The kiss last night with Ford was decidedly *not* forgettable since it's basically all I've thought about for the last twelve—nope, wait—thirteen hours.

It was the honey. Was it the honey? The fig? Some mind-bending alternate universe?

I don't know, but I'm not sure I ever imagined Ford and I would kiss again, and even if I ever *did* let the thought pop into my mind, I never could've possibly imagined how freaking *hot* it would be in reality.

But that's what it was. Hot. Hotter than hot.

Unexpectedly hot. Surprisingly hot. There's a chemistry there I wasn't expecting from a *friend*.

And now I'm a jumbled puddle using phrases like *hotter than hot* because I can't freaking think straight after what he did to me.

It was a *kiss*.

It was intimate and erotic, sexy and sensual, and now all I can think about is how if a kiss was that intense, what would *more* be like with him?

It's out of the question. Obviously. I mean, come on. He's Archer's brother. The guy I dated on and off for the last seven or eight years. God, was it really that long?

We started dating when we were sophomores in college. I needed a date to a formal, and he was my go-to guy. I asked him, we got a little tipsy, and he kissed me at the end of the night.

"We're doing this now?" I'd asked him. It was the one thing I always wanted, and he was finally giving in.

"Oh, we're doing this now," he'd said back to me, and then he went for it. Like, *went* for it. It was urgent and intense and hot, and the sex later that night was, too. It was *always* that way for us—urgent and intense and hot, but I think that's sort of just Archer's personality. Eventually all that fizzles, and then you're left with...

Well, you're left at the end.

We were only together for two months the first time we broke up. We were apart as long as we were together, and then we tried again. That time stuck. We were together for a couple years, and then I think I got scared when he graduated college and went to the minors. He spent a couple years in the minors, during which we were together. Eventually, he got called up to the majors and started with the Vegas Heat.

He's been there for four years now, and our relationship in-season was always more stable than out of season. Probably because we hardly had time to spend together. It's easier to stay together when you're never around someone. But put one fiery, passionate person against another, and sometimes things just explode.

Ford is milder. Calmer. Softer. Gentler. He makes me that way, too. He rubs off those good traits on me when I feel like I'm a hot freaking mess.

And somehow, last night, he showed me that he has that urgent, intense side to him, too. It was something I didn't see coming, but now it's something I want to explore. Only—I can't. Not with someone who's putting up with me when I needed to leave town for a while, and it's not just that we're friends on top of him being my ex's brother.

We're becoming business partners in a sense, and it would be far too complicated to introduce any sort of feelings into that equation.

And so we won't.

I'll set aside whatever this is I'm feeling. It was just a surprise. Maybe even just a show for Calla so she'd think we were a couple, just like we let Ms. Winston believe we were.

It's too soon anyway. Sure, things were over with Archer a long time ago, and yes, honestly, I'm pretty sure I've been ready to move on for some time. I stayed because things were comfortable and because I liked our life. We still had fun together even though the passion left, and I was content enough to stay if that's what he wanted. It wasn't. And now here we are, and I won't allow someone new to feel like a rebound because of some timeline imposed by societal standards.

Wait.

Is that why I set him up with Morgan?

What a confusing thought. Maybe those actual feelings I've relegated to the back burner were actually front and center much longer than I realized, and I tried to put him in a category of non-temptation by giving him a woman that seemed perfect for him. But she wasn't. And maybe she wasn't because *I am*.

Or not.

I can't let this become a mess, but it feels messy already.

I visit a few florists today, and I head home in Ford's SUV, a black Range Rover that errs on the side of conservative rather than flashy like a lot of his teammates drive, yet is still totally luxurious.

I'm wondering what tonight will be like when he gets home. I'm nervous, actually. Will we talk about that kiss? Will he bring it up? Will I? Will he do it again?

As it turns out, the answer to all of that is no.

He brings dinner in. He asks about my day as we sit on his terrace and eat out of takeout boxes. I ask about his as we sip wine together.

The kiss doesn't come up even though it's simmering between us.

Maybe it never will come up again.

But that would be a real shame since all I can think about is when the next kiss will be.

As the week ramps toward the end, Ford gets busier preparing for his matchup against the Titans this Sunday. He travels with the team, and I watch from his condo while I keep busy checking tasks off my to-do list.

I talk with my financial people and get the money ready for my half of Winston Manor. Ford's lawyer calls me to work out some of the details related to that, and I get in touch with my own lawyer to look over the contracts.

Snap DECISION

I book my flight back to Vegas for the day after Thanksgiving. I invite my family to Ford's place for the holiday.

I shop for a turkey and all the traditional sides. My brother's going to stop at a store on the way to bring the pies, and my mom's bringing her sweet potato casserole since they're driving up for the weekend. I'll be doing the rest, which will be…interesting.

And two days before Thanksgiving, on Ford's day off, we head to an office downtown to meet with Ms. Winston and her lawyer. We sign the paperwork, my hand trembling as excitement courses through me.

When it's all done, we're co-owners of a manor. A freaking *manor*.

"Want to go see it?" Ford asks after we leave the office. Ms. Winston stayed with her lawyer to finish up additional paperwork, but she let us know she didn't move a single thing since she was selling the manor as-is.

"Abso-friggin-lutely!" I practically yell, and he laughs as he picks me up and swings me around in a circle.

He sets me back down, and a heated moment passes between us.

He turns away first without a kiss this time, and I climb into the Range Rover as a jittery feeling settles over me.

I clutch the keys the entire way there, and once we pull in front of the gorgeous building, we walk up the sidewalk together toward the front door. I unlock it, and we walk inside.

I let out a breath, and I rush through toward the windows to take in the view.

"This is ours," Ford says, stepping into place beside me. "Can you believe it?"

I glance over at him, and maybe it's the way the light from outside is lighting his handsome face, or maybe I'm just nuts…but it feels like I'm seeing him in a whole new light.

This is *ours*. We own something *together*. We have this place that will tie us together for as long as we decide it will.

And it leaves me with a surprisingly giddy feeling.

I move away, breaking the spell holding our eyes together because I'm a little scared of what might happen if I don't.

I do a twirl across the large ballroom, and I imagine the beautiful weddings that will take place here. In a dream, maybe my own someday. In reality, likely not.

I push out the punch of sadness that presses in my stomach, and instead, I set off to explore my new property with my new business partner.

CHAPTER 14

FORD BRADLEY

Fake it for the Day

"Turkey, gravy, stuffing, mashed potatoes, cranberry sauce, dinner rolls, a salad...what am I missing?" Tatum asks me on Thursday morning. I had a short, early practice, and I'm already home with extra homework to review film ahead of Sunday's matchup.

"Green bean casserole?" I suggest. When she wrinkles her nose, I laugh. "You don't like it?"

She shakes her head vehemently as she feigns barfing.

"You've just never tried *my* GBC," I say, narrowing my eyes at her.

"They're all the same. Follow the directions on the can. Dump green beans, cream of mushroom soup, and the crispy onion things, add some milk, and pop it in the oven. Who the hell eats that garbage? The soup." She makes a face, and she actually does look a little green at the thought of it.

I shake my head with a laugh. "That's not how I make mine."

"Oh? Well, then. How, pray tell, do you make yours?"

"Can't tell you, but it's a secret family recipe." My grandmother on my mom's side used to make it before she passed, and it was a staple in my childhood. It's green beans mixed with a creamy garlic parmesan sauce and actual bacon pieces in it, and she always made it for me because of my love of bacon.

When my grandmother died, my mother gave me the recipe card, and I always make it on Thanksgiving. It's the dish I bring to the team gatherings, or sometimes I just stay home and make it for myself since I can't exactly fly home to be with my family given my career.

And that's why I happen to have all the ingredients on hand.

"What can I help with?" I ask.

"Besides your gross green beans, can you peel the potatoes?"

I shoot her a glare. "Hey, don't judge them until you've tried them."

She giggles. "Yes, chef."

"Your mom is bringing sweet potatoes, and your brother's bringing pies, right?" I ask.

She nods. "Yep. I need to toast the bread for my stuffing, too."

"I can help." We maneuver together around my kitchen, working in sync as we prepare the rather large meal. I move to put on some music, but she stops me.

"No music?" I ask.

She shakes her head. "Parade. Always the background sound of Thanksgiving. And after the parade, the dog show." She claps her hands together, and I remember her always having a soft spot for dogs.

I remember everything about her, and my feelings continue to grow despite everything.

It's been nearly two weeks since that kiss, over a week that we've co-owned the manor, and it *still* hasn't come up.

I want to do it again.

I haven't. I'm not sure the feeling is reciprocal.

"Are you excited to spend time with your family?" I ask instead, trying to make safe conversation that has nothing to do with kissing.

"I haven't seen Colton and Layla since Maddox's baptism," she says. "That was, oh…April. So seven months ago. Gosh, I bet Maddox has gotten *so* big since then. My parents came to Vegas to celebrate my birthday with me back in June, so still five months ago. It's always a good time to see them."

"Are you nervous?" I ask.

"How could you tell?"

I chuckle. "Because I've never seen an onion chopped as fine as that one."

She blows out a breath. "I haven't told them Archer and I broke up," she admits.

"Why not?"

She lifts a shoulder as she sets down the knife. "I don't know. I guess because it's been *so* on and off for us all these years, and I didn't want to hear the comments. *Again? For how long this time?* You know, that kind of garbage. I don't know how to express that it really is over this time."

"Is it?" I ask.

She lets out a frustrated sigh. "Not you, too."

"No, not me. I'm just trying to understand where your head's at so I can help you with them." I tell myself that's true. I ignore the nagging thought about how it's really for my own information.

"Yes, it is." Her voice is quiet, and she stares down at the onion while she talks. "It was over a long time ago, Ford. But after a while, if things aren't moving forward, and they're not moving backward, you're just sort of stuck. And we were stuck a long time. We were content, doing our own thing, not really communicating, not really together even though we were still together. So, in a lot of ways that are important to me, it feels like I've already moved on. But it's the optics, you know? They'll see that we *just* broke up, and they'll assume it means we'll get back together, and it's just…not a conversation I want to have today."

"Then tell them you've moved on," I suggest simply.

"With who?"

I lift a shoulder as if the answer is obvious because to me, it is.

Her jaw drops a little as she pieces together my meaning. "With *you*?"

I press my lips together. "Too wild?"

She snags her bottom lip between her teeth as she tilts her head and thinks it over. "It might be the only way to get them to back down so we can just have a relaxing, fun day and enjoy our turkey in peace."

"It's the perfect solution, right? We fake it for the day for their benefit," I say.

And maybe, just maybe, I'll get to kiss her again.

I don't push it, instead turning toward the fridge to grab the green beans once I've peeled all the potatoes. I start to wash and cut those, too, and I survey the mess on the counter.

It's a complete and total disaster. My kitchen has never seen a mess like this in all the years I've lived in this condo.

It's creativity at work, and I think I love it.

I love having a mess in here when I'm used to everything being neat and orderly. I love that Tatum breathes *life* everywhere she goes.

I love *her*, and I'm not sure what the fuck to do about it, so I'm waiting for her to twist that knife a little harder and tell me yes so I can at least act on my feelings for one day in the name of pretense.

"Let's do it," she finally says.

I school my expression despite the thrill racing through me, and I nod. "Okay, then. Let's do it."

I finish prepping the green beans, and I start cleaning the creative disaster without a word while she continues to work. Ten minutes before her family is set to arrive, she quickly changes her clothes and meets me in the kitchen once again.

She's stunning in a brown dress, her long, blonde hair tied up in a twisty thing, her blue eyes the color of the ocean on a sunny day, those freckles peppering her nose and cheeks adorably sexy even from across the room.

"So…exactly how are we doing this?" she asks.

"You tell me."

"I don't know. Just act natural," she suggests.

That shouldn't be too big a challenge.

My doorman calls up to let us know we have guests, and I tell him to send them up. A moment later, we hear a knock at the door. We exchange a glance, and I let out a breath while she smooths down the front of her dress.

And then we open the door.

Mr. and Mrs. Barker stand there with Tatum's brother, sister-in-law, and nephew behind them.

"Hey!" Tatum squeals, and the hugs and hellos commence.

"Ford, man, it's good to see you," her brother, Colton, says to me, giving me a bro-style hug. "This is my wife, Layla, and our son, Maddox."

"Nice to meet you," I say, shaking Layla's hand. "How old's your boy?" I ask.

"He turned one last month," Layla says. She looks at the boy and makes a silly face at him. "Such a big boy!"

He giggles, and it's clear they're a happy little family.

Snap **DECISION**

I greet Mr. and Mrs. Barker next, dressed in a matching floral dress (her) and button-down shirt (him), and they insist I call them Caroline and Larry.

The place seems to have filled with joy with her family here, and it's the sort of childhood I always wanted.

It's simple. It's small.

I see the way Tatum and Colton joke with each other, and I feel a twinge of jealousy. I love my family, of course. I wouldn't trade any of my siblings for only one single sibling.

But sometimes it was hard to feel like I fit in. Madden and Dex were six and four years older than me, respectively. I was close to Archer before we split paths and he chose baseball. Everleigh and I are close now, but we weren't always, with her being three years older than me. Liam was only three years younger than me, but it was a wide enough stretch that we were never particularly close growing up, and Ivy was a full nine years younger than me. My parents were too busy with work and charity events to bother with things that might bond their children together.

So here I am, twenty-nine and wishing for a family like Tatum's. It's just one more thing about her that seems ideal. Joining a family like hers would be a blessing.

"Come on in," I say once greetings are over and we've moved onto catching up in the entryway.

"Yes, right this way," Tatum says, and she links her arm around my waist. I toss mine around her shoulder, following her lead, and her family follows us into the family room. Her mom sets down her casserole dish, and Layla sets down a pumpkin pie and an apple pie.

"It smells fantastic in here," her dad says as we all take seats around the room, and all that's left once her family sits is the single recliner chair.

I nod to it to indicate that she should take it, and she shakes her head and gives me a look I can't quite decode.

"We've been busy prepping all morning," she says, and I take a seat. She plops on my lap, and oh, fuck, I wasn't expecting that. Being this close to her is *doing things* to me despite the fact that her family is here.

My hand sneaks up to her neck. I've always wanted to feel how soft her skin is there, and now I have my answer.

Soft enough to make my cock all the way hard.

I am so fucked.

"I'm just going to address the elephant in the room here," her mom says before we jump into another conversation. "What's going on between the two of you?" She circles a finger between her daughter and me.

Tatum glances back at me, and I chuckle.

"Oh, us?" I ask. I lift a shoulder as I try to casually act the way I think I'm supposed to act without looking like I'm acting.

"I guess I've always turned to Ford when things were tough, and I finally realized why. I've had feelings for him for a long time." Her eyes are on mine as she says the words, and Jesus, how I wish those words were true.

Those words rip me open and leave me feeling vulnerable. Exposed. Ruined.

She ruined me long ago.

She turns back to her mother. "So when I turned to Ford this time after my split with Archer was final, I decided to finally act on how I think I always felt. And this feels more right than anything I've ever felt." She leans forward and presses a soft kiss to my lips, one that's so gentle and feminine that it nearly kills me.

There's no way in hell she isn't feeling my erection digging into her ass.

Her words may be stretching the truth, but mine are sincere. "And I felt the same. All those years I spent pining for Tatum were well worth it."

Snap **DECISION**

Caroline clasps her hands together and holds them under her chin. "This is just so sweet! I always adored Ford," she says, her eyes bright with tears as they land on me.

She did? Tatum's mother always *adored* me?

"It's true," Larry says. "We've always been much more of a football family, right, big guy?" he says to Colton, slapping him on the back.

"That's right. We all did our best with Archer. He's a good dude, but I never saw it, you know? Not like what Layla and I have. I see that with you two." He nods over at us.

Is this for fucking *real* right now?

Her entire family was rooting for me this entire time when I didn't even know I was an option?

This is news to me, and it's the kind of news I can get on board with.

CHAPTER 15

Tatum Barker

I Don't Want to Fake

I don't really know what to say. Everyone in this room appears to have been rooting for me and…Ford?

Not Archer? The man I spent half my life loving, crushing on, pining after? But Ford? *Ford?* The man I'm *pretending* to be with to keep them out of my hair for the day?

What alternate universe have I stepped in?

They're careful not to say a bad word about Archer, which I appreciate. He's a good man, and I care about him. Besides, he's Ford's brother. It's not like they can sit here insulting him.

But they definitely play up how much they *always* thought Ford was a better fit for me. He's more outgoing than Archer, which is likely a better match for my personality. He's also analytical and strategic, focused and reliable, which are probably necessary traits in a partner to my complete and utter hot mess chaos.

But the truth is that my family probably *knew* Ford better than they ever got to know Archer. That's partly Archer's fault since he doesn't let *anybody* get to know him, but I suspect more of it has to do with the fact that Colton and Ford played football together. They were in the same grade. They were old friends who lost touch after high school.

But he'd eat dinner at our house once in a while. As he grew apart from his brother, he grew closer to mine—and other guys on the team. It's not like Colt and Ford were best friends or anything, but they played the same sport and spent plenty of time together.

And now I come to find out that my brother saw me ending up with Ford all along? Mom and Dad, too?

I'm so confused. So very, very confused. It's like I invited them in, and we all entered the twilight zone together.

Except we didn't. We're still right here in Tampa.

And is that a boner digging into my ass?

Is Ford *turned on* by the fact that I'm sitting on his lap? Or is that just my own wishful, lustful thinking?

What the hell is happening right now?

After that one kiss we shared when he pulled away, I focused on Archer. I didn't allow myself to look past Archer to see Ford standing right there, but suddenly, pieces start falling into place.

When I asked if I could come stay with him after Archer and I broke up, the answer was immediate.

When I asked if I should buy the Winston Manor, he did me one better by offering to put up half, pushing us together as not just friends but business partners.

When Archer took me to our senior prom and Ford was home from college on spring break, I didn't miss the somber look in his eyes. I didn't know it was because Archer asked him to snap some pictures of the two of us, oblivious to what might've been simmering between us. Maybe I was oblivious, too. I thought Ford wasn't interested. That he forgot about that kiss.

My God. Does it span that far back, and I just never knew? Or was there some other reason his eyes lit up when I walked in the room in my fancy purple dress but turned dark when I took my spot beside my date?

I won't know if I don't ask, but as instances such as these continue hitting me over the head, I feel the sudden need to get some space. I'm just not entirely sure if I need space from my family or from Ford and the boner by my ass as I piece together exactly what I'm feeling.

"I need to go check the food," I mumble as I push to a stand.

"I'll help," Ford says.

It's an open floor plan. It's not like we can whisper in the kitchen about how long he might've had feelings for me, or whether I'm delusional, or how I'm suddenly discovering that maybe I have feelings for him. And oh, by the way, was his cock hard while I was sitting on his lap, or did he just have a giant pipe in his pocket?

I'd never ask that last one, just for the record. No matter how freaking curious I am right now.

I mash the shit out of those poor potatoes, and Ford slices the turkey.

"Can I help?" my mother calls from the family room.

"It's all under control, but Dad, if you want to pour the wine, now's your time to shine," I say, and he joins us in the kitchen.

Ford bumps into me, and I nearly drop the potato masher thing at the sudden electric spark that passes between us.

"Oh, honey, use the hand mixer. It's so much faster," my mom says as she approaches us.

"I like them a little lumpy," I mutter. If I wanted her help, I would have asked her to bring the potatoes. I realize how bratty that sounds, but this fake thing with Ford was supposed to help keep my family out of my personal life today.

Not flip the script to make me see how I was with the wrong brother all along.

Sue me if I'm a little vulnerable after the last half hour sitting on Ford's lap in the family room.

"Suit yourself," she says, and she moves to help my dad with the wine.

Ford leans in closer to me, and I suddenly smell him. I *smell* him. I've never *smelled* Ford Bradley a day in my life, but he smells like a goddamn five-star resort on the beach somewhere. Clean and fresh and a little bright and expensive.

I push the thought away. So he smells good. Big deal.

He's done carving the turkey, I'm done mashing the potatoes, and we start carrying the dishes to the table. I gaze with curiosity at his green bean dish.

It looks…delightful. Not at all like that trash casserole everyone else brings to Thanksgiving dinner.

"Dinner is served," I call formally, and my family joins me in the kitchen. Layla has already strapped my nephew's booster seat to one of the kitchen chairs, and we all take our places around the table.

Ford and I are closest to the kitchen so we can grab whatever our guests might need, and after my father insists on saying a prayer, my mother says, "Let's all go around and say one thing we're thankful for this year before we begin. I'll start. I'm thankful for a year where we get to sit around a table together and celebrate this holiday. Larry?" She looks over at her husband.

"I'm thankful to be in Florida with this gorgeous weather. Sure don't miss digging out of an early blizzard on Thanksgiving back home in Chicago," he says. He looks to my brother next.

"I'm thankful for Layla and Maddox and the little family we're creating."

In the middle between them, Maddox says, "Gah!"

Layla goes next. "I'm thankful for the little one coming to us next June." She rubs her belly, and there's a moment of pause while the news hits us all. And then, suddenly, everyone is up and out of their seats with congratulatory hugs that my brother is growing his family by one more sweet baby.

He's only twenty-nine. Ford's age. He's turning the corner of thirty, and he's about to have two kids.

I don't even have a boyfriend anymore. I'm nowhere close to having a family, even though it's always been a dream of mine.

Instead, I'm starting to feel things for my ex's brother that I have no business feeling.

Once we're seated and the food is starting to get cold, I say, "Let's eat!"

"Well, wait a minute, honey," my mom says. "You and Ford haven't gone yet."

I nod at Ford to go first.

He glances at me. "I'm thankful we were finally given the chance to be together." He leans over and presses his lips to mine, and my thighs clench together involuntarily.

Whoa.

My God.

What the hell is happening?

And why do I keep having the same recurring thought with every minute that passes us by?

I'm starting to become fairly certain that I don't want to fake this with him at all.

I think maybe I want this to be real.

CHAPTER 16

FORD BRADLEY

Something Real Fucking Dumb

Thanksgiving is a success by all accounts, but mostly by mine because I finally got to pretend like the woman I've wanted to be with for a long, long time now is actually mine.

But when the last dish is dried and her family is long gone, the pretending has stopped, and I'm left with an empty feeling inside despite the very full feeling I have from eating way too much.

That's what the holidays are all about, I guess. Overeating. For most people. For me, though—I have to be up bright and early to practice football tomorrow morning, which means I'll be struggling since I partook in one of the luxuries I don't usually afford myself.

She's leaving in the morning.

She needs to be back in Vegas for a wedding on Saturday and a charity event next weekend—a charity event she's hosting for my brother, by the way. Her ex.

They'll see each other. They'll be together.

Any progress I think we've made is a delusion.

I can't be with her. She was with my brother, and he's still my brother whether he extracted himself from the family or not.

I'm leaving in the morning, too. For practice. We'll leave around the same time, but when I come home, it'll be to an empty house.

I'm not looking forward to it.

She gives me a hug goodbye in the morning, and I'm tempted to kiss her again.

I don't. I can't. She doesn't want me to, and while I got to have my fun yesterday, that's all it was. Pretend. A day to be thankful for, I guess—like I said at dinner.

I head to practice, and I guess I'm quieter than usual because Cole calls me out on it in his usual, eloquent way. "What the fuck's up your ass today?"

I grimace at his question. "Nothing. Just ate too much yesterday. Paying for it today."

"Been there. I ate with the team, and we had a hell of a time afterward." He throws out an elbow in his usual joking manner, but I can't muster up the enthusiasm for a return.

She's gone, and that's weighing me down today.

"It's really just the food? You weren't yourself out there on the field today, man," he says. He sits in his locker and leans forward so we can talk around the wall dividing us.

I glance over at him. One of the benefits of being clear across the country from my siblings is that I can share these sorts of talks with teammates instead of family. Some of my family are well aware of my feelings for Tatum—like Everleigh, for example. There are others—like Archer—who I hope never find out.

I blow out a breath and finally make my confession. "I, uh…have *feelings* for my brother's girl."

"The one staying with you?"

I wince as I nod.

"Thought you said she wasn't his girl anymore," he says.

"She's not. They ended things, and she asked if she could come hang out here a while."

"Did your feelings start before or after that?" he asks.

"Long before. I've known her since high school. Probably loved her since about then, too." I lift a shoulder. "I don't know. She's the chaos to my calm. We just fit. She makes me laugh like nobody else. She listens when I talk. We just have this connection I never saw with her and my brother."

"So you thought it would be a good idea to invite her to stay with you awhile after the breakup?" he asks, his brows furrowing in confusion.

"I'm a masochist, okay?"

He chuckles at that.

"The reality of it is that they've sort of always been on and off. I guess I assumed they'd figure it out someday and be on permanently, but this time, she tells me it's off permanently. And I guess things just sort of changed when she was here. It almost felt like she felt it, too. Like she wanted it. And then I did something real fucking dumb, and now she's back in Vegas, probably making up with him while I pine away for something that was never meant to be mine."

"Christ, you're dramatic. Pull it together, dude. Life's not so goddamn serious. But just so I can fully understand the bigger picture here, what was the dumb thing you did?" he asks.

I press my lips together. "She's a wedding planner. She's had this dream of creating this destination wedding brand, of owning event venues in different places. I went in on one here with her in Tampa."

"Oh, shit. You *bought* a place with her?"

I nod. "And it gets worse. Her family was over yesterday for Thanksgiving, and she didn't want to spend the day getting hammered with questions about whether it's really over with my brother, so we pretended *we* were together."

"I can't decide which thing is dumber. Going in half on a facility or pretending she was your girl," he muses.

"It gets worse. Instead of spending the day fending off questions about my brother, we spent the day listening to her family talk about how they always thought she and I would be perfect together."

He rubs his forehead. "I guess I can see why you were off your game today."

"It's complicated, but I'll pull it together for game day."

"You only have two days to prepare for that," he reminds me.

"I know. I got this." Except the truth is, I'm pretty sure I *don't* got this at all.

It gets worse when I arrive home to an empty place. There was so much light and joy here just twenty-four hours ago, and now it's back to being quiet. Dark.

I peek into the room where she stayed. The bed is neatly made, but three cups sit on the desk along with a few folders that remind me she'll be back.

A sense of loss plows into me.

She'll be back, but what will change between us in that time? It felt like we were getting close to something, like she was starting to awaken to the feelings I've had for years.

And now it feels like we're back to square one.

I need to focus on football. It's almost December, which means we're ramping up to the playoffs. What we do now on that field is more important than ever.

Who I am when I step foot onto the grass in two days could determine my fate for the next two months and my legacy beyond that.

I can't let this distract me from everything I've worked so goddamn hard for my entire career.

I leave her room and take a shower. I jerk off and moan her name as I come.

And then I slip under the covers…not of my own bed, but of the bed she slept in while she was here.

CHAPTER 17

Tatum Barker

Heart Versus Brain

I've never been *nervous* to see Archer.

But today, I am.

My flight landed in the early afternoon, and instead of heading to Kenzie's house, where I have a bed waiting for me, I head back to the house I lived in with Archer for the last four years since my car is still parked in the garage.

I think about ringing the bell, but I don't. Instead, I walk right in like it's my house—because it is. I may have moved out, but I texted him earlier that I'd be coming, and I still have the key.

For now.

It's something I plan to give back to him while I'm here.

"Archer?" I call out, and I walk toward the kitchen. I hear footsteps coming from the hallway where his home office is located, and then he appears there in the kitchen.

My chest tightens as I stare at the man I've loved for the last decade. Maybe we broke up a few times in there, but we also made up a few times in there, and I guess somewhere deep down, I always assumed we'd just...figure it out. End up together. We had an understanding. He doesn't open up to people, but he opened up to me.

And now it feels like I don't even know him anymore.

I've questioned more than once if he's an actual Bradley—to myself, of course. Never aloud.

The Bradley children all have dark hair and dark eyes like their father, Thomas Bradley, but Archer is the anomaly. He's got lighter hair and greenish-hazel eyes that sometimes pick up some gold depending on the lighting. And he's not built like a football player. He's tall and lean, made for baseball in the same way his brothers were made for football. Maybe he takes after Vivienne, his mother, but it's hard to tell with her since she's colored her hair since I first met her. It's hard to tell what's real and what's been altered.

As our eyes connect across the kitchen we used to share, he seems like a stranger. But I think that has less to do with him and more to do with the fact that my feelings might have changed in the last few weeks I spent away from here. Away from him. Away from what used to be *us*.

"Hi," he says, his voice soft. He doesn't make a move to come toward me, to take me in his arms. It sort of signals to me that it really *is* over this time. This wasn't some fight that we'll recover from. This is the end.

"Hey. How have you been?"

"It's been quiet around here without you." It's his way of saying he misses me. There's always subtext with him, and I guess I've gotten better about guessing what it is over the years.

I tilt my head and study him. "Can I ask you a question?"

His eyes meet mine, and he nods.

"What happened with your father?"

He scoffs before he asks, "When?"

"Before we broke up. The illegal casinos. How did your name get on them? When? Why?" These are the questions nobody can seem to answer.

He's all but estranged from his family for God knows how long—a decade, maybe? When he went off to college? Somewhere around there, or maybe before that, even when he was in high school. But suddenly, out of nowhere, he agrees to sign paperwork for his father? It's not adding up.

"My father came to me begging for my help with a family business," he says. "He claimed he wanted a reconciliation with me before we lose my mother. In a moment of pure weakness, I agreed. Heart won out over brain. I had no idea it was illegal."

"What did he tell you about it?"

"He said it was for tax purposes or some shit. I was stupid enough not to dig any deeper." He shakes his head. "I should've known better. Should've trusted my gut. Never should've trusted him. But he used my mother's illness, and I fell for it."

I feel like I should go to him, like I should rush into his arms and comfort him. But it's not my place anymore. "I'm sorry, Archer. What he did was so, so wrong, and he'll pay."

"Yeah." His voice is low and totally unconvincing, and even though I *say* that he'll pay, the truth is that bad guys like him know how to use loopholes to get out of trouble all the time.

There's nothing saying Thomas Bradley *will* pay for what he's done.

And he's evil enough to use his own wife's illness to garner the sympathy of his estranged son, ensuring his son will *stay* estranged. It's sick. It's awful.

He glances away from me, eyes toward the window, and his voice is low and raspy when he says, "I miss you."

Goose bumps break out on my skin at his words as a shiver runs up my spine.

"I know," I say, the volume of my voice matching his. "But we both know we're better off as friends. It's how we started."

He presses his lips together. "Is there someone else?"

I weigh how to answer that. The truth is no, there's not. Not really. But I'm starting to have feelings for someone else, someone related to him by blood, and given what I know about his relationship with his family, the words are hard to form. "There's not. Uh, not really. I've been staying with Ford."

He raises his brows. "He's in love with you, you know."

I gasp at his words. "What?"

He lets out a soft chuckle. "You didn't know? Everybody knows."

"Everybod…" I say part of the word, trailing off as a million questions plow into me.

Like, for example, exactly how long has Ford been in love with me? Why didn't he say anything? Who's everybody?

Before I can figure out how the hell to form words to respond to that bomb, he adds, "You should know the real reason I ended things with you. My father was about to be indicted, and I knew it could get messy for me since he put my name on that fucking place. I couldn't do that to you. I didn't want you to be affected by any of it. It's not over yet, Tate. Not by a long shot. I'm still being investigated. My father, too. But I want you back. I never wanted to let you go in the first place. But if you've moved on, fine. I want you to be happy. If it's with a Bradley, so be it. It's not like we'll be interacting at our weekly family dinners." He shrugs like he couldn't care less, and I'm not sure what to make of it.

His words are saying one thing. They're talking to the part of my brain that says *yeah, this makes sense. This is good. We love him.*

But for some reason, my heart is telling me something else entirely.

He's in love with me. Everybody knows.

Ford-Ford. Ford-Ford. Each beat repeats his name.

And I'm not quite sure what to do about that.

CHAPTER 18

FORD BRADLEY

Didn't Our Old Man Teach You Anything

When practice ends on Saturday afternoon, I think about calling Tatum.

We've been texting a bit—she let me know when she landed, I texted a check-in last night, and she texted me this morning to say good morning and to ask me to wish her luck on today's wedding. But I haven't heard her voice since she left, and I miss the hell out of her.

I did what I could to put her on the back burner of my mind at practice. I had to. I couldn't risk Cole calling me out on more shit, and today was a little better. I'm ready for game day, anyway.

But as soon as practice is over, the ache is back.

It's weird how quickly I got used to her being here.

My cleaning people stopped by today, and they washed her bedding and changed the sheets while I was at practice.

I'll sleep in my own bed tonight, I guess. That room won't smell like her anymore, but the one night I spent there was both admittedly weird and strangely comforting.

Snap DECISION

So I *think* about calling her, but I don't. She's at a wedding, and as much as I want to hear her voice, to talk to her about how the wedding went and whether the groom showed up hungover as she suspected he might, I leave her to concentrate on her own job.

Just because I had a hard time concentrating on mine doesn't mean I should inflict the same wish upon her.

I arrive home to an empty condo, pack up my shit, and head to the team hotel earlier than usual. We always spend the night before game day at a hotel, even when we're playing at home.

Being here is better than sitting around my place picturing her smile in one corner, her hot mess of chaos, her three cups on her desk—two now in the recycle bin since they were paper cups, and the third washed and ready for her to use when she returns since she left it here.

I look at it as insurance that she'll be back.

I shoot her a text once I'm checked into my hotel room.

Me: *Hope the wedding was a huge success and the groom wasn't still shitfaced.*

I see the bubbles appear that tell me she's drafting a reply, and I sit and wait patiently.

Tatum: *It's about as good as I could have hoped for considering I've been out of town for weeks. He was only mildly hungover. [smirk face emoji]*

Me: *Sounds like a win.*

I want to ask when she's coming back. I want to ask if she's seen my brother. If they got back together the way they always do when they see each other again after time apart.

I don't. I can't.

It's not my place to ask any of that. She'll give me what she wants to when the time is right for her.

The bubbles appear again, and then they stop. It's as I'm willing them to start up again that my phone starts to ring.

I glance up at the top of my screen, and my heart starts to race as I wonder whether I might actually get some answers to those very questions...just not from Tatum.

"Archer?" I answer, shocked that my brother is calling me.

We text upon rare occasions. I can't remember the last time I heard his voice over a phone line—at least when it wasn't in the background of a call with Tatum. He never calls me. Never.

"Hi." His single, short word feels like his entire personality.

"What's up?" I ask.

"Tatum said she's been staying with you," he says quietly.

"She was. But she's back in Vegas." My brows crinkle together as my grip tightens on my phone.

"I know. I just wanted to say thank you for being there for her."

"We've always been close. You know that."

"How close?" he asks.

"What are you asking?" I ask carefully.

"I know you're in love with her." His voice is an accusation, one I won't even pretend to deny.

"And?" I ask, not quite sure where this is going. It's a clear admission, and maybe it's my way of tempting him to tell me what the fuck I should do about it.

He's quiet a long beat, and in the time of his pause, I wonder why he bothered to call me at all. And then his words come. "I told her yesterday that I just want her to be happy."

"I don't know what you're trying to say."

"I'm saying I wanted to be that guy for her, but she assured me it's over. If that guy is you, I don't want to be the one who stands in the way for either of you."

"Oh," I grunt, not sure what else to say. What *is* there to say in response to your brother telling you that he knows you're in love with his ex and it's okay to give it a shot?

Snap DECISION

It's not exactly the call I was expecting.

"Anyway, I'm hanging up now." He sighs.

"Wait," I say, and the other line isn't dead yet.

"What?" he asks.

"What happened with you and Dad?"

"Ask Tatum. I told her. I shouldn't discuss it over the phone. Didn't our old man teach you anything?"

I can't help a chuckle at that—a chuckle at a tiny bit of understanding when it comes to Archer. He shut himself off because of our family, but maybe also because *he had to*. Madden, Dex, and Everleigh learned the hard way when they each almost lost what they cared about most because of their loyalty to our family. I'm not sure yet where I fall on that scale, but Archer managed to figure it out before any of us.

Longer than any of us ever even began to question things, I think.

"When did you know?" I ask quietly.

"Know what?" he asks.

"That we would be better off without him."

"The day I chose baseball over football. I need to go."

He cuts the call, and I think back to high school. I was two years older than him, and he played both football and baseball his freshman and sophomore years. He was good enough to make varsity for both sports, but junior year was when he needed to get serious about one sport or the other.

I'd already chosen football. I knew that was my path. I was a multi-sport athlete in my younger years, too, but colleges started looking at me more seriously my junior year, so that was the make-or-break time when student-athletes had to choose the path that would pave the way for college and beyond. Workouts got more intense, more strategic, more specific to help with training for particular positions.

I wanted to be a tight end, so I had to focus on my lower body for blocking, whereas a baseball player would be prioritizing upper body strength and shoulder mobility. It was these types of specific workouts that divided our paths.

And when Archer chose baseball, it looked an awful lot like our father froze him out. He wanted five football players, I guess. Maybe he gambled on it, something that wouldn't surprise me at this point. It was harder to get to his baseball games since the team played multiple games a week versus our football games that were once weekly.

So maybe they didn't freeze him out as much as they just couldn't put in the commitment to attend every one of his games.

And it wasn't just that. Baseball didn't have the same sort of social construct that football had, either. All the rich parents paying for their sons to be a part of the team were a community in and of themselves. The bleachers became a place where Mom could brush elbows with the other high-society women and where Dad could make his backroom business deals.

But Archer didn't see that. All he saw was that there weren't any Bradleys in the bleachers at his games.

And as I think about his lighter eyes and lighter hair, I can't help but wonder whether he was right to feel like an outcast. It's not the first time I've wondered about it. It's something Everleigh and I have even talked about before, but the more I think about it, the more it makes sense why my dad would have roped Archer into signing the paperwork for his criminal activity.

It makes sense why Archer would've chosen baseball when the rest of us chose football, when our entire family is a *football family*.

Maybe Archer isn't a Bradley after all.

CHAPTER 19

Tatum Barker

Full Planner Mode

The wedding was a success, and I sleep in on Sunday morning in Kenzie's casita only to wake up to the smell of bacon.

My first thought of the morning is of Ford.

Because of the bacon. That man loves his bacon.

I grab my phone and send him a text.

Me: *Good morning. My friend's place smells like bacon, and it made me think of you. [bacon emoji] Good luck at today's game! [football emoji] [flexed bicep emoji]*

His reply is immediate, and it has a photo of a plate with scrambled eggs and a pile of bacon.

Ford: *Team breakfast this morning.*

I giggle.

Me: *Looks perfect for you.*

Ford: *The only thing that would have made it better is having you here with me.*

I stare at his words as my chest tightens.

He means as a friend, right?

Archer's words come back to me again, likely for the millionth time since he spoke them. *He's in love with you, you know.*

No, I didn't know. And no, he's not. We're friends. Close friends. The best of friends.

But when I think about faking it on Thanksgiving and how I didn't really *want* to be faking it, well, I just end up in a pit of confusion that I can't seem to climb out of.

Me: *Lol. They wouldn't let me within a block of that place on game day. Score me a TD, k?*

Ford: *I'll do my best.*

I leave it at that and emerge from my casita, where the bacon smell carried, and head toward the kitchen.

Kenzie's two kids, a boy and a girl named Cassian and Kapri, are strapped into highchairs while Cody brings them milk in spillproof cups, and Kenzie flips pancakes at a griddle.

"It smells delicious in here," I say.

"Good morning," Cody says with a smile, and they really are just the sweetest family.

I look at the photos Kenzie often posts on her Instagram, and I can't help but wonder if it's really all as perfect as it seems. All blonde hair, blue eyes, wide smiles, the brightness levels turned up, and the exposure adjusted to perfection.

And as I walk into their bright kitchen that almost appears to have had the exposure adjusted this morning, it actually *is* as perfect as it seems.

Cody walks over and loops his arm around his wife's waist, bending to kiss her cheek, and she giggles as she flips a rocket ship-shaped pancake likely meant for Cassian and a star-shaped pancake that's probably for Kapri.

Then I spot the molds she used to create the space-themed pancakes beside her on the counter. It looks like I'll likely be getting a moon or a planet with rings around it if I don't get the rocket ship or the star. Honestly, when I've seen these things, I had no idea who might actually use them.

Kenzie and Cody, apparently. That's my answer.

"Can I do anything to help?" I ask.

"We've got it all under control, but thanks," Kenzie says. She flips the last few pancakes onto a plate, and Cody brings the plate to the table while she pulls a pan out of the oven with bacon on it. She brings the bacon over a moment later, and the adults sit to eat with the kids.

They pray first, and then they start dishing out the food.

"I've never seen a two-and-a-half-year-old eat bacon the way Cassian can," she says, setting a cooled piece on his tray. He grabs it and immediately puts it down, and she gives him a second piece while I watch Kapri, the fifteen-month-old, pick up the pancake and chew on the corner of it.

They're adorable. This whole entire scene is adorable, and it pulses something in me that I wasn't expecting. Something I wasn't planning on.

I want this.

I want the husband who kisses me on the cheek while I'm cooking pancakes, and I want the two cute kids with pink cheeks, and I want the pancake molds and bacon late on lazy weekend mornings. Out of season, anyway. I want the perfect exposure photos with the reality that backs them up.

I want a family of my own.

I felt the twinge when my brother visited Ford's on Thanksgiving, but this is now the second family with young kids I've spent time around, and it suddenly feels like time is running out.

I always wanted kids *someday*, and I guess I sort of assumed that Archer and I would get it together and have our own family eventually.

But that's off the table now, and that dream of my own perfect young family feels like it's slipping away.

Snap DECISION

I'm already twenty-seven. Even if I got pregnant today, I'd be twenty-eight by the time I had a baby. With the second, I'd be thirty or older. That's if I got lucky enough to get pregnant right away without the types of complications so many women face.

Maybe perfection is a fantasy. Kenzie got lucky enough to find it, but just because it's in my face right now doesn't mean it's the norm. It's more of an exception, I think. An anomaly.

I finish breakfast and help clean up, and then I tell Kenzie that I need to head into my little office to work.

I do, actually. I need to work. I have to finalize the details for Archer's garden party that's set to take place in five days. Kenzie has handled most of the details while I've been out of town, but this is still my business. My brand.

My ex.

But I also sort of have this need to get away from the happy little family. I want to give them their space to enjoy their usual Sunday activities without feeling like their fifth wheel.

I put Ford's game on my tablet while I mindlessly work through the details on my laptop. I have my three usual cups, but I left my favorite one at Ford's place on accident. Or maybe it wasn't an accident at all, and it was my subconscious leaving something physical behind as a way to pretend like that's all I was leaving there.

But the longer I spend apart from Ford, the more I can't believe that to be true.

The week feels long. I feel weird calling him now that Archer said Ford is in love with me, so I keep it to texts that somehow keep managing to turn flirty.

I bury myself in work. I plan all the details for the local weddings I have coming up, and I even spend a little bit of time on Devon and Lindsay's wedding as I schedule a time to take them to view Winston Manor next week. I've handed so many of the little details off to Kenzie over the last two years that I find I'm enjoying making these plans with Lindsay.

I guess that means I'm returning to Tampa next week.

Ford could take them. A little voice in my head reminds me of that. I mute said voice.

I want to get back to Tampa. I want to see him. I want to feel whatever it is I'm going to feel when I'm around him to see if it's real or some manufactured thing I'm feeling because I'm flailing after a breakup and being around *the perfect family* while I plan other people's weddings. It has to be that combination…right?

Ford calls me once on Tuesday evening to check in, and we chat for a while about the charity event I'm holding for Archer. We talk again on Thursday, but it's brief since he has an appearance.

Eventually Friday rolls around, and I'm busy all day with the final preparations for this evening's event.

I'm in my cocktail dress when the band arrives, and every last detail has been perfected. Archer's foundation creates scholarships and equipment donations for underprivileged kids, and tonight's party came with a pricey ticket and a selection of raffle prizes donated by Archer's teammates—not because *he* asked, but because *I* asked the girlfriends and wives of other players.

The atmosphere is warm and inviting with the string lights and the acoustic band warming up in one corner of the garden before the guests are set to arrive. We're serving hors d'oeuvres and champagne, and the gardens have high-top tables for guests to stand near with their food. I created two specialty cocktails for the event, both of which are quite expensive so we can wring every possible penny out of guests tonight. The Vegas Heat is a spicy margarita with a flair, and the Curveball is a whiskey and peach concoction.

Snap DECISION

Everything is ready, so I grab myself a Curveball to calm my nerves when I spot Archer walking in.

He beelines right for me, tugging at the buttoned collar of his dress shirt. He was always uncomfortable in a shirt at all, let alone a dress shirt. I never minded when he'd walk around the house shirtless with those gorgeous abs served up on a platter, to be honest.

"Thanks for your work on this. It looks great," he says. He orders himself a Curveball, too, and once it's in his hand, he holds it up. "To raising a bunch of money tonight for Archway."

I tap my glass to his, and we each take a sip.

"Anything you need me to do?" he asks.

I shake my head. "It's all under control."

"You're the best."

I shoot him a tight smile, not sure I really believe his words considering where we find ourselves at the moment.

Guests start arriving, and I'm in full planner mode as I keep tabs on catering, manage photo opportunities as I introduce guests to each other, and make sure Archer is mingling and always has a drink in hand.

Everything is going smoothly. Too smoothly. When it's going off without a hitch, I try to remind myself it's because of my careful planning. I never really believe it. My brain always goes to if it's too good to be true, it probably is.

Archer catches my eye from across the room.

It used to be so comforting when he did that.

We rarely ever spent time together at these types of events because he always put me up to the task of entertaining everyone while he sipped a drink quietly in the corner with one or two people at a time. I chalked it up to him being an introvert intimidated by events like these, but I'm not really sure that's true.

I'm not sure he's an introvert at all as much as he's just protective over his personal space.

He let me in there once.

He said he wanted me back, but it seems like the door is closed now. He gave me his blessing to be happy, and that's all I want, too.

And as Ford's face flashes through my mind, I think I'm finally untraining the years of practice I had assuming my happy ending would be with Archer.

CHAPTER 20

Tatum Barker

Butterflies

I stay the weekend in Vegas mainly to tie up any loose ends I have before I head back to Tampa for a while. It's open-ended, I guess. I'll be throwing myself into planning Devon and Lindsay's wedding, but my brand is destination forward, so I'm used to planning remotely. I guess I just want to plan remotely from the humid beaches of Florida for a while instead of the dry desert.

It's a three-hour time change plus a five-hour flight, and the direct options from Vegas to Tampa are few and far between. I book one on Monday afternoon that'll get me in around seven, and when I texted Ford my details, his response was immediate.

Ford: *Perfect. My place has been too quiet without you. I'll pick you up by baggage claim.*

That's Ford. Reliable. Dependable. Kind.

I don't know why I didn't see that before. I mean, I did, but not to the extent I seem to be studying it now. Before, I didn't allow it to be with anything other than friendliness as the motivator. But now, I look at everything through the lens of Archer's words.

He's in love with you, you know.

Those words play on a frustrating, endless loop in my mind. Interesting that *those* are the words on repeat and not Archer's own words about how he wants me back.

I keep trying to pulse those words into my brain, but I can't seem to muster them. I can only focus on the fact that Ford is in love with me, and everyone knows it except me.

And maybe I have feelings for him, too.

Feelings I pushed down and buried deep, feelings I never bothered to acknowledge because I couldn't.

But I can now.

And I am.

I want to kiss him again.

Excluding the one that happened when I was just a kid, the first one took me off guard. The second was for pretend.

But what if it was just for us? No sexy cakes or fake relationships to cloud what's happening, just an actual, real kiss. Tongue and everything. Maybe a little dry humping and feeling each other up for an extra win.

I intend to give it a try.

At least that's my plan as I board the flight back to Tampa.

Halfway through it, I chicken out. What the hell am I thinking? It's *Ford*. One of my closest friends. The guy who has been there for me for more breakups and makeups with his brother than I can count. He wouldn't have done that if he was in love with me, would he have? No. It's a ridiculous notion. He would've stayed away if only to protect his heart. Archer was just saying things. Trying to get into my head. Trying to confuse me.

But then…

I sigh heavily as I weigh it all over again.

He's been so flirty lately, and what *was* that kiss at the bakery? Or at Thanksgiving? And the boner...

God, I'm so confused.

And as we start our descent into Tampa International Airport, the butterflies start to kick up. They flap their wings heartily and strongly as I try to fight them off and keep them at bay, but they won't be silenced.

I text him when I land so he knows he can leave his place because soon enough I'll have my luggage, and then he can pull up to the curb outside baggage claim to pick me up.

Me: *Landed!*

His reply comes quickly.

Ford: *Welcome back.*

His two simple words feel like home, and I can't really explain why. Maybe because I'm staying at Kenzie's house back in Vegas, so it doesn't really feel like *home*. It feels like I'm crashing on a friend's couch.

I am here, too, in Tampa. That's what this is. It's not like I'm moving in with Ford. But it's different staying with a single friend versus a whole perfect, bright-exposure little blonde family.

The flight attendant opens the forward door, and the butterflies pick up a few notches.

I follow the signs toward baggage claim, the butterflies flapping around so hard that my stomach feels like it's twisting in knots, and part of me wishes Archer had never said those words to me. It's pulsing this anxiety in me that I never feel around Ford.

I turn a corner to head toward the carousels, and that's when I see him.

I didn't expect him to come inside, but he's here. He's waiting for me, waiting to help me grab my suitcase off the belt and walk with me toward his car and take me home.

Home.

Snap DECISION

His eyes move to meet mine, and my pulse kicks up, and my heart pounds at a thunderous volume in my chest.

He's wearing a hat to hopefully ward people off from recognizing him, but I'd recognize him anywhere. I freeze to the spot after I get off the escalator and move out of the way for a few beats as I study him, and it's like this rush of feelings washes over me.

And then my legs start to move. It's as if I can't even control them as they carry me across the space separating me from Ford Bradley.

I rush into his waiting arms, and I collide with him as he pulls me in. I tilt up my chin to look into his eyes, and I see it there now. All the love Archer was talking about. He has feelings for me, and I have feelings for him, and there's nothing standing in our way now.

I close my eyes and push to my tiptoes as his mouth crashes down to mine. It's a soft kiss at first, but it turns intense quickly as I kick up the speed, opening my mouth to his and feeling his tongue move with mine. We kiss there in the airport by baggage claim like nobody's watching, and I wrap my arms around him as he tightens his hold on me. He shifts a little, and that's when I feel his erection solid against my hip, more proof that he feels *something* for me.

We're in public, though, and he's a celebrity who's trying not to draw attention to himself. So I pull back first.

He looks a little dazed, and to be honest, I *feel* a little dazed. More than a little, actually.

His eyes come into focus on mine, and there's a question in them.

"I missed you," I whisper.

He hauls me against him again, not in a kiss but in a fierce, warm embrace, and his arms are full of comfort as they surround me. "God, I missed you too."

Now *this* feels like home.

CHAPTER 21

FORD BRADLEY

Permission

She missed me. *She missed me.*
She kissed me. *She kissed me.*
I'm trying to hold onto my shock, to keep a filter on it—unsuccessfully, I might add—because holy shit, she kissed me. It wasn't for show, or because of a sex cake, but because she *missed* me. Because she wanted to.

I wanted her to.

What the fuck is happening?

I'm nervous. I don't want to fuck this up. I don't know how to handle this, so I'm letting her take the lead.

I hold her close until the bags start to drop onto the baggage carousel. She rushes toward a bag, tugs at it awkwardly, and I reach in to help her with it.

"I have two bags," she says a little sheepishly, and I still can't believe she's here and she just kissed me. Would it be too soon to take her back to my place and offer her a spot in my bed beside me rather than in the guest room?

Jesus.

Snap DECISION

I've been waiting for this moment for far too long, and I'm afraid I'm going to scare her off. The intensity with which I want her is scaring *me* off, to be honest.

Her second bag comes, and I take the lead toward my Range Rover, parked close by in the parking deck.

It's on the way home when I can stare out at the road and not feel the awkward rush of eye contact when I get up the nerve to ask the one thing I need to know. "Can I ask you a question?" I begin. I'm leaning on the console armrest, and I reach over and take her hand in mine.

"Anything." She laces her fingers through mine, and she rubs the back of my hand with her other hand.

"What changed?" I can't help but glance over at her, and she's staring down at our hands.

She twists her lips before she answers. "I realized that I have feelings for you." Her voice is soft.

"What made you realize?" I press.

She clears her throat. "Archer. He, uh…he said he wanted me back, and I said we were better off as friends. And then he wanted to know why I kept running to you, and he told me you've, um…had feelings for me for some time. It made me realize that I've pushed away my feelings for you because I thought I had to. But when he gave me permission to be with you and said he wanted me to be happy, even if it was with a sibling, then he was okay with that, and I guess that made me think about what I want."

"And you want…" I ask, trailing off as I wait to hear what I've wanted to hear for far too long.

"You."

My breath hitches, and I wish I wasn't driving right now so I could kiss her again. As if she can read my thoughts, she pulls our joined hands to her lips, and she kisses the back of my hand.

"I want you, Ford," she says softly.

She can have me. All of me.

"I want you, too," I rasp.

I pull into the parking garage, and we get her bags out of the back of my SUV. We head to the elevator and take it up to my floor, and the moment my front door latches shut behind her, her mouth is on mine again, initiated by her for the second time. Her hands are on my jaw, and I loop one arm around her waist to haul her to me as my other hand curls around her neck.

She moans into me as I deepen the kiss, our tongues moving in a slow dance together, the urgency and need there even as we take our time and hands start to move and explore. One of my hands stays around her neck while my other fingertips move under her shirt and along the warm skin of her back. I shift my hips as my cock becomes painfully hard, seeking her out as I push against her.

She moans at the feel of me, and one of her hands trails down toward my waistband, sending a shot of need up my spine as my cock gets somehow even harder.

Fuck, I want this. This is all I've ever wanted, for her to realize there's something here between us, that it's not just me hopelessly in love with someone I can't have but that there's a real chance for us to be together.

I need this. I need *her*.

I slip my hand around to the front under her shirt and up toward her tits, and I cup one of them over her bra as she gives me a soft moan. I want to hear more. I want to make her moan while she's naked beneath me, her lips parted and her head tossed back in pleasure as I drive into her over and over.

Night after night, for a lifetime.

It's that exact thought that forces reality to plow into me.

Snap DECISION

I reluctantly drop my hand from her tit, and I slow the kiss before I end it. I rest my forehead to hers as I draw in a shaky breath.

"Why are you stopping?" she whispers, and her hand curls around my neck to pull me back down to her.

I kiss her lightly and pull back again, straightening as I draw in a breath. She lets me go, and I think this might be the single hardest thing I've ever done.

"Fuck," I mutter, running a hand through my hair as I walk over toward the windows.

"What are you doing?" she murmurs.

I glance out the floor-to-ceiling windows spanning one side of my condo, and then I turn back to her. "We shouldn't need someone else's permission to be together." My voice is soft and raspy as I choke out the words.

"We don't," she says.

"You said it in the car. You said Archer gave you permission to be with me. Like that somehow makes it all okay."

She lifts a shoulder. "Well, it does. It lets us be together without the guilt of having to hide something from one of your siblings."

It's a logical enough argument, sure. But for me in this moment, it's the wrong one.

"If it's right, there shouldn't be any guilt. I can't be some rebound for you. It's not how I pictured any of this."

"You pictured it?" She seems well and truly surprised by that.

"Archer wasn't wrong when he said I have feelings for you."

She moves toward me and wraps her arms around me. I feel my resolve weakening as my eyes meet hers, as I study those gorgeous freckles up close.

"What kind of feelings?" she whispers as she stares up into my eyes.

I'm quiet a beat, and then I eviscerate myself, choosing to turn my gaze to the window as I make this confession. "I've been in love with you for ten years. Maybe more. Fuck, maybe since I met you almost half my life ago."

I glance at her, and her eyes soften as if in understanding. "You've waited that long for me?"

I clench my jaw, the muscles working back and forth as I contemplate how to answer that. "No. I couldn't wait. I had to try to find some connection like I felt with you. I'm still looking."

"But I want this, too, Ford. I see it now. I see *you*."

"Then let's take our time. As much as I want to take you to my bedroom, strip you naked, and fuck you until morning, I won't allow this to be less than everything it is."

She pushes up to press a soft kiss to my mouth. "I'll wait until you're ready."

She has no idea how fucking ready I am. How ready I've been. It's a contradiction to the words I'm speaking.

The right thing is often the hard thing, and this feels like the right thing. I finally nod as I try to search for what it is that will be the signal to me that she's ready, the moment I know she's well and truly over my brother and ready to move on.

I'm not sure I have an answer for when that will be, but I feel like I'll know it when I see it.

"I'll wait until you're ready, too," I say softly, and I press one more kiss to her lips before I let go of her. I carry her suitcases back to the guest room—her room, now—and then I head to my own room to take a long, cold shower where I can give my cock the release he so desperately needs.

CHAPTER 22

Tatum Barker

Manila Envelope

I'm not mad, but I'm definitely…something.

Hot, for one thing.

I tear off my jeans and bra, and I change into just a T-shirt for bed, not bothering with shorts.

I slip under the covers of the bed in the guest room. All alone.

I don't think he realizes how ready I am to move on. Or how freaking horny I am after all that hot kissing.

Archer was a good kisser, but there's something totally different about Ford's kisses. They're all-consuming, like our souls are somehow connecting.

This feels big. Important. Different.

I'm trying not to make comparisons to Archer, but it's hard since he was my first love. My first…well, everything. I don't have a big basis for comparison outside of him except for one hookup after one of our breakups. He had one, too. We both thought it was well and truly over that time, and when it wasn't, we were honest with each other about it when we got back together.

And I get it from Ford's perspective. We *thought* it was well and truly over in the past, and it wasn't. He's waiting for us to get back together since we have every other time.

He doesn't want to be the hookup I have to confess to my partner when we patch things up. But that's the thing—we're not patching things up this time.

The past week in Vegas *felt* different. Of course I still love Archer. He's a great guy, and I spent half my life either wanting to be with him or actually being with him. And I think that's part of why we held on so long. It was comfortable. It was easy. But it was also nothing more than friendship for far too long despite trying to pretend like it was more.

And nothing made me more aware of that fact than seeing him in the flesh and not feeling those old feelings I once felt. I didn't have butterflies when I landed in Vegas. Instead, I had dread.

But when I landed back in Tampa, I had butterflies. I had excitement to see Ford. My pulse thundered so loudly I could hear it in my ears. My legs felt weak. I felt nervous. It felt like the start of something *new*. Exciting. Different.

And that kiss?

God.

I touch my fingertips to my lips as I think about that kiss, and then I can't seem to help myself as I lie in the bed in Ford's guest room. I picture the surprise in his eyes at the airport as I moved in toward him, just before I closed my own eyes and pressed my mouth to his.

I lick my fingers, and then I push them into my panties. I stroke my clit softly at first, and I open my thighs to give myself more room. I push my finger into my pussy, and I didn't need to lick it first. I'm plenty wet after Ford warmed me up with all that kissing. It was deep, sensual, sexy. Fucking hot.

I pump my finger in and out as I remember the feel of his mouth on mine. The way he smelled, the way he tasted. The way he felt.

I slip my other hand under my T-shirt and grip onto my nipple as I slide my finger out of my pussy and furiously rub my clit. I feel the wave wash over me as something gives way, and I clamp my legs together as the pleasure undulates over me, pulse after pulse. I do my best to stay quiet through it, but my God, did I need that release more than I realized.

The only problem is that as soon as it ends and I lie panting alone in the guest room, the ache presses in on me again.

I want Ford Bradley, but it looks like I'm going to have to wait for him.

I'm not used to waiting. I'm used to getting what I want because I go after it.

And I *could* go after it. I could walk into his room, tear my shirt off, and slide into bed beside him, and he'd give me exactly what I want.

But I can't do that to him. I can't do that to *us*. He's right. If we're going to make it past a one-night hookup, we need to wait until the time is right.

It feels right for me, but it looks like maybe it's not right for him.

* * *

Ford agreed to accompany me to *our* manor to show Devon and Lindsay around the place on Tuesday. I walk into the kitchen after I'm ready for the day, and he nods toward some takeout boxes on the counter.

"I ordered breakfast."

"Thank you," I say, and I open the top box to find an omelet with two sides of bacon. I pass that container over to Ford, and I open the second one to find waffles and sausage.

The man knows me well, I'll give him that. "This was really sweet of you." I grab a sausage from the box and take a bite, and I tip my head back in ecstasy. Something about the salty goodness of breakfast sausage just can't be beat.

He shifts a little, and he shoots me a wry look. "You sure know how to torture a guy."

I make a little show of it, moaning loudly with my second bite. "You're the one who wants to wait."

He chuckles. "I'm ready."

My lips lift into a smile. "I know. So am I. But I get it, Ford. We'll give it a little time to be sure it's going to work. After all, we have an investment together to consider."

"There are no guarantees it's going to work no matter how much time we give it," he points out.

I open the syrup container and dump it all over my waffle. "I'm just saying, we have the manor to consider. And as a friend...I can't lose you."

"So you'll never be ready?" he asks. "Or am I worth that risk?"

I glance up at him, and a heated beat passes between us as our eyes connect. I think of his lips on mine last night. "You're worth the risk. When you're ready, we'll jump together, okay?"

He nods, and I hope he's ready sooner than later.

We spend the rest of breakfast talking shop about Winston Manor, and then we head out to the place itself to get ready for our first couple's site visit.

It's exactly as we left it, and my chest fills with excitement as we walk through the front door. I don't think that feeling will ever go away. This is *ours*, and that's pretty damn exciting.

Ms. Winston moved some personal effects out but left mostly everything. We find a manila envelope sitting on the little table in the corner of the kitchen, where we're set to meet with our first potential clients in a few minutes.

As we get closer, we both see words written in small handwriting on the outside of the envelope. *To the New Owners.*

Ford and I exchange a glance, and he picks up the envelope and turns it over in his hands before he offers it to me.

I shake my head. "You do it."

He tears it open and pulls out a sheet of paper. His eyes move over the words on the paper, and they widen at one point as his breath hitches.

"What is it?" I ask.

He shoves the paper toward me, and I grab it and start reading.

Ford and Tatum,

Thank you for agreeing to my terms about the manor. Selling it was never about making money. I don't have anybody to leave the money to, anyway. I thought about a charity, or splitting it among the workers who have been with me for decades, but ultimately I wanted it to go back to the manor. To that end, the money has been put in a trust in your names. The money will be released to you upon the conclusion of your wedding ceremony here at the manor. The only requirement is that the first wedding at the manor after ownership has transferred is between the two of you. There are no other strings attached to this. You don't have to stay married for a certain amount of time or anything like that. I already know you will be together forever based on the way I saw you interacting the day I showed you around the manor. You share a bond that's rare, but it's obvious to anyone looking for it. I've searched for it in the couples who wed here in the sixty years I planned weddings, and I hope that you'll find it in the weddings you plan, too.

Snap DECISION

Here's to forever love and the future of Winston Manor.
-Edith Winston

"She's leaving her money…to us?" I ask.

His eyes are wide. "If we get married."

"Holy shit, Ford. We could invest in *more* properties. This is incredible!" I fling my arms around him without thinking about how maybe this *isn't* so incredible.

She thought we were a couple. We're not. We've talked about it, sort of. But marriage? The *first* wedding here at the manor now that we're the owners?

That's when we hear a knock at the front door.

I pull back, and I don't have time to process any of this because we have guests. We have a tour to give. A wedding to plan. A wedding that will have to take place after ours if we want to see that money.

"Let's, uh…let's talk after we show them around, okay?" Ford asks carefully.

I nod, and we rush to the door to let them in. "Welcome to Winston Manor," I say, sweeping my arm out to showcase the grand ballroom.

Lindsay gasps as she takes it in. I think Devon gasps, too. This place is a hidden gem that's not going to be so hidden now that I'm here.

We'll have events every weekend. We'll make enough to hire a staff to manage it so I can keep building toward my dream.

And we even have the chance to get our investment back. I just have to find some way to convince Ford that it's the right thing to do.

CHAPTER 23

FORD BRADLEY

Six Weeks

*T**he only requirement is that yours is the first wedding at the manor after ownership has transferred.*

We let her think we were a couple. That was our first mistake.

Or was it?

I'm stuck somewhere in the middle on that, to be honest.

This is my chance. My shot to prove we belong together.

But literally *last night*, I rejected her advances and told her we needed to wait until she was ready. It's barely been twelve hours since that conversation, yet here we are, considering planning a wedding to each other because someone else told us to.

Who would say no to marrying the only woman they've ever loved for a cool five mil?

Nobody in their right mind, that's for damn sure.

And she *does* need the money so she can invest in her business.

It's quite the conundrum. Quirky old people and their quirky conditions.

I do my best to put it out of my mind as we give the tour to Devon and Lindsay.

"I need to move up the date a bit," I hear Lindsay say to Tatum as we stand in the backyard overlooking the dock.

"Move it up?" Tatum squeaks, clearly losing her cool at that.

Lindsay rubs her stomach. "I'm pregnant!"

"Congratulations," Tatum says, and I can hear the anxiety in her tone. I'm sure she's happy for the happy couple and their upcoming baby news, but this is going to force a timeline on us that we certainly weren't expecting. "You had mentioned in the offseason before, around June, which gave us six months to plan. When are you thinking of moving it up to?"

"I don't want to be showing in photos, and I'm already eight weeks. So we were thinking no later than six weeks."

"From now?" Tatum squeaks again.

"From now." She pulls out her phone and taps around. "So say...no later than January nineteenth."

"But what about playoffs?" Tatum asks. "You won't be showing *that much* yet if you wait until, say, mid-February, right?"

"I mean, I'll be eighteen weeks by then, so yeah. I might be pretty bloated." She shrugs. "It's one day out of the week, and Dev won't care. Actually, let's do that Monday before the nineteenth so we can have one night off together."

"So six weeks from yesterday," Tatum says flatly.

"Yes. Six weeks from yesterday, and definitely here. This is the most romantic, perfect venue we've seen. Can you pull that off?" Lindsay asks.

I'm trying to catch Tatum's eye. I'm trying to give her some sort of signal to tell her *no*, to plainly express that we cannot possibly pull off a wedding *here* in six weeks.

"Yes, of course," Tatum says, and my heart drops down into my stomach.

If she wants that money, which I know she does, then that means she needs to marry me in less than six weeks.

Fuck.

My phone starts to ring, and it's my realtor back in Chicago. "I'm so sorry, but I need to take this," I say, and I head inside to take the call in privacy. I wander upstairs to the top floor as I answer. "Ford Bradley."

"Mr. Bradley, it's Sonny Russo. I just got an offer on the mansion and wanted to share it with you."

My chest tightens.

"It's a little lower than asking, but I don't think it's unfair. There are a few pieces of furniture they'd like to keep as well as the appliances and built-ins."

"What's the offer, Sonny?" I ask, staring out the window at the view here.

"Fourteen."

"That's a million dollars lower than asking," I say. It's definitely unfair. They're lowballing me, and I know what that place is worth.

"So negotiate," he says. "If I were you, I'd take it. But I understand the attachment."

"I'm not attached," I hiss, and I know he only said that to get a rise out of me. "I'll give them their concessions for fifteen."

"I'll take it back to them, but I think this is a mistake," he says.

"I'm not paying you for your opinions, Sonny." It's more curt than I'm used to being with him, but this isn't some backyard deal. This is a fifteen-million-dollar mansion.

Snap DECISION

"No, Mr. Bradley. You're right. You're not paying me *at all* until there's a sale. That's what I'm trying to get for you."

"Fifteen," I say. "Not a penny lower."

"Yes, sir."

I cut the call and draw in a breath as I contemplate what the fuck I'm supposed to do here, and I'm coming up short.

I know I should wait, but I need to process this through before I make a decision, and with less than six weeks to spare, I don't have the time to make an informed decision.

Before I even realize what I'm doing, I press the button to call my sister. She's one of the few people I can confide in when times get tough, and if this isn't tough, well…I don't know what is.

"Ford?" she answers.

"Hey. Is this a bad time?"

"Not at all. What's going on?"

"I just got an offer on Mom and Dad's place."

"How much?" she asks.

"Fourteen million."

"I hope you said no," she says.

I chuckle. "I did."

"So why are you calling?"

"I'm, uh…" I trail off as I try to find the words. "I'm in a bit of a situation here."

"What is it, and how can I help?"

"I kissed her."

"Kissed who?"

"Tatum," I murmur.

"Oh. Oh! And?"

"She kissed me back. She told me she has feelings for me, and I fucking blew it."

"What? How?" she asks.

"She just got back from Vegas, from visiting Archer. She said they're done, and she also said he gave her permission to be with me." I stare down at her, below me in the yard. She's laughing with Lindsay, and she flips her hair over her shoulder as if we don't have this huge weight settling between us at the hands of some quirky old woman.

"Wow. That's big," she says.

"Yeah. I guess. But it just felt...I don't know. Wrong. Like we shouldn't need someone's permission to be together. So I backed off and told her I wanted to wait until she was really ready."

"Oh, Ford." She sighs. "You're such a good guy."

"It was selfish, Ev. I didn't do it to be good. I did it because I didn't want to be a rebound," I say.

"Who could blame you for that? It was the right thing to do. When the time is right, it'll work out." Her words feel like generalized platitudes that anyone could say about anything at any time.

I blow out a breath. "You know how Tatum and I went in on a wedding venue together?"

"Mm-hmm," she prompts.

"There was a letter from the owner today. It said the money we paid for the mansion is in a trust that will revert back to us if ours is the first wedding that takes place here," I blurt.

Everleigh is silent on the other end of the line.

"Well?" I prompt.

"Shit, Ford. I don't know what to say. How much money are we talking?"

"Enough for Tatum to invest in other properties. Enough to make her dreams come true. Enough to make mine come true, too...just not the way I want it."

"That's the problem with dreams," she murmurs. "Either we get it and it's not everything we thought it would be, or it comes around in a way we never could have expected."

"How is that true for you? You've got it all."

Snap DECISION

"Yeah, *now*, sure. Everything's been great for the last month, but it was a hell of a road to get here. Remember a few months ago when I said I'd never work with an athlete?" She laughs after she says it because now she *only* works with athletes. "I got what I wanted in the end, but not at all how I expected. And maybe that's what this is for you, too. Maybe instead of taking it slow and dating, you marry her and then get her to fall for you. Just, like, pick up around the house, okay? Nobody falls for the guy who leaves dirty socks on the floor."

"Duly noted," I say dryly. It feels strange having this conversation here in this place, like Ms. Winston is watching and can hear me, like she'll know that even if we do go through with it, it'll be a sham. Except…will it be? "Well, thanks, I guess."

She laughs. "You'll make the right decision, Ford. Of all the Bradley siblings, I feel like you're somehow the one who ended up with the strongest gut instincts."

I hope she's right because wherever my gut leads me this time has the potential to change my life forever.

CHAPTER 24

Tatum Barker

Twenty-Two Days

I'm not going to turn away business. That would be stupid.

But six weeks? Six weeks! She wants to move the wedding, I'm trying *not* to freak out, Ford disappeared, and six weeks?

Six weeks.

I'm still wrapping my head around it, but I can't seem to find a reason *not* to get that money back. The note said there were no other strings attached to the money, that we just had to be the first wedding there. An idea sparks in my mind.

"What about holding the ceremony somewhere else? Like maybe at your church? And then just having the reception here?" It could be the loophole I've been searching for.

She shakes her head. "I want the ceremony here. Right here, actually." She nods to the yard where we're standing, and she spreads her arms around to indicate what she means. "A quick one. No chairs, even, except one for my grandmama. I want our guests to be in a circle around us instead, and then the reception inside where the tables are already set up. We'll keep it simple since we cut planning time."

"I can make that work," I say weakly. I feel like I'm going to throw up.

Could I really marry my ex-boyfriend's brother in some crazy bid to get the money back from this place?

Yes. The answer is yes.

It's five million dollars. Twice as much as the trust fund I blew through to put up my half of the capital for this place.

This is my future. These are my goals and my dreams being served up to me. This is a gift from the universe. You don't reject gifts from the universe, or you may never get another one.

And that's what I tell Ford after Devon and Lindsay cut us a check for the deposit to hold their date here at the manor.

I close the door behind them and lean on it, and his eyes meet mine.

"What are you thinking?" he asks carefully.

I don't want to go first, but I do. "The universe is giving us a gift, and we can't reject that gift even if the way to claim that gift is a bit nontraditional."

"So you're a yes, then," he says flatly. It's not a question but a statement.

"What are you?" I ask.

"I don't know," he admits. "I'm trying to think it all through. Would we tell Archer the truth? Would we invite our families? Tell them? Would we need to start being seen publicly so it's not such a huge shock when we show up married?"

I bite my bottom lip as I contemplate his questions—all things I didn't consider at all with those dollar signs in my eyes, but he's a public figure, and so is everybody else in his family. "We should tell Archer. It would be too big a shock for him to find out from the media that we're suddenly married. We could tell everyone close to us, and they can decide if they want to attend, or we could just do it and tell Winston's lawyer that we had to make it quick since we had a wedding booked."

"What if it got back to Ms. Winston that we're not a couple?" he asks.

"She said no strings attached." Besides…what if we *do* become a couple? We're in a weird timeline where that could actually happen.

"I can't just get married," he points out. "My life is under a microscope. You sure you want those headlines?"

I sigh, not sure how to answer that. I don't care about the headlines, really. I'm more focused on what would happen if we got married and then things started to work out for us. Is it a possibility? Maybe. We already have feelings for each other. Maybe I was with the wrong brother the whole time, and this was always meant to be where I'd end up.

I won't know if I don't give it a try. The money is the motivator here, obviously. But there are other reasons to marry Ford. There doesn't have to be an expiration date on us.

I turn toward the windows like the answers will be out there. They aren't. It's still just a gorgeous yard overlooking a dock and water beyond that.

Eventually, he sighs. "Doesn't it feel like dirty money if we're doing it for the wrong reasons?"

His logic is both something I love and hate about him.

"So, what do you suggest, then?" I ask. "It's a lot of money to leave on the table, Ford. Maybe I could even find a way to use my portion to finance the Bradley Mansion, or we could invest together in that like we did this one."

His jaw works back and forth as he clenches it, and it's really fucking hot when he does that.

Snap DECISION

We have feelings for each other. We've known each other a long time. Would it really be so bad to jump into this with him?

No. The answer is definitely *no*, it wouldn't be so bad at all. At least I don't think it would be.

I wish I had someone I could sort through this with that wasn't as invested as Ford is. But the truth is that I have Kenzie, who wouldn't understand because she's in the perfect marriage already, my brother, who I don't talk to about things like this and would pick Ford for me anyway, and…Ford.

He's who I would call.

I throw myself wholly and totally into my projects, and since college, my projects have been Archer and my business. It's why I don't have close girlfriends except for the woman I hired who works in the office next to mine.

So now that one project has ended and the other has the chance to accelerate at a high rate of speed, what am I supposed to do? I can't talk to Archer about it, that's for damn sure.

So where do I turn?

I'm staring at the answer, and we're talking it out. Still, it would help to have an opinion from someone with no skin in the game.

His eyes edge over to mine, and we stare off for a few beats as we each think this thing through. I've gotten by on my own instincts just fine up to this point, and something is telling me yes. It's like it's pumped through the air vents in this place or something. I was sure when I brought Ford upstairs and talked him into going halfsies on this place with me.

And I'm sure about this, too. "I think we should do it."

His brows shoot up in surprise. And then, as if there's also something pumped through the air vents that causes practical people to make absolutely impractical decisions, he nods. "Then let's do it."

My jaw drops at his words. "Are you serious?"

He narrows his eyes at me. "Do you not want to?"

"No, I do. I just thought you'd be the one to talk some sense into me."

"When it comes to you, I'm not sure I have any sense at all."

I rush at him and fling my arms around his neck.

His response is a soft *oof* even as he loops his arm around my waist. "You ready to be Mrs. Bradley?"

The name sends a shot of something down my spine.

I've been ready to be Mrs. Bradley since I was in high school. It's just not the Bradley I thought it would be.

And I'm starting to think this one's even better…even though I'll likely have to keep my name since it's attached to all my branding.

He's been standing right in front of me this entire time, and I was too blinded by Archer to see.

But I see him now, and I can't wait to get planning for the future I never saw coming.

It feels like I have a ton of big decisions to make, and it's not just cake flavors and guest lists and choosing the best date for us.

It's about where to live. Where to work. Where to place my next investment.

The day after we agreed to get married, I can't stop pulling up the listing for the Bradley Mansion. There are just so many precious memories there in that house—and not solely with Archer, but with Ford, too.

It's a piece of our history. It's that fallen kingdom imagery, and I want to be the one who steps in and gives life back to a place that seemed to have lost everything.

Snap DECISION

I flip through the photographs on Zillow. I labor over every single one. I envision the walls we could knock down, working with the Bradley Group—my *brother-in-law*—on a project that would be close to his heart, too, since it's where he grew up.

I can't stop looking at the view of the Chicago skyline, either. It's *so* gorgeous from the mansion's backyard, an image that nearly looks photoshopped.

I see a bride and a groom standing there, two people who adore their hometown and chose this city as the backdrop of the most special day of their lives.

I force myself to close the window.

I have a shitload of work to accomplish now that I'm planning not one but *two* weddings set to take place in a town I'm still getting to know, and the last thing I should be doing is staring at Zillow.

And to that end, once Ford is home from practice, I bring up my living situation over dinner.

"Have you thought about our living arrangement at all?" I ask.

He shakes his head. "I assumed you'd stay with me. Are you moving somewhere else?"

"Well, yeah. I mean, I don't have a home back in Vegas anymore. I moved out of the house I shared with Archer, moved my stuff into storage, and crashed with a friend when I went back for the charity event and the wedding. But what are your thoughts on me moving here?"

"Like *here* here? Permanently?" he asks, indicating his condo with a fork.

"Ideally, yes. *Here* here. In Tampa. With you. Since we're getting married." The words still feel strange coming out of my mouth. I can't believe this is really happening as quickly as it is.

He looks a little dazed. "Right. Yes, of course. Move in. Bring whatever you want. I can arrange a moving truck to get your stuff here if that's what you'd like so it feels like your home, too."

"I don't want to overstep." I pop a french fry into my mouth.

"Don't be ridiculous. I love having you here, and you're right. If we're getting married, we should live together. It makes the most sense."

None of this makes any sense at all, but I keep that thought to myself.

"When should we do this?" I ask quietly.

"Move in?"

"Get married."

"It has to be before…" He trails off, prompting me.

"January eighteenth is Lindsay and Devon's wedding."

His eyes widen. It's December ninth now. That doesn't give us a whole lot of time.

"New Year's Eve." He says it with finality rather than as a question.

"New Year's Eve?" I ask.

He lifts a shoulder. "It's always seemed like such a meaningful holiday to me, don't you think? It's a chance to celebrate the good stuff and leave behind the bad stuff. It feels like a new marriage is sort of celebrating the same thing."

"Ford Bradley," I taunt. "I didn't peg you as a romantic."

His eyes are hot when they meet mine. "You never gave me the chance."

His vulnerable words pulse a pit deep in my stomach.

According to his brother, Ford has had feelings for me for a long time. And now I'm jumping straight to marriage with him without any of the other stuff first. I can only imagine what's going through his mind right now.

Snap DECISION

I bite my lip, and then I say, "I know we said we'd wait, but what if I don't want to wait? What if I want to experience life with you *now*? The ups, the downs, the joys, and the hard stuff. All of it."

He looks surprised at my words, and then he surprises me with words of his own. "Go out on a date with me."

"What?"

"Let's go out on a date. A real date, not some charity event. Though I do have tickets to a black-tie event next week if you want to make our red-carpet debut. But I mean something just for the two of us. Date me. Let me take you to dinner and a movie. Let me hold your hand in public and kiss you goodnight. Let's see how it goes for the next twenty-two days, and we can decide if we want our wedding night to be *the* night."

"*The* night?" I repeat.

"The night I finally get you naked in my bed," he says darkly.

A tight ache throbs between my legs.

And suddenly, just like that...I don't know if I can wait twenty-two days.

CHAPTER 25

FORD BRADLEY

We're a We

I'm not sure why I said New Year's Eve. Maybe so I'll always remember our anniversary, but deep down I know that's not something I'd ever forget no matter what date we chose.

We.

We're a *we*.

It's just to get the money, but it also feels like it's *not* just to get the money.

Lines are blurring, and we're about to hyper speed this whole *dating* process during the time of my season when I'm supposed to have my focus on the field. We're making a playoff run, and we're currently in second place in our division. Every game matters now, and if we win against the team in first place when we play them in week sixteen, we have the best shot of a playoff spot without having to fight in the wild card game.

This is the toughest time of the year. We're all under an immense amount of pressure.

Snap DECISION

We need to stay healthy, and that includes not just avoiding injury but our mental health as well.

I don't need these dates and this impending wedding clouding my focus right now, but it's not like I can pass up the chance to be with the woman I've loved since high school…to make her fall in love with me, too. What if marrying her is the thing that keeps my mental health in balance?

I text her before I pull out of the parking lot at practice on Wednesday.

Me: *Put on shoes you can walk in and meet me downstairs in fifteen minutes.*

She's there when I pull up in front of the building, and she hops right into the passenger seat.

"What's all this?" she asks, and she's a little breathless, like she spent the last fifteen minutes running around getting ready for the mystery location where our first date will take place.

"It's our first date," I say.

She laughs as she buckles in. "Is it?"

"I don't really count the cake tasting, do you?"

"I suppose not. It wasn't intentionally a date. But then you kissed me and started this whole thing." She waves a hand between us.

"I think we should definitely have the honey and fig sex cake at our wedding, don't you?" I tease.

"Definitely," she squeaks.

I chuckle as we head toward our destination. We arrive, and I pull into a parking lot.

"Where are you taking me?" she asks.

"The Riverwalk," I say, nodding ahead of me. "They have food trucks tonight, so I thought we could grab a bite to eat and walk along the water. You know, like a real date."

"I love it," she says. She's always been the type of person who's up for anything, and maybe she appreciates the simplicity of this date. It's showing her that we can just be a normal couple even though there's a chance I'll be recognized. It's a little easier to stay incognito at night with a ball cap on than during the day without one, so I grab a hat from my backseat and slip it on.

We get out of the car, and I walk around to take her hand in mine. And that's how we walk along the Riverwalk. The sun is sinking into the Hillsborough River, and the backdrop of Tampa is stunning at this time of the evening. We walk along and see a variety of shops and bars along with statues and parks.

It's a reminder of why I love this town. That even after my playing days are over, maybe I'll stay. I have a reason to stay since I own a property here now—or half of one, anyway—and it's just convincing enough to keep me here.

And it's far, far away from my brother…my future wife's ex.

The thought comes thunderously unbidden into my mind, and it clings on.

I need to tell him that I'm marrying Tatum. Or she needs to tell him. One of us needs to. He deserves that much.

And we will. We're still three weeks out. We have time…sort of.

We stop at a food truck, and she orders fish tacos while I opt for a chicken and quinoa bowl to keep my diet as healthy as I can while I'm out on a date.

I kiss her goodnight at the front door, and I don't make a move beyond that.

It takes exactly one hundred percent of my willpower not to ask her if she'd like to join me in my bedroom.

Snap DECISION

And so I fist my cock in the shower, pumping up and down until the cum spills out onto my hand with her name a breathless whisper on my lips.

I'm not as sensible with my eating the next night after we go miniature golfing and get ourselves an ice cream treat afterward.

Or the next night when we head to a drive-in movie theater and opt for hot dogs and popcorn.

I know what I *should* be doing when it comes to my eating habits—and my dating habits at this time in the season, for that matter. But I can't seem to stop. I have zero self-control when it comes to her, and these dates are bonding us closer than ever. Why would I possibly want to stop that?

And once the movie starts and the lights go down, she leans her elbow on the console. I do the same, and soon my arm is around her, and we're turning in toward each other, and then we're making out as we miss the entire movie in favor of kissing. And a little over the shirt tit action.

It's another night of jerking off in the shower.

On Saturday morning before I have to leave for practice, I ask over breakfast, "Do you want to come to the game on Sunday?"

She tilts her head as she thinks about it. "Where would I sit?"

"I can get you tickets pretty much wherever you want."

"And I'd just go…by myself?"

"You could probably sit with Lindsay."

"I could…but she's a client, and if I go, I don't want to talk shop. I want to watch the game." She twists her lips and sighs. "I really need to make some friends here in Tampa."

"No better way to get that underway than to attend a game," I suggest, and she agrees.

Saturday night is spent away from each other, and I use the time at the team hotel to catch up on the film I should have been studying all week. All games matter, but none are as important as our matchup next weekend against the Fury in Nashville. We should easily be able to beat the Falcons this weekend, while the Fury has a harder matchup against the Forty-Niners.

We need them to lose. We need to win this week and next. It's simple math. That's our path to the playoffs.

I'm focused as I take the field on Sunday. I know Tatum is here somewhere, and that makes me feel a little lighter.

Everything is off to a good start. A *great* start, really. But it all sinks down the drain in the third quarter.

Our quarterback, Grant Landry, snaps the ball, and I'm being used as a blocker on this play. I do my job, carefully keeping my weight balanced as I explode off the line to meet the defensive end. I'm keeping him back using every tool in my arsenal, and that's why I don't see the defensive tackle slant on the outside.

He rushes right for Grant and takes him down.

Sacks are common in this game, averaging two or three per game. Some have none, some have seven. But what it comes down to is that someone didn't do his job correctly. It wasn't me. I kept Darius Briggs away from Grant.

So sacks are common. It's common for the quarterback to get taken down and pop right back up to keep playing. Sometimes the wind gets knocked out of them, and that's the worst of it. But on some rare occasions, the quarterback gets taken down, and he doesn't get right back up.

This is one of those times. He's grabbing onto the shoulder of his throwing arm, which is bad news for us.

Real bad news.

We've still got a chance to win this game, and we still have a shot at the playoffs. But if Grant's injury is more serious than a bruise, we're fucked. We're not going to get past the teams waiting to beat us if we don't have our starting quarterback.

The training staff rushes over to help him off the field, and he lifts to a stand to the thunderous roar of the crowd. But his arm doesn't look right, and it's a sharp reminder that none of us are invincible.

We finish the game with our backup, Reggie Maddox, and we were far enough ahead that we still win even though we don't put more points on the board. He's not a bad player, but he's young, and his nerves are incredibly apparent each time he steps onto the line of scrimmage.

As we gather in the locker room, Coach looks emotional as he says, "Looks like Landry's dealing with an AC joint sprain." A collective groan rises up from the group, but Coach talks through it. "We're looking at three to six weeks."

Fuck. At the earliest end, that puts us at Wild Card Weekend. At the later end…we'd be out of contention.

Everyone in this room knows it's a team sport, but if we don't have a quarterback who can put up points the way he has all season, we're fucked.

Coach gives us some encouraging words before he heads out to his presser. I take a shower and change into my clothes before I head out of the locker room.

Tatum is waiting for me in the hallway. She's standing beside some of the other girlfriends of players, and a wide array of emotions comes crashing into me. Disappointment that my season may be down the drain. Gratitude that she's here. Frustration that we can't heal Grant's shoulder any faster. Love for the woman standing here waiting for me.

I rush toward her and take her in my arms, and not a single bit of what I'm feeling is fake—except if you count the fact that I'm holding back how much I actually feel for her.

She wraps me in her arms, and I force myself to remain the stoic man I'm known to be. I feel it, though. All of it. It's plowing into me from every angle, but mobile phones are out, and plenty of people are around to catch my reaction to what went down on that field today.

I'm not here to comment on it. It's Coach's job to share what happened with Grant, not mine. So I pull out of our embrace, grab Tatum's hand, and lead her toward my car in the player parking lot so we can head home.

CHAPTER 26

Tatum Barker

Peppermint Schnapps

Once we're on the road on our way back home, I ask, "What happened with the quarterback?"

Ford clenches his jaw, and I watch as it works back and forth. "He sprained his shoulder."

"Ouch. What does that mean?"

"Torn ligaments. He'll push to come back sooner, but if it doesn't heal completely, he won't have the range of motion to throw deep balls."

I force away the rather immature inclination to make a joke about deep balls.

"But if he doesn't come back sooner, our playoff run is fucked before we even get underway," he finishes. He glances over at me. "Nice sidestep on the deep balls, by the way."

I giggle. "You like that?"

He chuckles as he reaches over and grabs my hand, keeping his other hand on the steering wheel. At least he can laugh about it.

Snap DECISION

"I'm sorry, Ford," I say quietly, and I squeeze his hand. "This must be so hard for you, but isn't there still a chance you could make the playoffs?"

He lifts a shoulder. "There's always a chance, I guess. But Reggie isn't as seasoned as Grant. He doesn't have the accuracy or the instincts. He's nervous on his feet because he's young and inexperienced."

"Guess that means the tight butts have to work harder," I say, and my cheeks burn when I realize my mistake.

"Tight butts?" he repeats, calling me out on it.

"Sorry. I know you're a tight *end*. I know that's what it's called. In my head, though, I see those tight, white pants over your cute little butt, and that's where my head goes." So much for resisting those immature urges.

"You think my butt is cute?" he asks.

"Adorable."

He chuckles, but the levity doesn't last long. He lets out a heavy sigh.

"How does this time of year usually go for you?" I ask, genuinely curious. Christmas is a week from Friday. In my part of the world, we're hanging wreaths and decorating trees and hosting office Christmas events. In fact, I should be in Vegas now, but I have Kenzie on it. She's taking care of several Christmas events while I run away from my life in Vegas and attempt to create a new one here. Same last name, different brother.

He lifts a shoulder. "Depends on our record. There's nothing predictable about December. Sometimes we've already secured our playoff spot, and other times we already know we're out. And then there are the times like this year where every second on the field counts."

"Which do you like best?" I ask. It's a ridiculous question, right? Of course he's going to prefer the year where his spot is secure.

He surprises me when he says, "Years like this one—minus the injury. I'm a competitor at heart, and there's nothing more frustrating than being in a locker room with people who have already given up or, worse, who get cocky because the rest of the season doesn't matter. I'm leaving everything I have out there each week, but you find all kinds in a locker room."

"Are you close with your teammates?"

"I'd call most of them friends, but I'm probably closest to Cole, TJ, and Kellan."

"Who, what, and where?" I ask.

He laughs. "Cole Andrews is a tight end. TJ Brooks and Kellan Price are both wide receivers. We hit the town together sometimes."

I'm not sure why my chest tightens a little at that. They *hit the town*, and everybody knows that has to mean they're out picking up women.

I don't like the sound of that. It makes me wonder how many women he's been with. It's not my business, not *really*, but at the same time, if we're getting married, it kind of is. And my big mouth opens before I get the chance to stop it. "What does *hit the town* mean?"

He shrugs. "You know. Go out. Get a few drinks together."

"Pick up ladies and head home separately?"

"Sometimes," he admits carefully.

"Is that what you do?"

"I can't say I never have. But what I can say is that the last time Cole talked me into going out, even though I technically went home with the girl, I never stepped foot into her apartment and instead caught an Uber home."

My brows dip down. "Why?"

Snap DECISION

He stares straight ahead, and his voice is low as he says, "Because it wasn't fair to her that I was thinking of someone else."

My breath catches in my throat.

Oh.

He means me.

I'm not quite sure how to respond to that, and I mumble something about how that was gentlemanly before I switch back to the topic at hand. "So do you even celebrate Christmas?"

"Depends what day of the week it falls on. If it's a Monday or Tuesday, I'll fly to Chicago for the day. Any other day, I either have practice or a game."

"So this year it's a Friday," I say. "What are your plans?"

"Breakfast with my fiancée, maybe exchanging a gift if that's something you'd like to do, and then it's practice and preparing for Sunday."

I press my lips together. What do you get the guy you're going to marry that hails from a billionaire family and can get anything he wants at the snap of a football?

I'll have to think about that, but I'm curious enough about what he'll get me that I say, "I'd love to exchange gifts with you."

He nods. "Then we'll do it."

"Can we get a Christmas tree tomorrow? It doesn't feel like Christmas at your place, so we need to decorate."

"Absolutely." A cute little crooked smile plays at his lips. "But Tate?"

"Hm?" I ask, glancing over at him.

"It's *our* place now."

My heart melts a little at that.

We arrive at *our* place, and I pull up a cheesy Christmas movie as I settle in on the couch. "Watch with me," I say, and he grabs some popcorn and settles in beside me.

Our thighs are touching.

I know we're getting married. I know we're in this trial dating phase. But he usually doesn't sit this close to me, and I can't help but like it.

A lot.

I want to touch more than just those thighs.

Our hands meet in the popcorn bowl, our eyes meet before either of us moves our hand away, and it's as cute and as cheesy as the movie we're watching.

We haven't even made it to second base, but I'm definitely feeling some feelings.

Those feelings only intensify as we head to the store the next morning, and he tells me to pick out whatever ornaments I want. We drive to the Christmas tree lot next, and he lets me take the lead. He doesn't balk when I pick out the biggest tree, as I imagine how perfect it will look in the middle of his floor-to-ceiling windows overlooking the bay, and he doesn't complain with a single word as he wraps it in twinkling lights the moment we get it unloaded and set up.

Instead, he hums Christmas carols along with the random playlist Alexa blares for us while I sing at the top of my lungs as I take the ornaments out of their protective packaging to get them ready to hang on the tree.

He pours two glasses of some sort of liquor, and he hands me one.

"A Bradley tradition," he says, holding his glass up.

I must look confused because he clarifies as I tap my glass to his.

"I've had a glass of this every year around the holidays since I was fifteen, usually while I'm decorating or doing something festive."

"Fifteen?" I repeat, taking a whiff of it.

He chuckles. "Yeah, well, when you have two older brothers and an older sister, you get started early. It was something Madden drank in college, and he brought a bottle to our family holiday gathering. Dex was home, too, and they got wasted on it. They offered me some, and I chugged a full cup. Needless to say, it wasn't long before I was puking my guts out."

"Most people would never drink it again, but that made it a tradition for you?" I tease. I take a sip and wrinkle my nose. It's strong, whatever it is, and I take a look at the bottle. "McGillicuddy's peppermint schnapps," I read.

"I always keep a bottle around for the holidays. Reminds me of simpler times with my brothers."

I'm tempted to ask if Archer got drunk on it, too, but since he never kept a bottle of it around, I'd venture to guess he wasn't part of that tradition.

And besides, I don't particularly want to talk about my ex right now.

I tip the glass to my lips and take a sip, and it's actually pretty good. It warms my chest and leaves me with a minty taste in my mouth.

"Hot chocolate was a tradition in my family, and honestly, I think this stuff would be pretty good in a cup," I say.

He nods. "It is. I've had that many times. But straight is still my favorite."

We sip on our drinks slowly, so nobody winds up puking his or her guts out. Once I finish the first glass, I pour a second as we continue to work on decorating the tree together.

I'm a little tipsy an hour later when I take a break to make us some hot chocolate. Only…I can't find any.

"Ford?" I yell, and he's behind me a second later as I stand in the pantry.

"Yes?"

I chuckle. "Do you have any hot chocolate?"

He twists his lips with a bit of disappointment. "I don't think I do."

"It's a holiday tradition. I don't just *want* some. I *need* some."

He laughs. "There's a restaurant downtown that has hot chocolate and churros."

"Hot chocolate and churros?" I ask, tilting my head. "I think it just might be the combination I never knew I needed."

"Then let's go," he says.

"Wait," I say, and I grab his arm.

His eyes land on my hand first before moving up to meet mine. He raises a brow, and I yank on his arm to pull him closer to me, but he's a huge football player who doesn't budge from my efforts. He looks confused, so I make it clear.

I toss my arms around his neck, and I rise to my tiptoes so my mouth can collide with his. He responds immediately, moving his arm to hook around my waist as he opens his mouth to mine. Heat pools between my legs as I move a hand to cup his jaw, to feel the rough hairs there to remind me that this is really happening between us.

I grip onto his bicep with my other hand, afraid my knees will buckle, and I'll fall to the floor as his tongue teases mine. I hear a soft groan escape him as I taste the hint of mint the schnapps left behind on his tongue, and when his hand moves under my shirt to splay on my back, I shiver at the feel of his skin on mine.

It's a kiss filled with intensity, of this passion and need that seems to be growing between us as we wait for some self-imposed deadline.

He pulls back first, breathless, and I'm panting as I wait for him to take it to the next level.

Snap DECISION

It has to. We can't keep fighting this, and there's no way in hell I can wait seventeen more days for the thirty-first to get here so we can finally be together.

"Ready to go get that hot chocolate?" he asks.

I have no clue what the hell kind of brutal self-control this man has, but it appears to be something I don't possess.

I shake my head. "I want to keep kissing you, only I want us to be naked beneath the tree while our bodies find the same sort of rhythm together that our mouths seem to have. I don't want to wait seventeen more days, Ford."

I don't know where those words came from. If I wasn't halfway to tipsy-town, I'm not sure I would've had the nerve to say them.

His eyes are hot on mine as he takes a step toward me. He lowers his mouth to mine, and he kisses me slowly.

It was his idea to date to see if there's something between us. It's working. I'm falling for him as we bond over Christmas trees and food trucks and stolen pantry kisses with the promise for more.

Instead of taking me over to the tree, he slides a hand under my shirt. This time, though, his hand doesn't stay on my back. He moves it around, and his fingertips glide along my torso, up my ribcage, and toward my breast. He cups it over my bra, and then he yanks the fabric to the side so my breast is free. His thumb moves over my nipple, which immediately responds to his touch, forming a tight peak.

He moves us so I'm pinned against the only wall in this walk-in pantry that isn't covered in shelves, and he shoves his hips against mine. I immediately feel him. He's hard. He's always hard. He's always ready, and it seems like he's been waiting for me to give the green light.

I just did.

He moves his hand from my breast down to my hip, and he slides his hand down into my jeans. He bypasses my panties and cups my mound, teasing me, petting me, feeling me.

He groans as he breaks from our kiss to trail his lips down my neck. He's panting as he buries his face in my neck, and he hisses loudly as he slips one of his fingers into my folds to feel how dripping wet I am for him.

He sinks a finger into me, and he grunts as I wrap one arm around him, riding his finger as we stand right here in the pantry. I reach down with one hand to stroke him over the outside of his jeans, too. I run my hand along his long, hard erection, and he grunts.

"You're fucking soaked," he murmurs, and I'm at a complete loss for words. My mind is blank, fully focused on the pleasure he's giving me as he adds a second finger. I tip my head back, clunking it against the wall with a thud as he works his fingers in and out of me, pleasure curling all around me and warming me from the inside out.

"Oh, God," I yell, and he sucks on my neck as he increases the speed, my pants and panties no barrier for his movements as he gives me exactly what I need.

I yank on the button of his jeans, and I pull down the zipper. I reach into the opening and pull out his cock as his mouth slams to mine, and I start to stroke him as he fingers me.

He groans, and he's breathless as his mouth moves toward my ear. "Make no mistake, Barker." His fingers seem to move in and out of me in rhythm with his breathless, raspy voice, and I stroke him at the same pace. "I'm going to fuck you. I'm going to give you exactly what you need. What I need. What I've needed for an entire decade. But I'm not going to do it because we're both horny and half drunk off McGillicuddy's. I'm going to do it when I can worship your body. When we're ready for it. I'm going to do it when you're my wife."

Snap DECISION

His words, *that* word, *wife*, send my body crashing headfirst into a catastrophic orgasm.

I whimper his name with a moan.

It's brutal as he works my pussy with his fingers, the pleasure tearing through me in a way I've never felt before. I'm going to be his *wife*. He's going to be my *husband*.

And apparently my body really, really likes the sound of that. I keep pumping my fist along his shaft, my moves jerky and out of rhythm as my body hits the climax I've needed for far too long at the hands of someone other than myself.

I cry out, moaning, gasping, my body shattered as I ride out this pleasure, and once the wave starts to slow and warmth fills its place, I continue to stroke his cock in a more measured manner. I open my eyes to see his eyes right on mine as he watches me, and as our eyes connect, his are fiery and hot. They cloud over for a beat, and then he growls out my name as he starts to come. Pulse after pulse of his hot cum spills out of the head of his cock and all over my hand. He hasn't pulled his hand out of my jeans yet. His finger is still inside me. And watching me come made *him* come.

If that isn't some beautiful forecast for the sort of glorious sex life that lies ahead of us, I'm not sure what is.

And I, for one, can't wait for it to get started.

In seventeen long, achingly painful days filled with yearning, pining, and need.

CHAPTER 27

FORD BRADLEY

Sunset Cruise

Hot chocolate and churros are great and all, but they've got nothing on a midafternoon pantry hand job.

I'm not usually one with my head in the clouds, but right now, I'm pretty sure that's where my head is.

I wanted to fuck her. Jesus Christ, it's everything I want.

But I've waited this long. I'm not going to fuck it all up by getting her drunk on peppermint schnapps and giving in when the time isn't exactly right.

No matter how much I want to.

I want her to be sure—not drunk. I want her to want me, not to just want to get off because she's tipsy and horny. I meant what I said.

I've never been one to worry about waiting for marriage for anything, but with her, it seems right.

And there's another factor, one I've kept at bay but one that's important to consider. I don't want to hop into bed

Snap DECISION

with my brother's ex unless I'm positive that what we have is real.

Archer and I may not be all that close, but this would seal the fate of our brotherhood. There are unwritten rules as brothers, and one is that you don't touch what doesn't belong to you. And Tatum belonged to Archer first. For my own emotional safety, I need to know for sure that she's ready to sever that tie forever.

Because once we fuck, there's no turning back. Once we're married, whatever she had with him is done and dusted. For good. Even if the initial intent behind our marriage is one of convenience rather than of reality.

That doesn't mean it won't become our reality, and the more we *date*, the further I fall. The further I fall, the more I want this to work.

The risks are terrifying, but sometimes the greatest things in life come from the risks we take. And this is a risk that could potentially give me everything I've ever wanted.

After hot chocolate and churros, instead of taking her home, I take her downtown. I pull into the parking lot of a jewelry store, and my future bride glances at me.

"What are we doing here?"

"I realized you're my fiancée, but you're not wearing a ring. You should be wearing a ring."

Her eyes light up.

"As a wedding planner, I feel like you probably have some idea of what you want—" I begin, but she interrupts me.

"Oh my God, oh my God, oh my God. A compass cushion center stone with a platinum band. My dream ring, Ford. My dream!"

"A compass what?" I ask. I have no clue about diamonds.

"So, a cushion cut is basically a square with rounded edges. The compass is how it's set, so it's not flat but rotated to point to the four directions. It's *so* dreamy, like the groom is the bride's compass and vice versa. Come on, let's go look!" She's squealing as she explains it, and she throws open the door, possibly slightly denting the car next to us, and then she skips toward the front door of the jeweler. I have to practically run to keep up with her, but her words roll over in my mind.

Like the groom is the bride's compass and vice versa.

I suppose I've sort of always seen her like that. She's home. She's always felt like home to me. I let myself believe it was because of our strong friendship even though deep down I knew it was so much more.

And now...this. It's really happening.

"I can't believe this is really happening!" she squeals, echoing my thoughts and hugging my arm in hers once I catch up to her.

She tells the jeweler what she wants, and they show us a selection of diamonds that fit her request. I point to the largest one.

They'll need to set it into the band, but they assure me it'll be ready by tomorrow.

When morning comes, I head out to pick up breakfast, and when I return, I knock on her doorframe. "Breakfast is here."

She turns and glances up at me, a little guilt in her eyes.

I glance at the screen behind her, and the listing for the Bradley Mansion is pulled up.

I don't bring it up. She does.

"I can't stop thinking about what a perfect venue this would be," she admits quietly. "And now, once we're married, it would stay in the Bradley family. Are you *sure* you have to sell it? Can we just figure out some way to keep it in the family?"

My chest tightens. It would stay in the Bradley family.

Is she using me to get to the mansion?

I mean...in one way, yes. Absolutely, she's using me to get to the money from Mrs. Winston. It's the whole reason we agreed to this wedding. But when we bought the manor, part of me thought that took the mansion off the table.

She's mentioned Madden to me before and how she asked Archer to help set them up so she could use his development company to help with her vision, but he wanted her to stay away. So the first thing she does when they end things is run to...*me?*

Is she only here to make Archer mad? Is she only with me to get back at him?

It feels like she and I have bonded. You can't fake feelings. You can fake orgasms, but the way her cunt gripped my fingers greedily in the pantry yesterday sure as fuck didn't feel fake to me.

Still, it's in my head once again that maybe there's more to the story than what I'm seeing.

I've been lucky enough to be chosen to play professional football for my career—with hard work, determination, grit, and a bit of natural talent, I suppose.

But lightning doesn't strike twice. I don't think I'm lucky enough to *also* get the girl.

Logic tells me that it's not about luck, but something in the back of my mind is telling me that indeed it is.

"Liam and I have money tied up in it. It's the right thing to do," I say softly. "Though to be perfectly honest with you, Liam told me not to sell it."

"Then don't," she says softly. A quiet moment spans between us, and then she adds, "I wish I had fifteen million dollars."

I chuckle. "Don't we all?"

She glances wryly at me. I do. She knows I do.

But I'm trying to get rid of the place. Not buy it myself.

She turns back to her screen and closes the window as I turn to leave her room. "Hey," she says, stopping me. I turn back and look at her, and she asks, "Do you think we need a prenup?"

Something about *her* being the one to ask makes me feel a little more at ease. Like she's not in this for my money or my connections. It started because of the mansion, but it feels like it's going somewhere else now.

I shake my head. "I think we've known each other long enough that I can trust your intentions."

She rushes over to give me a hug, and then we spend the afternoon making wedding plans. After we finish an early dinner, I tell her, "Grab your coat. I have plans."

She narrows her eyes even as they light up at my surprise, and we head out for another date night.

This one is going to be special, though.

We drive about thirty minutes to St. Pete, where we board a private boat for a sunset cruise. I rented out the entire cruise, which wouldn't have been crowded given the time of year, but it gives us privacy. The temperature is fairly moderate, but with the wind whipping by us on the boat, it'll be chilly.

I have something that's keeping me warm, though.

My nerves.

I shouldn't be nervous. We've already made the agreement.

Still, I've never actually asked anyone this question before, and a big part of me never thought I would. I thought the woman I loved was happily in love with someone else, and I'd forever be reduced to the man who couldn't have her.

Yet here we are.

It's a bit surreal, and given my status, I likely should have warned my brother this would be happening.

I didn't. I don't know if she did. We talked to each other about it, but I don't believe either of us talked to him about it.

Snap DECISION

It's possible news will break since I'm doing this on a boat with workers present, but the chances are slim. I'll get ahead of it. I'll talk to him before it gets out.

The cruise sets sail, and even though it's just the crew and the bar staff, I'm recognized almost immediately.

I just ordered a glass of champagne for each of us when the bartender asks, "Are you Ford Bradley?"

I smile. "I am."

"Huge fan," he says. "I'm Carl, by the way."

"Nice to meet you, Carl. Thanks for cheering us on."

He passes our glasses over to us, and we head out to the deck to look out over the water.

The sun is starting its descent into the water, and that's when I decide to do it. I set my glass on the ledge under the railing, and I reach into my pocket, where I feel my phone.

Wrong pocket.

She's rubbing off on me.

I reach into the other pocket, unzip the little secret compartment there, and finger the box.

I get down on one knee, and Tatum's eyes widen as she watches me.

I hold the ring up. "Tatum Barker, will you marry me?"

Just as her mouth forms the *y* in "Yes," I hear someone yell, "Oh my God! Look at all the dolphins!"

Our attention is pulled away from my proposal—one that's as good as locked up, all things considered—and we spot a pod of dolphins leaping through the sunset not far from the side of our boat.

It's a gorgeous view. It feels somehow lucky to be here in the presence of these magical creatures just as I asked Tatum to marry me.

She leans into my side. "Yes," she says close to my ear, and I turn and catch her lips with mine.

We break apart, content as we watch the dolphins, and I allow myself to dream of what comes next.

So yes…I had planned to give Archer fair warning ahead of the news getting out.

But what I never accounted for was a viral video.

CHAPTER 28

Tatum Barker

Carl and Mindy 47

"Oh no," I whisper.

I'm rotating between scrolling TikTok and staring at the diamond on my hand when I should be going to sleep since I have a full day of planning for my own wedding tomorrow when I come across the video.

The video.

It was posted four hours ago. It already has close to a million views.

It's from the sunset cruise we were just on, and the username is carlandmindy47.

Wasn't Carl the bartender's name?

Once he recognized Ford, he must have had his phone glued to us the whole night. We were a little distracted to notice.

It's him. It's me. I'm going viral. He's going viral. My brain is short-circuiting.

I have to admit, though, it's a beautiful video.

Snap DECISION

It's literally Ford getting down on one knee, holding up a ring, and dolphins dancing and leaping out of the water behind him in the glow of the sunset.

The words across the video say, "Tampa Bay Beasts star proposes with dolphins watching!"

No wonder it went viral.

It continues on as he stands and I lean into him, watching the dolphins with him.

The caption reads, "But did she say yes?"

The comments ask and answer who the star is.

It's making our announcement for us.

We're really doing this.

I leap out of bed after watching it a full eight times, and I knock on Ford's door. I don't hear a reply, so I try the handle. It opens, and the room is dark. I walk over to the bed, and I find him fast asleep.

This could maybe wait until morning. I don't *have* to wake him. It's not like we're going to do anything about it in the middle of the night.

But I also can't sit with this by myself until morning.

I shake him awake. "Ford?" I whisper, and then a little louder, "Ford!"

"Huh? Wha—?" he mutters, and I can't help a tiny nervous laugh.

"Ford, wake up."

He's clearly groggy, but I shove my phone at him anyway.

"Wake up and watch this video."

He's half-asleep still as he squints at the screen that's replaying the video over and over on a loop, and he watches all fifty-four seconds of it a full three times before what he's looking at seems to register. "Can't this wait until morning?"

"No. Watch it," I demand.

"What is it?"

"Apparently it's our engagement video as filmed by Carl and Mindy forty-seven."

"Who the fuck are Carl and Mindy forty-seven? And how did they get your number to send this to you?"

"They didn't send it to me, Ford," I say, not bothering to hide my frustration that he's not snapping out of sleep quickly enough to understand what's going on right now. "It's on TikTok. It's going viral. Everyone is going to see it if they haven't already, and we haven't told anyone anything yet. Including my family. Including *your* family. Including my ex, *who is your brother.*"

He sits up straight as the realization hits. "Oh. Fuck."

"Right. Oh. Fuck."

He rubs his forehead, and he reaches for his own phone. He taps around on it, and then he curses again.

"What is it?" I ask.

He flashes his phone at me, and I see he has seventeen unread text messages and five missed calls.

"Yeah? So?" I ask as I flash my own screen at him with my forty-two missed calls and two hundred thirty-one unread text messages. Don't even get me started on the number of unread emails I have in my inbox. I just thought this was how people operate.

"I don't usually have the little red bubble notifying me of how many missed messages I have. I always respond as soon as I'm able to," he says quietly.

"So those are all since you went to bed?" I ask, and he nods.

"Well, are you going to deal with them?"

"Dammit." He rubs his forehead. "I should've known better than to do something in front of other people that we weren't ready to announce."

Snap DECISION

"Who would've thought *this* would happen?" I ask, shaking my phone. "There was hardly anybody even on that boat. What are the chances?"

"Apparently pretty good." He sighs. "I just wanted to get ahead of it and tell Archer first."

"Then let's call him and tell him," I suggest.

He nods, and he picks up his phone. He dials his brother, and my heart pounds as I wait for him to answer.

He doesn't.

That's not unusual for Archer. He often ignores calls, especially from his family. But deep down in my heart, I have a pretty strong feeling that he already knows. He's seen the video. Someone showed it to him.

Someone *had* to have shown it to him. Someone close to him who knows we were together for as long as we were.

He hangs up rather than leaving a voicemail. "There's not much we can do tonight, so let's just try to get some rest, and we'll deal with it in the morning. I'll check the texts and listen to the voicemails then."

Right. We'll deal with it tomorrow. Because surely I'll go straight to sleep and not freak out at all over this. My parents might find out before I can tell them. It's late here—after midnight now, and I don't want to call them in the middle of the night and wake them up. What good would that do?

Tomorrow. He's right.

"Come here," he says softly. He pats the bed beside him, and I climb in.

I should go back to my room and turn off my light.

But as I settle into the bed and Ford wraps me in his arms, I'm finding I don't have any motivation at all to get up and walk out of here.

And so I don't. Rather than tossing and turning in my own bed, I feel safe here in Ford's arms. And as I drift off to sleep, it feels like everything's going to be okay.

Only…it's not.

Ford's not in bed when I wake up. He's an early riser, and he's usually at practice by now, so being up early isn't exactly out of the ordinary.

I pad out to the kitchen, and I find Ford sitting there at the counter with his head in his hands. My brows dip together as I realize how much this is affecting him.

I wonder how many views that video has now.

I walk over to him, and I set my hand on his back. He startles a little, and when he pulls his head out of his hands and turns to look at me, I see that his eyes are rimmed in red.

"Ford, what is it?" I ask quietly.

"Those calls and texts last night…they weren't about the video."

"They weren't?" I ask.

He shakes his head. "My mother died." His voice breaks a little as he says the words.

"Oh, no. I'm so, so sorry, Ford." I wrap my arms around him as I feel torn between comforting him, being here for him…and being there for his brother.

I've never felt torn between them. Not in the time since Archer and I broke up, and not in the time since I've been doing…whatever this is with Ford.

But right now, they both need me. They'll both be hurting, both be keeping it on the inside even though it's okay to show it.

Ford doesn't need this now. He's got enough on his plate.

And Archer…he's more sensitive than he lets on. Just because he wasn't close with her doesn't mean this won't hurt. He'll almost certainly go to the funeral, where he'll have to see his brother, who's newly engaged to his recent ex.

It's too much, and for as much as none of this is about me at all, I have no clue how to handle it.

Snap DECISION

I want to be there for everyone, but I no longer fit where I used to. And now I'm wearing my dream ring from the brother I never expected to give it to me.

I pull back and go into planner mode. "What can I do? Have arrangements been made? Do you need me to notify anyone?"

He clears his throat. "Arrangements have been made. Next Tuesday. Everybody's day off. Three days before Christmas." His voice is flat. No emotion. Apart from the red-rimmed eyes, I have no real clue what he's thinking or feeling right now.

But what I do know is that he needs to get back to Chicago a week from today, and he'll have to face his family.

"Come with me," he says softly.

I nod. "Of course."

Scratch that. *We* will have to face his family. Together.

The next week passes in a flash in the whirlwind of wedding planning and funeral travel arrangements. That viral video topped out at a little over two million views, and Ford has spoken to every member of his family except for Archer and his dad. Well, and his mom, obviously. He's the one who said it. Dark humor for the win, I guess.

We'll be staying at the Bradley Mansion together in Ford's old room, and I wonder how many of the other Bradley siblings will be staying there as well. As far as I know, Madden has a place in the city, and so do Everleigh and Liam. But Dex, Ford, Archer, and Ivy don't.

I don't allow myself to imagine how awkward it'll be to share a space with Archer when I'm sleeping beside Ford, nor do I allow myself to imagine the looks I'll get from the other Bradley siblings as we stay in the mansion.

It already feels messy, and we haven't even boarded the plane yet.

I watch the game on Sunday from Ford's couch since he's away in Nashville. The Beasts fight hard, but without Grant Landry in the game, they come up short.

Ford is in a *mood* when he arrives home on Sunday night.

I leap off the couch to greet him at the door, and he gives me a halfhearted hug. I know they lost, which sucks, but usually he greets me with a bit more enthusiasm than *this*.

"What's wrong?" I ask. It's a stupid question, I know. He lost his mother. We have to fly to Chicago in the morning to help with her estate and be with his family and attend her funeral. On top of that, his team lost.

"We fuckin' lost," he mutters.

"I watched. You played so hard, Ford. You were amazing."

"What good did it do?" he mutters. "Another season down the drain."

"It's one loss," I protest. "It's not the end."

"We lost, the Fury won. They won last weekend, too. Our playoff spot isn't secured, so we'll have to play Wild Card Weekend, and without Landry, we will lose. No doubt about it. So, yeah. It's the end. It's over."

I don't really understand how it all works, but what I do understand is human emotion. I slip my arms around him. "I'm sorry. I know this is hard. But your team has amazing talent, and maybe you'll surprise even yourself at the wild card game. And if not, there's always next year."

He sighs. "Yeah. Always next year." He lets go of me and heads toward his bedroom, and I guess that's it.

We sleep separately, and when morning dawns, I wake with a heavy weight on my shoulders and nerves constantly moving up and down my spine.

I guess it's time to face Archer with this engagement ring on my finger.

CHAPTER 29

FORD BRADLEY

Ransacking

It's drizzling in Chicago when we land. It's often gray here. I heard on the radio once that nearly half the days of the year are cloudy. I guess that's why when I was drafted by a team in the Sunshine State, I was ready to pack my bags and get the fuck out of here.

I love Chicago. It's home, and a part of me will always feel that way. But with more of my family members in Vegas now than here, and after having lived the last seven years in Tampa, it's really *not* home anymore.

Still, as the car we took from the airport pulls up to the mansion for the second time in the last two months, I can't help but let the nostalgia wash over me.

My mother wasn't around much when we were kids. She hired a nanny who took care of us, and that nanny had a helper when our brood expanded. Mom was always off at some charity event or gala opening, some premiere or launch, or even just an event at the country club.

Snap DECISION

She worked hard to be something I'm not sure she ever was, and I can't help but wonder how the people in her social circle really felt about her. She tried her damn hardest to fit in, so much so that it cost her her very life. She refused to allow anyone to see her as anything other than what she wanted to project, and that meant avoiding doctors until she no longer could.

And here we are, gathering together as a family so we can celebrate the life of a woman we hardly knew yet to whom we should all feel the most fundamental connection with.

As I step out of the car while the driver gets our luggage out of the trunk, Tatum and I both stare up at the house. She's probably reflecting on how she's back here at the very place she wishes she could buy, and I'm here reflecting on how much money is tied up in it.

I glance over at Tatum once the driver sets our luggage beside us and I've tipped him.

"Ready?" I ask.

She hesitates as if she wants to say something. But then she presses her lips together and nods, and we head toward the front door.

I ring the bell, and I find Ivy on the other side of the door.

"Ford," she murmurs, and she pulls me into a hug. "And Tatum. Good to see you," she says, the first of my siblings to gracefully sidestep the fact that Tatum is here with me and not Archer. I'm hopeful she won't be the only one. "Come on in."

"Who else is here?" I ask.

"Everyone's rolling in today," Ivy says. "Liam's in the kitchen with Madden and Kennedy. Dex and Ev are on the same flight from Vegas with Ainsley and Maverick, and they're landing any minute. I haven't heard from Archer." Ivy's eyes dart to Tatum at the mention of him. My chest tightens, and I suck in a breath.

I'm going to have to face him eventually with Tatum by my side.

I head into the kitchen and find Liam, Madden, and Kennedy standing around the rather large kitchen island—the very same one that Tatum stood on not so long ago. I almost laugh at the memory.

Liam turns first at the noise in the doorway, and he grins as he moves over to greet me.

"Congratulations, man," he says. "I saw the viral video." He gives me a bro-style hug complete with an aggressive pat on the back, and then he moves to Tatum while Madden makes his way over to greet us, too.

"We all saw it. It's been fucking everywhere," Madden says as we hug in greeting next. "I already texted you, but let me say it in person, too. Congrats, bro."

"When did you two get in?" I ask.

"About an hour ago. How are you doing after Sunday?" he asks.

"We don't have a chance with Reggie," I say.

He presses his lips together. "Stranger things have happened. Keep fighting."

I know he's right, but it's hard not to give up when our quarterback is hurt and we're the underdogs.

We all stand around the kitchen island bringing up memories from this very kitchen. The time Dex tried to microwave a shirt to dry it faster and ended up starting a fire. Leaving empty cereal boxes in the pantry to disappoint a sibling. Stashing a particular snack only to find our secret stashes had been raided. The time Madden and Dex dented the stainless-steel fridge during a Nerf war. The time Archer and I convinced Liam the egg was hard-boiled so he'd crack it on his forehead.

The list goes on.

Snap DECISION

We may not have had Mom and Dad around much, but we had each other, and that was enough.

"Where's Dad?" I ask.

"He was taking care of some details at the funeral home," Liam says. "Should be back soon."

It's a sobering reminder of why we're here. Not a single one of the memories we've been laughing about has included our mother.

But maybe they don't have to. Even if we weren't close to her, she still gave us life. She still gave us *this*. These are memories we can stand in a kitchen and laugh about all these years later.

"Do we, um...need to go through Mom's stuff at all?" Ivy asks.

We all glance over at her. She's probably the closest out of all of us to our parents. She's the youngest, and she still lives here when she's not away at college—for now, anyway. Liam said in passing that she might stay with him instead of here all alone once Dad's locked up, but once she graduates in a few months, I wonder where she'll land.

"You take what you want," I say quietly to her.

Madden and Liam nod.

"I don't need anything," Madden says.

"Neither do I," Liam adds.

I press my lips together. I feel like I should take *something*. Like I'll regret leaving here without a single scrap to remind me of my mother. I have the memories, but they're not memories of *her*. They're *sibling* memories that she helped facilitate but wasn't present for.

Trips we took where the seven of us siblings looked out for one another because our parents were off attending events.

Kitchen wars and fort nights when they were out.

Five brothers messing around with each other while Everleigh joined in, and Ivy peered in as the youngest back when we were all home at the same time. Madden getting mad because he thought he was in charge. Dex starting a food fight, Archer joining in next, Liam in general causing chaos. Me somewhere in the middle trying to maintain fair, orderly rules to a food fight that was never meant to be orderly.

What the hell has become of this family? And what will become of our future if we don't make the effort to get together outside of weddings and funerals?

And how does what I'm doing with my brother's ex contribute to any of that?

Nerves strike through my chest as I wait for his arrival.

Nobody knows when he's coming. Maybe he won't come at all, or maybe he'll just attend the funeral. Maybe he doesn't want to deal with the questions from his siblings or the betrayal of his brother. But there's also that slightest slice of possibility that he'll knock on the door next. Nobody ever knows with him.

"I don't *need* anything. But I want something. I just don't know what," I admit.

I take the suitcases upstairs with Tatum trailing behind me and Ivy leading the way. I drop our bags in my old room, where Tatum grabs her laptop to answer some pressing emails. I join Ivy in Mom's closet.

Rows and rows of designer dresses and pantsuits. Racks and racks of designer shoes, size seven. Cases and cases of designer jewelry. Ivy tries on a pair of shoes, and like Cinderella, they're the perfect fit.

Suitcases, handbags, and tote bags with names even I have heard of. Dior, Chanel, Fendi. I'll let Ivy and Everleigh take first pick, but maybe there's something in here Tatum would like. Or maybe our mother already allocated who gets what.

"How's life?" Ivy asks when we're alone.

"Life-ing," I say.

She laughs. "Same. You and Tate now? Is she getting passed to Liam next?"

"Fuck no," I say, an unexpected darkness in my tone. She better not, anyway.

She purses her lips as she tilts her head at me. "Is it real?"

"It is for me. Always has been," I admit.

She nods a little. "Thought so. And her?"

"Getting there."

"So why are you marrying her if she's not there yet?"

"It's complicated."

"Relationships always are." She sighs, and we both silently survey the contents of the closet. "Why didn't they take this stuff?"

"Who?"

"The investigators. Why aren't these assets frozen?"

My brows draw down. It's a great question—one I hadn't considered. "If I had to guess, I'd think that the investigators didn't see these as big-ticket items. They're looking for Aston Martins, not something fresh from last year's runway." As I look around, I think that what's in this closet has to be worth millions of dollars. But only if someone took the time to catalog all of it.

As I glance through what's in here, I can't find a single item that bears any connection to my mother at all.

It's as I'm about to leave the closet when I hear footsteps approaching, and then my father's figure fills the doorway. "Already ransacking for your inheritance? You should know your mother wanted each of you to have something. The lawyers will be here tomorrow after the funeral to share who is getting what."

I hold up my empty hands. "Just keeping Ivy company and trying to find…something." I'm not sure what. A connection. Some *feeling*. I felt sad when I heard she died, the way you feel sad when you hear *anyone* died. I didn't *cry*. I hadn't slept that night as I wondered about the viral video, about Archer, about Tatum, about all of it, and my eyes were red-rimmed in the morning because of it.

But I can't seem to dredge up the sort of emotion I *should* be feeling over losing my mother. Maybe because I never *had* her, so it doesn't feel much like I've *lost* her. I feel more upset over losing against the Fury last weekend than about being here for a funeral.

It'll hit me eventually. Surely. I feel like a monster for even thinking that. Admitting it is a nonstarter. But I'm sure I'll hear the same thing from everyone: everyone processes grief differently.

Is this even grief? I'm not sure.

"What are you looking for?" he presses.

"There's nothing here I want," I finally say. I make a move to step around him, but he stops me.

"Don't sell this house," he demands.

"Why? My own money is tied up in getting your ass out on bail."

He raises his chin and sniffs, but he doesn't thank me. As if he ever would consider it. "I was able to be with your mother in her final hours because I was out."

I guess that's all the thanks I'll ever get. "I'm glad. I want my money back, as does Liam, so the house stays on the market. What's the latest with your case?"

"They're already asking for a continuance. It'll be six months minimum before I head to trial. I need a place to live until then."

"I heard Liam has a spare room," I deadpan, glancing at Ivy.

"Actually, that's where I'll be staying for the time being," Ivy says curtly to our father. "Sorry." She's flippant, and I love her a little more for it. It feels like it's us against him. All of us. All seven of the Bradley siblings tied together against one common enemy.

"I think Kennedy's old apartment is available," Madden says, appearing in the doorway. "She lived a little south of here for a while with a friend. Not a great part of town, but she managed to make it out alive."

For some reason, having Madden here feels like we have the voice of reason. Maybe I see him more as a father figure than I ever saw my father as one, even though he's only six years older than me. He took care of us in ways our father never did—sort of like Everleigh cared for us all in ways our mother didn't.

"I'm selling the house," I say, my voice cold and firm.

"No, you're not," my father hisses.

"You don't have the money to stop me." I leave those as my parting words as I push past him and head toward my bedroom, only to find that Tatum is no longer alone in there.

Archer's here.

And he's hugging my future bride.

CHAPTER 30

Tatum Barker

History and Future

"I don't know what you want me to say," I whisper to Archer.

His head is on my chest as he leans into me, and I cradle him against me as he attempts to shutter his emotions the way he always does. Just like usual, though, he can't hide them from me. We may not be together anymore, but that doesn't mean I stop knowing who he is. You can't just erase a decade of friendship with a breakup. The muscle memory remains.

I rub his back gently, and my heart stutters in my chest.

I always had a soft spot for Archer Bradley.

"I know this is tough, and I'm sure that's where it's coming from," I say gently.

He pulls back a little, his head tilted as those clear, hazel-green eyes land on mine. "The only thing that's tough is that you're not here with me. That I have to go through... *all of this* alone." His voice is low. Raspy. Sexy.

Snap DECISION

He doesn't mean losing his mother. He means dealing with his family.

I close my eyes against the heat pinching behind them.

"You told me it was okay to move on," I say softly.

"Saying it and meaning it are two different things entirely."

"I can't read your mind, Arch. You know that's something I've never been able to do."

"That's not true," he protests, hitting me with a little lift of his lips. It was an argument we had often, one that usually ended with us both naked since the truth is that in some ways I sort of *could* read his mind. After a while, anyway. I learned to.

I blow out a breath, and he settles his head on my chest again. It's familiar, that's all. It's comforting, and I'll be here to comfort him. But I also need to make space for Ford.

"Is this real with you and him?" he whispers.

"I think so," I admit.

"If I would've asked first…" He trails off.

"I would've said yes." But that's the problem. He never *did* ask, and knowing what I know now, it would've been wrong anyway.

He lets out a strangled sound. "The dolphins were a nice touch."

"You saw the video?"

"Why do you think I didn't answer his call?" he asks. "Of course I did. I couldn't fucking escape it, and all I could think about was how that should've been me standing there with you. It's all wrong."

"Why'd you end it with me, then? Why'd you let me move on?" I ask. "Why'd you give me permission to be with your brother?"

"The feds were coming, Tate. I couldn't let you get mixed up with that. I couldn't let it tank your business, your livelihood, everything. I thought I was the smart one separating from my family all those years ago. But it turns out that one mistake meant that I wasn't, and so you weren't, either. I thought it would just be like all the other times, and we'd find our way back."

"Do you still think that?" I whisper as I brush away a tear that splashes onto my cheek.

"Until you've signed a marriage certificate, I think I'll always hold onto that hope."

"It wasn't just that, Arch," I say quietly. "There were other things wrong with our relationship. With us. We weren't perfect."

"You're right. I was trying to keep you away from my family. I didn't know what else my father was doing that we didn't want to get tied up in, so I thought it was simpler this way. If saying no to letting you work with Madden was our downfall, I still stand by what I did."

"He's here now," I point out.

"Then go talk to him. What are you doing here with me?"

"It's you. You and me, Arch. Just like it always was."

"Except it's not. There is no you and me anymore." He takes my hand, and he threads his fingers through mine. He turns our hand so he can study the ring Ford slipped onto my finger. "Compass cushion center stone with a platinum band. Your dream." He sniffs, and then he mutters a curse. He stands, and he walks out of the room.

I don't know where he goes, and I don't chase him down. I've been sitting here crying by myself for a few minutes when Ford walks into the room. He closes the door, and he sits on the bed beside me. He takes my hand in his. "Are you okay?" he asks.

His mom just died, and he's here with all this family drama, yet he's asking *me* if *I* am okay.

I swipe at the tears, and he gets up to grab the box of tissues, which he hands to me. I wipe my nose, and I nod. "I'm okay. You?"

He lifts a shoulder. "I saw you in here with Archer, and I didn't want to interrupt. I went downstairs until he came down."

"Was that hard?" I ask, my voice guarded.

"You have no idea."

I press my lips together.

"It's been hard my entire life, Tatum. It's always been you for me, but I resigned myself to the fact that it wasn't me for you. Except...now it is. It's happening, and my heart wants to believe it's real, but my brain keeps telling me that if you had the chance, you'd go back to him." He's quiet as he waits for my response to that, and again, I'm at a loss for words.

"Say something," he says softly. "Are you going back to him?"

I clutch his hand in mine. "I told you once that he and I had our problems. It wasn't perfect, but now he wants me back. He wants to try again. I think maybe it's losing your mom...realizing life is short and unpredictable. I don't know."

"Or it's just you, Tate. Your stunning beauty, your kind heart, your perfect chaos. There's something about you that we both fell in love with."

My chest hurts. I thought I already made this decision, but it feels like he's asking me to make it again.

"And I love you both, too." In very different ways.

I love Archer as the man I was with for the last eight years—give or take, on and off—and as the man I had a crush on for four years before we ever even got together. He makes up nearly half of my life's history.

But Ford is my best friend. He's been there to pick me up when I fall more times than I can count. He's my business partner, too. He's home. And I think he's my future.

I knew it would be tough coming here, that seeing Archer would dredge up old feelings. But what I didn't expect was to see him and be so sure that what I'm building with Ford is actually what I want out of life.

I thought it would be different.

I lean my forehead to Ford's, and then I say the words softly. "But you're the one I want a future with."

I hear a soft exhale, and then I feel his lips as they collide with mine.

We both hear the doorbell, and he pulls back.

It's brief. Too brief. I want to lean into him, to feel him. For ten days to pass in a flash so we can get married and ride into the sunset toward a future together—a future I never expected and never knew I wanted until I experienced the last month and a half with a man who wants to give me everything.

"Come on," he says, and he grabs my hand to lead me downstairs to greet whoever's at the door.

I take a deep breath in the front hall as he opens the door, and for just a split second that belongs only to me, I take it all in. This entry, this mansion, this family. The legacy here in the walls, the memories that even I have here that I don't want to let go.

It's not my mansion to make those decisions with, but it seems like Ford is the only one of the Bradley siblings who actually wants to sell it.

Everleigh's best friend, Penny, is at the door with bags of takeout. Ford grabs the bags from her hands, and we all head into the kitchen only to find the rest of the Vegas residents of the Bradley family standing around the large counter. It's more hugs hello, this time with Dex, his wife Ainsley, and his son Jack, along with Everleigh and Maverick.

We unpack the food—salads, a few different types of pasta, and garlic bread—as Everleigh gathers plates and silverware. It's chaos as the eleven of us in here (discounting the baby who just turned one) reach for food to fill our plates.

"Where's Archer?" Ivy asks, and everyone glances around, but no one knows.

I notice Mr. Bradley is also missing, and I can't help but worry what he'll try roping Archer into next. And if Archer feels like he's left out in the cold, I worry that he'll sign more papers that'll only get him into more trouble.

We all take our plates filled with food to the dining room, the place with the table big enough to accommodate all of us, the place where we always gathered for the famous Bradley Monday night dinners.

Eventually Archer, Mr. Bradley, and another man I don't know walk into the room with food on their plates, too. They sit at the far end of the table, and a beat of quiet passes.

Dex breaks the silence by belting out "Sweet Caroline," Neil Diamond's most popular song, and the rest of the family follows with "Bah-bah-bah!"

Everyone laughs, and it breaks the awkward spell. I glance across the table at Archer, and even he has a small smile playing at his lips.

"God, I miss this," Everleigh says. "All of us together, here in this place. How long has it been?"

"Not quite long enough," Dex cracks.

"I think the last time all seven of us sat around this table at the same time was Liam's college graduation," Madden says.

Archer shakes his head. "I was in season. Didn't make it."

Madden tilts his head and nods as he thinks back. "Then maybe Archer's college graduation? That would put it at...Jesus, like six years ago? That can't be right."

It probably *is* right. Archer is in season when the rest of the pro athletes are out, so to get all of them gathered around this very table would've taken either a miracle or a catastrophic event...like losing their mother, for example.

"I think it is," Ivy says quietly. "You all got busy once you went pro."

Everyone glances at her. She would've been fifteen back then, and it was *my* college graduation, too. I remember how boy crazy Ivy was back then, and I remember her trying to kiss one of Archer's buddies who was a full seven years older than her.

I saw it all go down. I saw the rejection. I remember how distraught she was, and I remember talking to her—like she was my own little sister. I told her how it was just a crush for her, but for him, it was illegal.

Archer and I had been together for two years at that point. I thought we'd be together forever. And now I'm here engaged to a different member of the same family.

It feels weird. It feels like I don't know my place.

So I sit quietly as I listen to the conversation around me. Ainsley and Ivy are close, and they bend their heads together every so often. Everleigh is next to me, and the man who just proposed to her is on her other side. I glance over at him. We're sort of in the same boat along with Kennedy. We're all engaged to siblings, but none of us are members. Yet.

And then there's Archer, an outsider in his own right because he wanted it that way.

"Did anyone ever realize our first initials spell MED FAIL?" Liam asks out of the blue.

Everyone turns to look at him.

"Huh?" Dex asks.

Snap DECISION

"Madden, Everleigh, Dex, Ford, Archer, Ivy, Liam. MED FAIL," he says. "I'm guessing that's why none of us became doctors."

"Or mathematicians," Madden says. "It also spells FAILED M, and I figured M meant math. Or MAD LIFE, which is me. My life. The Mad Life."

"You guys are weird," Everleigh says. "Everyone knows it's MAID ELF."

Laughter erupts around the table, and it's reminiscent of days gone by. Days when I was here for Monday night dinners and the brothers would tease each other while Everleigh bossed them around, when they'd all gang up on Liam because he was the youngest, when they'd prank each other with silly things like replacing the sugar with salt or hiding the best cookies and pretending like they ate the last one.

I wonder how many of those memories include Vivienne Bradley, or if she was just a shadow who was here but never really present. Sort of like Thomas Bradley now, whose head is bent closely to the man beside him as they partake in their own whispered conversation.

I glance across the table at Archer, and his eyes are on me. At the same moment, the man on my right reaches down to squeeze my knee.

I feel a bit torn. They all seem to be dealing with their mother's death in much the same way—except for Ivy, who's quiet as she picks at the food on her plate.

Madden brings up last weekend's games, and the men gathered around the table—except for Archer—all join in on the conversation.

Everleigh is beside me on my left, and she leans in toward me. "It's good to see you. How are you doing?"

I nod. "All right. You?"

"It's weird being here, even weirder seeing you with Ford. But weird in a good way, you know?"

"Yeah. He told me he's felt this way a while."

"A long while, Tate. He and I are close, you know."

"I know. I feel bad, though." I'm whispering as I glance over at Archer again.

"About Arch?" she correctly guesses, and I twirl some spaghetti around my fork as I nod. "He'll be okay."

"I know he will." I glance down as something glints and catches my eye, and I see the rather large engagement ring on her finger. I nod toward it. "Congratulations, by the way."

She stares at it, too, a goofy grin on her face. "Thanks."

"Have you made any plans yet?"

She shakes her head. "It's all brand new."

"I'm happy to help." I glance around the dining room, and I decide to take my chance. "Actually, I have this wild dream to create a brand of luxury destination wedding venues, and I just invested in a property in Tampa."

Her brows rise. "You did? That's amazing! And I love the offer, but I'm really looking to get married here."

I glance around the dining room again. "Here, here?" I ask.

She twists her lips. "I mean, ideally, yes. I always wanted to get married here at the mansion. The views of the city, the gorgeous backyard. Perfect for a May wedding, or, oh God, imagine the snow in a winter wedding. But Mav's in season, so likely April, May, or June. But with Mom gone and who knows what's going on with Dad...and Ford's selling it, anyway." She winces a little as she says the words, and it makes me want to confess my dream to her.

"Can I tell you a secret?" I whisper.

Her eyes light up. "Always."

"I want to buy it."

She gasps a little. "The mansion?"

I nod. "I want to buy it and gut the first floor to create the wedding venue of every bride's dreams. A gorgeous ballroom, maybe even a smaller room for ceremonies. The bedrooms could be converted to bridal suites for the wedding party to gather and get ready before the event." I sigh. "I just have this clear vision of what I can do with this place, but I can't afford it. Fifteen mil plus the reno work is too far outside of my budget."

"Damn," she murmurs. "Well, maybe we'll move up the wedding and have it here anyway before Ford closes on it, but only if you promise to help."

"Excuse me?" her fiancé beside her asks. "What's this about *moving up* the wedding?"

I giggle. It seems like a point they haven't discussed quite yet.

"Oh, that's right," Madden says across the table. "When's the big day, Ev? Congrats, by the way."

"You guys, he literally proposed two days ago. We haven't even gotten engagement portraits done yet. Give a girl a break," Everleigh huffs.

"As if you don't have the entire thing planned already," Dex teases. He glances at Ford. "What about you, Sunshine?"

"Sunshine?" Madden asks.

"Yeah. You know, because he lives in Florida," Dex explains, and we all laugh again.

Ford glances at me.

"Oh, no you don't," Everleigh says. "Don't you *dare* say you're getting married before me."

"Um," Ford says, and he clears his throat. Are we doing this? I think we might be doing this. "We, uh, decided to make it quick."

"How quick?" Liam asks.

"New Year's Eve," Ford murmurs.

The table goes silent.

Like…completely silent. I think I actually hear a pin drop. Except for one noise.

The sharp intake of breath across the table from Archer.

"New Year's Eve?" Everleigh echoes. "Like…as in ten days?"

I bite my lip as Ford nods.

"Why the rush?" Liam asks at the same time Everleigh asks, "Were you planning to invite your family?"

Ford clears his throat again, clearly feeling awkward about having this conversation. We never exactly decided if we were going to be honest about our reasons for a quick wedding or not.

"It's just what we decided," he says quietly.

Archer stands up and quietly walks out of the room, and tears pinch behind my eyes. I wasn't expecting to have to deal with all of this. I thought we'd just quietly get married and surprise everyone with it.

But I guess fate had other plans.

CHAPTER 31

FORD BRADLEY

This Means War

I need to talk to Archer. I know I do.

I'm dreading it.

So when he walks out of the room, I walk out behind him a moment later, my heart thundering as I face the guy who's not just my brother but who was once one of my best friends.

It's been a long time since those days.

I find him in the kitchen, his palms flat on the counter and his elbows straight as he leans forward, staring down at the countertop.

"Hey," I say quietly, breaking into whatever thoughts he's having.

He glances up at me. "What the fuck, man?" he asks. "Ten days?"

"I'm sorry. It's…complicated."

"She's marrying you in ten days," he says flatly. "Doesn't sound very complicated to me."

Snap DECISION

"We invested in a property in Tampa," I blurt. "The woman who sold it to us wanted our wedding to be the first to take place when the estate changed ownership. If it is, the money we invested in the property comes back to us."

His brows knit together. "You can't stand there and tell me it isn't real for you."

"I'm not pretending it isn't. But she wants the money, man. She wants to invest in more properties. Build her brand. And from what she's told me, I'm the first member of this family who's actively working to help her make that happen."

He presses his lips together. "All I ever wanted was to try to protect her." His voice is strangled as he straightens and backs up, so he's leaning on the counter behind him. He folds his arms over his chest. "I wanted to keep her away from the toxic mess this family is. I thought that precluded you. I suppose not."

I place my hands on the counter standing between us and lean forward a little. "I'm not going to fuck her over, Archer."

"Neither was I." He sounds defensive.

"Yeah, but you two broke up enough times that she didn't see that. She was hurt that you weren't supporting her."

"So she ran to you to get what she wanted? You don't see that?" He's playing on my biggest insecurities when it comes to her.

"That's not what this is," I say quietly. Carefully. Evenly.

"Then what is it? Because you came in here to tell me it was all a ruse to get your money back, but it feels like there's a big *but* in there somewhere." He sighs. "And yes, I realize I just said *big but*, but I didn't mean *butt*."

"You know as well as anyone that I've always had feelings for her. That hasn't changed unless you count the fact that they've gotten stronger and more intense over the last few weeks. I want this, and I think she does, too. She's a fucking wedding planner. Of course she wants her own happy ending.

And you had her for seven years and couldn't give it to her. Don't you think there was a reason why?"

"Yeah, there was," he says bluntly. "This family. I tried my best to get away, and I still get dragged back in. Dad's bullshit. Mom's funeral. Everleigh's wedding. The expectation to be present even though nobody really wants me there. I'm on the outside looking in, and Tate was my one lifeline to feel some sort of connection. I let her go to help keep her away from this mess, thinking it was only temporary, and she ended up even deeper in it."

"Everybody wants you here, Archer," I argue. "Every single one of us. And what Tatum and I have…it's not a mess. I love her."

"Enough to marry her for money," he spits back. He shakes his head. "It's fucked up, and it shows me exactly where I fit into your life."

"You're putting me in an impossible position. You want me to choose you, who pulled out of this family years ago, over the chance to give both her and me everything we've always wanted."

He shakes his head. "You two don't want the same things."

"You don't know that."

He lifts a shoulder. "I guess that's for you to discover on your own." He leaves that as his parting shot as he walks out of the room, and now it's me leaning forward on the counter with straight elbows when Tatum walks in.

"I was dying out there. Everything okay? Where's Archer?" she asks.

I blow out a breath. "He stormed out. It didn't go well."

She reaches up to touch my arm. "I'm sorry. I didn't expect it to."

"Yeah," I mutter.

Snap DECISION

When we head back into the dining room, my father and his lawyer have disappeared. I pull a chair out as I remember something from long ago, and instead of sitting on the chair, I pull it back until I'm right in front of the large glass cabinet displaying family heirlooms here in the dining room.

I stand on top of the chair, and conversation ceases as everyone looks over to see what the hell I'm doing.

I reach on top of the cabinet and over the lip on the outside. It's tall enough that I can't see on top even standing on a chair, but I feel around, and sure enough, it's still there.

I pull it down, and Madden, Dex, and Liam start to laugh. Archer would, too, if he were here—or in a laughing mood.

I turn the ancient Nerf gun over in my hands, and I see it's still loaded. "I hid this up there when Archer and I were in a war back in seventh grade." Jesus, that was…sixteen, maybe seventeen years ago.

I aim it at Madden.

"Don't you dare," he warns.

There aren't enough of these to start a fight—at least not a fair one.

When it comes to Nerf wars with brothers, though, it's never a fair fight. It's an old instinct that calls to me when I pull the trigger just after I switch my aim to a completely and totally unsuspecting Liam.

I nail him right in the forehead.

"What the fuck, man?" he yells, jumping up out of his chair as he rubs his forehead. He lunges toward me, and I take off running.

I need more ammo. This gun holds five darts, but it only had three in the chamber.

I'm hiding behind the curtain in the formal living room that we weren't even allowed to step foot into when I hear a whisper.

"Psst. Ford!"

I peek around the curtain, and I spot Ivy.

"There's a trunk in the garage with some old stuff, and I know there are more blasters and darts in there," she says.

I narrow my eyes at her. "Why are you helping me?"

She twists her lips. "Because I just want us all to have some fun. Make some new memories together."

My chest tightens for my baby sister. She's always worn her emotions on her sleeve, and I think this whole thing is hardest on her. And if this will make her smile, then that's what she deserves.

I step out from behind the curtain and move toward her to hug her, only to get pinged in the arm with a dart.

My eyes widen and my mouth drops as I trace the path the dart had to have taken to get to me, only to find Madden holding a blaster and aiming it in my direction.

"He sent you as a decoy!" I accuse, and she giggles as she takes off running.

This means war.

I aim and fire my two measly darts at my oldest brother, and it's moments before the others join in—including Tate, Kennedy, Maverick, Ainsley, and even Penny. We're all darting around the house, hiding behind furniture, and firing when our target least suspects it.

Even if Ivy was sent as a decoy, she joins in on the fun as we actually do have fun and make new memories together. I feel like a kid again as I skid across the tile, run up the stairs, and peek around corners looking for anyone coming to attack.

I laugh. God, do I laugh. We all do, and we meet up in the dining room over an hour later with red cheeks, sweaty hair, and panting from exertion as Madden walks in with a stack of shot glasses and a bottle of McGillicuddy's.

Snap DECISION

We don't toast to anything specific, but I see the longing on everybody's face. I've heard the quiet remarks when the others don't think I'm listening.

Nobody wants me to sell this mansion. Nobody is ready to let go of these memories.

It's my decision, though. We won't lose the memories just because I sell it, and I think that's something they're all forgetting. It's just because we're here. It's an emotional weekend.

It's the last time we'll have a Nerf gun fight under this roof, perhaps.

Consistent with history over the last ten or so years, the only one missing from all this family bonding is Archer.

CHAPTER 32

FORD BRADLEY

Inheritance

When I wake in the morning with Tatum in bed beside me, my first thought isn't how today is my mother's funeral.

My first thought is that it's nine days until I marry Tatum.

We were all a little tipsy last night after shots, and to be perfectly honest, I didn't get much sleep. Instead, I spent the night fighting my urge to give in to the heat between Tatum and me well before the already agreed-upon date.

She kissed me goodnight, and it wasn't just a quick peck. It was lips, tongue, hands caressing jawlines. We didn't take it further than that. I wanted to. It felt like she did, too.

But Archer is in the next room. It wouldn't be right, no matter how strong the pull is between us.

I take a cold shower, and when I get out, she's sitting up, leaning against my headboard and scrolling on her phone.

"Good morning," I say. Her eyes edge to my abdomen and then to the towel wrapped around my waist—the only thing currently keeping me from showing her all the goods.

Snap DECISION

"Morning," she murmurs.

"Stop looking at me like that, or you're going to get the kind of good morning I'm supposed to be waiting nine more days for."

She glares at me, but then she giggles as she climbs out of bed and walks toward the bathroom. "Fine. But just for the record, I'm no longer convinced I want to wait nine more days." She closes the door behind her with those words, and then I have to fight with my boxers to get them over the enormous erection she just caused.

I slip into my suit, and I'm dressed when she exits the bathroom with a towel wrapped around her hair and her body. I allow my eyes to dance down to that towel, too, and she fingers the edge like she's going to drop it.

I walk over toward her, and I grab her to pull her against me. I drop my lips to hers, and I pull back to whisper, "Don't tempt me. I'll fuck you right here."

She gasps at my words.

I let her go even though I'm reluctant. "I'm going downstairs for breakfast. Come join me when you're ready."

She's gorgeous in a black dress when she joins me twenty minutes later, and Penny provided food for us once again. This time it's a buffet of breakfast items, and I'm grateful that she's nearby to help.

We fill our plates, and I suppose I take more than my fair share of bacon. Eventually, it's time to leave for the funeral.

My mother thought of every last detail, and this is less of a sad event bidding goodbye to a loved one and more of the event of the season. The funeral itself is going to be held at a cathedral downtown, and then there will be a procession to the cemetery followed by the reception at Mom's favorite country club.

Limousines have been arranged to take the family to each event, and Archer slips into ours at the last second, taking a seat beside Tatum.

I let go of the slice of jealousy that forces its way through me. She's choosing me, and she has a history with him. She *should* be there for him during this difficult time. We may not have been close to our mother, but that doesn't mean we didn't lose someone important to our family—no matter how much Archer claims he isn't a part of it.

And that's where I find myself torn. If I go through with this wedding, Tatum gets the money back to put toward another venue. She gets to keep building toward her dreams. I get everything I've wanted for a decade. But I also put my already fragile relationship with my brother into even greater jeopardy.

If we *don't* go through with it, though, we don't get that money back. We weren't expecting it, but it's an awfully nice bonus. If we don't go through with it, maybe we'll build toward this same place eventually, if we're truly meant to be. But maybe we won't. Maybe we'll lose each other. Maybe I'll lose everything...not *just* a brother who I already lost anyway.

I blow out a breath.

The decisive piece that makes up my personality wants to make a snap decision. Marry her. It's what you want anyway.

But the pragmatic side wants to weigh the options carefully and make sure we're doing the right thing.

Only...we don't have that kind of time.

We have nine days.

We have a funeral to attend.

I have practice tomorrow.

I have a game this Sunday.

It's a lot. All of it. It's weighing on me. Heavily.

Can I really do this to my brother?

Snap DECISION

I think of her standing in the towel this morning as I pulled her in for a kiss.

Can I really *not* do this and give up the only thing I've ever really wanted?

I don't think I can.

She sits between us at the cathedral. She walks with Kennedy as my brothers and I carry the casket out of the church and help load it into the hearse. She sits between us in the limo as we travel to the cemetery. She holds each of our hands as we say goodbye.

Ivy cries. The rest of us are stoic, Everleigh included.

We make it to the reception, where we're forced to mingle and dine with the members of high society my mother considered friends—or associates, at least.

We take pictures. A lot of them. The seven Bradley siblings are all in the same place, and apparently that's big news when it comes to town gossip. Four pro football players, a pro baseball player, a brand strategist engaged to a pro football player, and the baby sister still finding her way in the world. We're all in the same place at the same time, and we're all dressed up. It's the photo op of the century.

We make it back to the mansion one more time to gather our belongings and meet in our father's office, which looks like it did long before the feds upturned it not so long ago. It's a big office, but it's still crowded with our father sitting behind the desk, his lawyer standing behind him, and the rest of us gathered around.

Madden sits in one of the chairs facing the desk with Kennedy standing behind him. Ivy sits in the other chair.

Dex, Ainsley, and Jack are on the couch with Everleigh and Maverick beside them.

Archer and Liam lean against the wall next to the couch. Tatum and I stand near the door.

"Your mother left you each something she thought would be meaningful to you," Dad begins. He nods to his lawyer. "Paul has an envelope for each of you. She also wanted Everleigh and Ivy to take whatever they wanted from her closet. She specifically wanted Everleigh to get anything red and Ivy to get anything blue."

Maverick lets out a little chuckle at that.

It's the first sign that maybe our mother knew us better than we thought she did.

Each of us gets our envelope from the eldest to the youngest, and we all open them at the same time.

Mine is a letter from my mother.

Dear Ford,

As I reach the end of this journey, I can't help but reflect and wish I had done things differently. You are smart and strategic, and you always loved science. Those are the things on the surface that everyone knows about you. I never allowed myself to know you deep down the way a mother should. I regret that, but I do hope that you'll learn from my mistakes. To that end, I've set up a trust for any future children you may have. I had my hand involved in many foundations over the years, and I've decided to create new foundations for each of my children. Enclosed, you'll find all the details regarding the foundation that's already in your name.

All my love,
Mom

Emotions plow into me for the first time as I glance around the room and see similar reactions to the letters.

She gifted each of us a foundation. A way to make a better impact on the future.

I glance through the attached paperwork to find the Ford Bradley Foundation. The details say that I can do whatever I want with it. She laid the groundwork and fronted quite a bit of capital, so now it's up to me to run with it to help people however I choose.

"Your mother set up trusts and foundations years ago for each of you," my father begins.

I glance up at him, and I narrow my eyes. Did she? Or is this another *thing* he's done to protect the *legacy* he's so fond of mentioning?

It appears I'm not the only one thinking those thoughts.

"Did you have anything to do with this?" Madden asks quietly. Frankly, I'm surprised he's asking in front of everyone here. While everyone in this room is important, not everyone is officially a member of this family.

Dad holds up both hands. "I had no hand in any of this."

"But where did the money come from?" Madden asks.

"Your mother's inheritance." He glances around the room at each of us only to find we all look like guppies, our mouths dropped wide open. "As you know, she didn't get along with her own parents. What you might not know is that they demanded she marry someone in the same social class as her. She married me anyway. There was love between us once upon a time, believe it or not." He sighs, and I sense a bit of regret in its heaviness. "When her parents died, they left everything to her. She refused to touch it, insisting we make our own path. I suppose that was the point for me when greed took the place of love, and that's something I have to live with. Regardless, she wanted the seven of you to have the money. You'll see when you look further into both the trust and the foundations that the trust has five million in it for each of you to use for your future children, and each of your foundations has an account with two million in them to start your bankroll."

"That's almost fifty million dollars," Madden murmurs, echoing my own thoughts. "Her parents were worth that much?"

He shakes his head. "Her parents were worth double that."

I mean...I don't want to sound greedy, but—

Before I can finish the thought, Dex asks, "Where's the other half?"

Dad glances out the window, guilt playing on his features.

"Oh, no. Dad, no," Everleigh says.

"He has admitted to nothing," Paul reminds us, but we all know where the money went.

He pilfered it for some underground operation, or for gambling, or for...*something*. He took it. It didn't belong to him.

Add it to the list of crimes.

"What's all this nonsense about the fucking legacy when you continue to prove that all you care about is yourself?" Archer asks, surprising everyone in the room with his question. It's one we were all wondering, but probably one that none of us had the nerve to ask.

"Judge me how you want, but understand that there's a lot you don't know," he answers. "I made investments to build this family's wealth. I did it to create something that would last, to give us the type of wealth and power we deserve."

Madden stands and shakes his head in disgust. "You're not fooling anybody," he hisses. "You did this to serve yourself. To pretend like you fit in with some social class, like you were good enough for Mom. But there's more to that class than wealth. It's not just how much you have. It's how you make it. Mom apparently came from old money." He shakes the papers in his hands to prove his point. "You come from dirty money."

He walks out of the room, and Kennedy looks around a little helplessly, a little lost, before she follows him out of the room.

The rest of us glare at our father and give him our own looks of disgust as we each follow suit, walking out of the

Snap DECISION

room and leaving him alone with his lawyer...which is likely a mirror image of how he'll be spending most of whatever time he has left on this earth.

CHAPTER 33

Tatum Barker

Home

I haven't seen Archer since we all left Mr. Bradley's office.
    I want to say goodbye. I want to say…something. To defend why I'm marrying Ford, maybe. I don't need to defend myself, but I want to. Only, I'm not exactly sure why I'm marrying him.

Because he asked.

Because I want the money.

But also…

Because I think I'm falling for him.

Ford is angry. All the Bradley siblings are, and they all have a right to be. He's angry-packing after he changes out of his suit and into jeans and a T-shirt for the plane ride back home. Putting things into his suitcase with a little more force than necessary. Throwing his toothbrush back into his toiletry bag. That sort of thing.

It's definitely *not* the time to ask him about how we can work out a deal on keeping the mansion in the family.

Snap DECISION

"Can I do anything to help you?" I ask softly.

He sighs, and he backs up to lean against the wall. He shakes his head. "This was just...a lot. You know? I need to get my focus back on football since we *have* to win this weekend or we won't even make the wild card game. But my head is here with my family. With my dad and his lies, how it affects all of us, this fucking *legacy*. With Archer and how he's reacting to this. With you. Wanting to take the next step. Solidly not where it should be."

"So how do you get your focus back?"

He shrugs. "No idea. I've never gone through this before."

"Losing a loved one?" I ask, and I take a step to close the gap between us.

He twists his lips. "I mean...yeah. We weren't close."

"But it still hurts." I take another step, and I reach out to touch his heart. He reaches up to rest his hand over mine, and I feel how fast his heart is racing.

"Yeah."

"It's okay to be sad. It's okay to feel all the things. It's even okay if you don't feel anything. If you're numb and just want to get the hell out of here. Everyone processes grief differently."

"What if I don't feel like I'm grieving?" he whispers.

"That's normal, too. Ford, she just died last week. It's going to take some getting used to, and maybe you'll never truly grieve her. Maybe one day down the line, you'll be sitting at a table, and a memory will pop up that will take you down at the knees. However you react, however you feel...it's all normal. It's all okay."

He loops an arm around my waist and rests his forehead against mine. His breathing picks up the pace, and I think he's about to kiss me when I hear a voice at the door.

"Knock knock."

"Ugh," Ford mutters in disgust. "Who's there?"

"Ev," Everleigh says.

"Ev who?" Ford asks, playing along as he straightens, and we both turn to look at her.

"Ev-eryone from the Vegas side is heading out if you want to come down to say goodbye."

I giggle at her little joke even as my heart seems to constrict at the thought that *everyone* from the Vegas side is leaving. Does that include Archer?

"Our flight is soon, too," Ford says. He zips his suitcase, and mine is already standing by the door. "Can we hitch a ride with you to the airport?"

"We're full. Sorry."

"Is Archer going with you?" Ford asks.

She shakes her head. "He already left."

My heart drops down into my stomach.

Oh.

He's already gone.

I didn't get to say goodbye.

I didn't get to say *anything* at all.

I blow out a breath, and then we head downstairs to bid Ford's siblings goodbye—sans Archer, obviously, and also without Mr. Bradley. I wonder where he went. Maybe he's still in his office with the lawyer.

The Vegas crew's car arrives, and they head out. Our car is next, and we say goodbye to Liam and Ivy.

I stare at the mansion as we pull away, regret filling me that this may be the very last time I ever visit this place. It cracks my chest in two, and I'm not sure why. It was never meant to be mine, even though it feels like such a deep part of my past.

When we land in Tampa, it *feels* like I'm going back home. It's a weird feeling since Chicago was home first, then Vegas.

But now, being with Ford, walking into the penthouse that overlooks the bay…this feels like home. This feels *good*.

This feels like my future.

Snap DECISION

It feels like we made it over the first obstacle, and now we can do anything.

I move to drag my suitcase to my bedroom, but Ford's voice behind me stops me as I hear the door click shut behind him.

"Wait."

I'm standing near the kitchen counter when I turn back toward him, and he abandons his suitcase by the door. My brows push together as he strides across the room toward me. "What?" I ask.

He stops mere inches from me, and he takes me in his arms. His eyes bore down into mine, his full of heat and need and something much stronger. His lips move down to meet mine, and I reach up to cradle his jaw in my hands. He deepens our kiss, his tongue brushing against mine, and then he pulls back suddenly. His eyes move down from my lips, tracing the curves of my body, branding me with heat in each place they land as I wait for his next move.

I'm wearing a skirt paired with a knitted ugly Christmas sweater, and suddenly I feel *hot*. Like I need to take the sweater off. But I don't dare move.

He makes the first move instead as he moves toward me and lifts me up, setting me on the counter. He moves in between my legs, and I have just a tiny bit of height on his six-three frame when he usually towers over me by eight or so inches. He presses a kiss to my neck, and then he sucks on the skin there. I lean my neck back to give him more space to work with, and he trails his mouth from my neck back to mine, kissing me tenderly as I wrap my arms around him.

He trails his lips down again, this time from my neck to my collarbone and over my sweater. Down, down, down he goes, until he's kissing my hip over my skirt. And then he reaches under said skirt and lifts it up. He tugs on my panties, and I lift one side of my ass off the counter at a time so he can work on slipping my panties off.

His eyes meet mine, and his are full of need as he tosses my panties to the ground. He presses kisses along my thigh and pushes my thighs apart, exposing my pussy to him.

Then his mouth is on me.

I gasp as I feel his tongue dipping first into me before moving back toward my clit, and I lean back on my palms and close my eyes, my head tipped back as I give in to the pleasure.

He pushes a finger into me as his mouth covers my clit, and he picks up a punishing, pounding rhythm as he swirls his tongue around. I gasp, and my body clenches tightly as he drives his fingers in, his tongue working my clit as he hums against me, sending shockwaves of pleasure through me.

His mouth is pure heaven as I feel my body give way, and I rock against his face as I start to come. I moan, the sound strangled as the force of pleasure whips through me, my legs clamping around his ears as he forces his way through to ride it out with me.

When the scruff on his jaw tickles against my thigh, I open my legs again, thrusting my fingers in his hair as I pull him back a little to stop, my body too sensitive to go on.

"Holy fuck, Ford," I murmur as he tilts his head back, so our eyes meet. He wipes his mouth with the back of his hand.

"I can't tell you how long I've wanted to taste that cunt," he murmurs.

Holy hell. I practically come again just from those words.

He groans, and then he reaches into his jeans, and he pulls his cock out. The tip is dripping, and he only pumps himself twice before he starts to come. I watch with rapt fascination as he grunts through his release, and I don't know that I've ever watched a man jerk off before, but it's oddly the hottest thing I think I've ever seen.

Snap DECISION

His neck is corded, his head tipped back as he gives into the pleasure. Cum erupts from his cock, and he was obviously so turned on by putting his mouth on my pussy that it nearly made him have an orgasm in his pants.

Why is that the sexiest thing ever?

I have no clue, but I'm so turned on right now that I want his mouth back on me. I want his fingers driving back into my pussy while his tongue swirls around my clit, giving me everything he has to give.

My God. There's no way I'm going to be able to wait nine more days for the main event.

CHAPTER 34

FORD BRADLEY

Best Man

When I walk out of my bedroom in my practice apparel on Friday morning, I find Tatum sitting on the floor near the tree. She's wearing some ridiculous pajamas with reindeer wearing Santa hats, and she has the lights on the twinkle-blinking setting. She's sipping from a mug of hot chocolate as she stares down at the boxes under the tree.

There are only a few. It's certainly not the spectacle the Bradley Christmas mornings were, back when there were at least ten presents per kid, all bought and wrapped by assistants and hired help. We didn't know it back then, but even if we had, I don't think we would've cared.

I care about what's under this tree, though.

The woman I love, for one thing.

"Merry Christmas," she says. "Just so you know, I'm starting the day with your McGillicuddy's."

I chuckle. "I'd join you, but I have practice in an hour."

She makes a pouting face, and I laugh.

Snap DECISION

"Open that one," I say, nodding to the small box directly beside her.

She tears the paper off, and when she flips open the little box, she stares at the contents inside before she glances up at me, her eyes shining.

"This is gorgeous, Ford."

She takes the necklace out of the box it's nestled in, and she holds it up to inspect it. It's a silver chain with a delicate pendant on the end, a diamond outline of a dolphin shape. She immediately puts it on.

"I love it. That was so sweet of you." She stands, and I meet her halfway to press a soft kiss to her lips. "Your turn!" She grabs a box and shoves it at me, and I chuckle.

I open it, and it's a bottle of McGillicuddy's—the big size.

"I figured I've gone through probably a bottle of this shit all on my own, so you deserved a new one."

I laugh. "That was very thoughtful."

We each open a few more gifts, and the final one is a large one hiding in the back that she got for me. I can't begin to imagine what it is, but when I open it, I can't help but laugh even as the meaning hits me.

"This is amazing," I say, studying the two-by-three-foot canvas print that's clearly a screenshot from the viral video where I proposed to her while dolphins danced behind us.

I kiss her softly, tenderly, and then I need to get going to practice.

By some miracle, we just barely grab the victory on Sunday even without Landry. The other team was riddled with injuries, too, and I guess they were down more starters than we were.

That means we're in for Wild Card Weekend. We'll either advance to a longer season, or it'll all be over.

Except for Christmas morning, I've been forced to keep my distance from Tatum since we got back, barring the one indiscretion on the kitchen counter—one that just so happens to make me hard every goddamn time I walk into my kitchen. We've been tasked with extra film to study along with extra meetings to prepare for our opponents. I don't *want* to keep my distance, but in order to focus on football, it's been a necessity.

But with that said, I'm getting married on Thursday.

I've done zero preparations for it. She's done everything.

I'm not quite sure what to expect other than the fact that Tatum has told me I need a best man.

I know exactly who to ask, and I do it on Sunday after the game.

We traveled for this one, so we're on the plane back to Tampa when I turn to the guy in the seat beside me, closest to the window...my closest friend here in Tampa.

"I have a question for you," I say to Cole.

He narrows his eyes at me. "You wanna go out *tonight*? I'm beat after that game, man, but I guess I can force myself to—"

I hold up a hand. "No."

He narrows his eyes at me. "Okay. Then what?"

"I'm getting married, and I was wondering if you'd be my best man."

His eyes go from narrowed to wide so fast that I think they might pop right out of his head. "What?"

"You heard me."

"When?"

"Thursday."

He chokes. "Thursday, like as in four days?"

I nod.

"New Year's Eve. There better be some premium pussy there for me to give up my plans for this shit," he mutters.

Snap DECISION

I laugh. "You don't have to give up any plans. I just need you for an hour to witness. Then you can be on your way. We're not doing anything over the top."

"I didn't even know you were seeing anybody, let alone serious about somebody," he says.

"Her name's Tatum—"

"Wait a minute. Tatum? I saw the viral video, but I figured it was AI or some shit. Wasn't your brother serious with her like five minutes ago?"

I grimace, and he lets out a low whistle.

"Premium pussy," he murmurs.

"Huh?"

"It's the only explanation." He shrugs as if it all makes sense.

"I mean, yeah. It's premium. Definitely. But there's more to it," I say.

"Of course there is."

I'm quiet as I debate how much to give away.

"Well, out with it. What am I agreeing to here?"

Fuck it. I decide to tell him everything. He's an impartial third party, so maybe he'll have some insight I haven't thought through yet. "I love her, and I think she loves me. But there are reasons we decided to fast-track this."

"She's pregnant," he guesses, his voice flat.

"No! I haven't even fucked her yet."

He makes a face of horror. "And you're *marrying* her? Are you saving yourself for marriage, Bradley?"

I roll my eyes. "I don't know why I bothered talking about this with you."

"Okay, okay," he says, holding up both hands. "I'll stop. Go on."

"She's a wedding planner. We invested together in a property. The woman who sold it to us is elderly and has nobody to leave her money to, and she said she'd return our investment to us if we're the first couple to get married at the estate after it switched ownership."

"To the tune of..." He trails off as he waits for me to fill in the blank.

"Five million dollars."

He lets out another low whistle. "Fuck, man. I can see why you'd fast-track it. But isn't that messy with your brother and your feelings for her?"

I nod. "Incredibly messy."

"And not like you at all."

I shake my head. "Zero percent like me. But I've loved her since I was a teenager, and I'm not passing up the opportunity to have everything I've ever wanted."

"Damn, bro. I didn't peg you for a romantic."

"Make no mistake, I'll still kick your ass."

He laughs. "Right. Text me when and where, and I'll be there. Oh! Should I wear my tux?"

I tilt my head. "I have no idea. I'll get back to you on all of that."

He laughs. "You're an idiot."

"Thanks," I mumble, and then I text the actual boss to get all the details.

* * *

I glance through my schedule one more time for the rest of this week. We have practice tomorrow morning that gets out in the early afternoon, I'll get married, and then we have a late start on Friday since we've already secured our wild card spot and it's the morning after a night when we'll all be up later than usual.

Tatum informed me that we have a rehearsal on Wednesday evening, so Cole and I head out of practice together and drive toward the Winston Manor so I can show him around.

When I walk in, I find Tatum chatting with Ms. Winston, and a perky blonde woman stands beside Tatum.

"Oh, you're here," Tatum says, and she beelines for me. She presses a kiss to my lips, and her eyes edge over to Cole, who's eyeing the blonde woman up and down like he's never seen a woman in the flesh before.

"This is Cole, my best man," I say, elbowing him in the ribs to get his attention. I'm pretending to introduce him to Ms. Winston, not Tatum, since I don't particularly want to raise Ms. Winston's suspicions, and learning that my best man is just meeting my bride might just do that.

"Nice to meet you," he says to Tatum. I elbow him again.

Tatum plays it smoothly, though. "Oh, stop, Cole. Good to see you again. You remember Kenzie, right, Cole?" She's playing that we've all met and hung out before. Well done, future bride. "My best friend from Vegas. She's my matron of honor."

I'm trying to remember if *matron* versus *maid* means married or single when I spot the giveaway on her left-hand ring finger, and I hope Cole notices it, too.

That's when a dude walks through the kitchen doors and straight up to Kenzie, slipping his arm around her waist. He must be in the know, too, because he nods at me. "Ford, man, great to see you again." He holds out a hand, and I slap it first, and then we fist bump as if we're old friends. Bro code for the win.

"What did you think of the kitchen, Cody?" Tatum asks, clearly so we can figure out this dude's name.

"It's incredible." He does the hand-slap, fist-bump thing with Cole, too, pretending to know him as well, and Ms. Winston seems fooled enough.

We run through the ceremony. It'll take place at sunset, and Cody is going to officiate. We'll share a small catered dinner afterward, and provided all goes to plan, I'll be home fucking my wife when the clock strikes midnight.

Jesus.

I can't fucking wait.

CHAPTER 35

Tatum Barker

The Right Investment

"You're *sure* about this?" Kenzie asks. It's just the two of us left here. Cody went to the hotel to check in, and Cole and Ford walked Ms. Winston out and headed their separate ways.

Kenzie's kids are with her parents back in Vegas, and she and Cody were all too eager to take a New Year's Eve trip for themselves while helping me out here in Tampa.

I nod. "Look at this place," I say, spreading my hands out. "It's mine basically for *free* provided I do this one thing."

"What about Archer?" she whispers.

I glance away from her. "I saw him last week when I went back for their mother's funeral."

"And?"

"And it was…weird. But my heart landed squarely with Ford."

"And you're sure you want all this?"

The wedding-planning optimist in me has zero inclination to walk away now. I can't even imagine it.

Snap DECISION

I know she's talking about the venue and the wedding rather than the man, but I twist it anyway. "Of course I want this, Kenz. I wouldn't be getting married if I didn't think there was a chance it would last. How romantic, right? We've known each other for years, and we're falling for each other, and I was just with the wrong brother all those years."

"What if you weren't?" she asks.

"Look, I've seen this before. I'm a *wedding* planner. I've seen it all at this point. Most brides get nervous before they get married. Most grooms do, too. Even the ones who are absolutely certain. There's still that little asshole in the back of their minds picking away, planting seeds to make them question whether what they're doing is right. And you know what I tell them? To trust their gut. The gut is almost never wrong."

"And what's your gut telling you?" she presses.

"My gut is telling me to do this."

She nods. "Great, then. But if you need to talk through any of it, you know I'm here."

I lean in and give her a quick hug. "I know, and I appreciate you so much."

"I'm not just the matron of honor. I'm here for whatever you need."

I first met Kenzie when I planned her wedding to Cody a little over four years ago. I was there for her, too. Even she of the perfect family had chilly feet the morning of her wedding.

I remind her of that. "You were nervous, too. Remember? But your gut told you it was right, and now you're glowing with happiness."

She nods, and she snags her bottom lip between her teeth as she walks over to the windows, staring out at the gorgeous view of the water.

"Kenz?"

She sighs heavily. "It's not perfect, you know."

"What's not?"

"My life. There are days when the kids are bonkers and Cody is pissing me off, and I just want to pack up and run away from it all. Toward someone like that Cole Andrews."

"Would you?" I ask.

"Run?" she asks, and I nod. She shakes her head. "No. Of course not. But even when it's right, it's not perfect. It's not easy. So I can't imagine how much harder it would be if it *wasn't* right from the start. You get me?"

I nod as I glance down at the floor. Yeah, I get the message loud and clear.

But it's not going to stop me.

I stay at the same hotel as Kenzie and Cody, just in my own room. We have an entire spa day planned here at the hotel while Ford attends practice and gets ready at home for our sunset wedding.

I'm not surprised when my phone rings just as I slip beneath the sheets and find it's Ford calling.

"Hi," I answer.

"Hi."

"You okay?" I ask.

"Yeah. You?"

"Yeah. Kenzie was trying to talk me out of this, I think. Or at least, like, force me to examine why we're doing this."

"Why are we doing it?" he asks softly.

"At first, it was because of the money."

"And now?"

I sigh. "And now…it's more."

"Is it love?"

I'm quiet a long time as I contemplate that. We haven't even slept together, but I have these enormous feelings for Ford. They started as friendship. We have a solid base. We can talk about anything. We can laugh together. We've had a few intimate, sexy moments together that tell me the vibe is right there. And the man can kiss. Holy hell, can he kiss. So good that just the thought of his mouth on mine has my toes curling.

But is it love?

"I think it is," I finally whisper.

"But you also love someone else," he says flatly.

"Of course I do. Those feelings don't just go away."

"Yeah," he mutters, and I think he's tried fighting his feelings for me for longer than he's ever admitted to me. "We can't help who we fall for."

"What if I love two men?" I ask quietly. Two men who just happen to be brothers.

"Then you choose one. And I hope you choose me, Tate."

I feel the heat of tears pinch behind my eyes. I want to choose him, and marrying him tomorrow will be a big outward sign to the world that I am.

But first, he deserves the inward sign between the two of us.

"I do," I whisper. "I choose you."

He lets out a breath of relief. "Don't change your mind."

"I won't. I'll see you tomorrow."

"I love you," he says softly. It's the first time he's said those words to me, and my heart fills.

"I love you, too." I do. I'm sure of it. I just hope it's the intimate kind of love you have for the man you're marrying and not just the love between two friends who can't live without each other.

CHAPTER 36

FORD BRADLEY

I Do

Practice is interminable.

We run the same drill forty-seven times. That may be an exaggeration, but it doesn't feel like one. We need to be perfect on Sunday, according to Coach. The game doesn't matter in terms of playoff berth, but every play still matters. We're fighters here in Tampa, and we're not going to throw in the towel just because the outcome doesn't have an effect on playoffs.

I'm exhausted by the time we're excused at one, and I eat a quick lunch at home, take a long shower, and get ready for tonight.

We're meeting at the manor an hour before sunset so we can take photos both before and after. The photographer that Tatum hired is one she's already put on her short list of favorite vendors, and I can't wait to see how they capture this day.

It's a day a decade in the making. One I never thought would happen for me. Yet here we are, and I'm fucking ready.

Snap DECISION

Cole arrives a little before four o'clock, and I leave him in my family room so I can finish getting ready.

He's already dressed in his tux, and I'm not quite sure how Tatum worked her magic to get him a properly sized tux when I just asked him to be my best man a few nights ago, but that's her. She gets things done. It might take three drinks and a bunch of chaos, but she gets it done.

It's one of my favorite things about her, along with the smell of her hair and the taste of her cunt. That one taste that left me wanting more. An appetizer for what's to come. It was fucking perfection.

And tonight, that cunt will be mine.

Fuck.

It's hard to believe that I'm about to get everything I ever wanted, and I feel better after our conversation last night. I didn't want to go into a marriage that was based on a fluke. I didn't want to get everything I wanted because of someone else's strange request.

And when she said she loves me too, that she chooses me...well, that was everything I needed to hear.

I find Cole sitting on my couch watching SportsCenter once I emerge dressed and ready to go.

"Looking good, bro," he says.

"Thanks."

"You sure about this?"

"Yes," I say. "Never been more sure about anything in my life."

"That's the exact sort of enthusiasm I was looking for," he says.

"You ready to go?"

He nods, and we head down to his car. He drives us to the manor, and Ms. Winston greets me at the door.

"Good evening, Mr. Bradley," she says, opening it wider to let me in. I wasn't sure she'd be here, but I suppose it's better for her to greet me than my future bride since we're not supposed to see each other before the ceremony.

"Ms. Winston," I say, and I give her a short hug as I enter.

"Why did you two rush this wedding?" she asks.

I glance at Cole, and then I give her the most honest answer I can. "Well, we have a wedding scheduled for mid-January, so we were trying to abide by your terms."

She narrows her eyes at me. "Would you have married her without those terms?"

I nod solemnly. I didn't think it would happen, and maybe the stars aligned and I got lucky. But hell yes, I would have. In a heartbeat.

"Okay, then," she says. She holds up her hands, her palms facing me. "Treat her well, and I bless you with many happy years of marriage."

"Thank you," I murmur, feeling surprisingly choked up at her words.

"You may go out to the gardens, where the photographer is waiting for you," she says, holding a hand up toward the windows.

Cole and I head in that direction, and we pose for the photos, doing whatever the photographer asks. I wonder if Tatum is up in the bridal suite looking down at me. I wonder what she's thinking. What she's feeling.

I miss her.

It was strange waking up to an empty house before practice today.

I wonder if she misses me, too.

We head up to the groom's suite, and shortly after that, Ms. Winston tells me it's time. I head downstairs, and I walk into the ballroom to find that a few of the chairs are occupied.

She had once asked me for a guest list, and we both kept it small. All the same, I spot her mom occupying one of the chairs with the one beside her empty—likely for her father,

Snap DECISION

who's about to walk his daughter down the aisle. Her brother, his wife, and their baby take up others. Everleigh sits beside them.

That's it. She's the only representative from my family, and she's here alone.

I wasn't expecting her to be here, and my chest warms that someone cared enough to show up.

It makes sense, really. My brothers are in season, so they can't just hop on a plane to Tampa in the midst of playoff runs. Archer could have, but he wouldn't have.

My father isn't here, most likely because he's not allowed to leave the state since he's out on bail.

I wouldn't have wanted him here anyway.

I didn't invite anyone from the team aside from Cole. I'm close with many of them, but this was never meant to turn into a spectacle, and inviting pro football players would have made it one.

So that's it. A few witnesses. We'll dine together afterward, and everyone can head home. Maybe they can even make it home before the clock strikes midnight, ringing in the new year.

I walk down the aisle as my eye catches Everleigh's, and I take my place up at the altar. The pianist begins with some instrumental piece I recognize but can't name as Cole escorts Kenzie down the aisle.

Once they're in place, there's a soft pause that causes my heart to thunder. The music changes, and another instrumental piece begins. I think it's "Clair de lune." I remember Tatum saying once that she always dreamed of floating down the aisle to that song.

The front doors burst open, and Tatum appears on the arm of her father.

She's positively breathtaking. She's wearing a white lace dress, simple and elegant, with long sleeves. Her hair is pulled back into a low bun with romantic waves and delicate flowers woven in.

My chest tightens, my heart thunders, and my nerves race. She's about to become my wife.

My *wife*.

The door closes behind them as she walks along the aisle toward me, and as her eyes connect with mine, a feeling of calm settles over me.

The thundering subsides, the nerves quiet.

It's just the music, her, and me in this room.

She stops in front of me, the flowers in her hands trembling a little as if she's trembling. She smiles at me, and it feels like everything is going to be okay.

We're really doing this.

"Good evening, and welcome to the wedding ceremony celebrating Ford Bradley and Tatum Barker. Who gives this bride to be married to this man?" Cody asks.

"Her mother and I do," her father says, and he reaches over to shake my hand. I pull him in and give him a hug.

This man is about to become my father-in-law. I don't know him all that well, but I know he raised one hell of a daughter, and I know he's a better father than the one I got.

He hugs me back before he joins his wife, and Tatum hands her flowers to Kenzie before turning to me and taking my hands in hers.

"Today Ford and Tatum will begin the next chapter of their relationship. They've known each other since high school, over a decade now, and they have spent much of that time getting to know one another. When you know, you just know." Cody glances at his wife, and she smiles. He turns back to us. "Let's get to it, shall we?"

He flips the page in his book, and he starts to read from the script. "Do you, Ford, take Tatum to be your lawfully wedded wife?"

Snap DECISION

We decided to forego the formal vows, the old clichéd *to have and to hold, in sickness and in health*, and all that. We're making a promise, and we both know what we're promising.

"I do," I say, and Tatum's lips tip up into a smile.

God, I can't wait to kiss her.

"And do you, Tatum, take Ford to be your lawfully wedded husband?"

She opens her mouth to form the words just as we all hear the front door as it's thrown open and a voice yells, "Wait!" The figure is silhouetted against the light coming in from the front door, but I'd know that voice anywhere.

And as he rushes up the aisle to where we are, it's confirmed.

"Archer!" Tatum gasps. "What are you doing here?"

He's panting. "Tell me I made it on time. Tell me you didn't go through with this."

I'm still holding her hands in mine while my brother tells her not to marry me.

She glances at me, her eyes full of horror, before she turns back to him.

Nobody knows what to say.

A million thoughts race through my head. I should come up with something, anything, to say. To apologize for taking the woman that was his first. I want to be sorry for that, but I can't seem to find it in myself to apologize for finally getting the one thing I've always dreamed of.

I keep my mouth shut.

"Am I too late?" he begs. "Tell me I'm not too late."

He's standing opposite Cody. The room is silent as Tatum looks from him, back to me, to Cody, to the small group gathered here to celebrate this day with us.

He's not supposed to be here.

He should be back in Vegas. He ended it with her. Whatever his reasons were, he ended it. Too many times. She deserves better. Am I better? I'd like to think so. Better for her, anyway. I'll treat her the way she deserves. I'll help make her dreams come true. I won't break her heart.

Although…he's not too late. Not technically. She hasn't said *I do* just yet.

I have.

I wait.

I hold onto every last shred of my patience as Tatum's mouth opens and closes, as she tries to form the words, as she fights with what to do here, faced with her history pitted so clearly against the future that I can and want to give her.

Finally, she finally turns back to me, and I see the determination in her eyes, as if she just made a snap decision that she's completely confident in. "I do." She clears her throat and turns back to Archer. "You're too late."

He closes his eyes and tilts his head back, his head pointed toward the ceiling instead of toward us, as if he's trying to draw strength from the heavens.

"You're welcome to take a seat and join us as we celebrate our commitment," Tatum says quietly, her voice surprisingly even despite the tremble in her hands.

"Fuck," he mutters, and instead of taking a seat, he walks straight out of the manor.

Everleigh looks wildly between us and the front door that he left open, and she gets up to chase after him.

We'll be fine. She knows this.

But Archer? That's another story entirely.

CHAPTER 37

Tatum Barker

Mrs. Bradley

We exchange rings, and that's it.

The ceremony is over.

Everleigh was only outside for a moment before she came back inside, and I'm curious what happened. Maybe he had a car running at the curb, and he ran out and made his escape. Maybe he thought I'd pick him, and he'd whisk me away to some destination.

But in the moment when I had to choose, everything suddenly became very clear.

He's my past. I love him, but Ford is my future.

He's the one I want.

I don't see Ford ever throwing in the towel on us. He's dependable, and he's the type of man who's going to continue to try with me. He's going to continue to work on it. He'll fight for me.

We both will.

And now it's done.

𝒮𝓃𝒶𝓅 DECISION

Ms. Winston only stays long enough to witness the ceremony, and she leaves an envelope on the small table with gifts from our few guests.

I always thought I wanted a big wedding. It's what I do, after all.

But this feels intimate. It feels perfect. I want our lives to be a reflection of this…except, you know, that whole *getting interrupted by my ex* thing that happened in the middle.

That's it. I made my choice, and he needs to accept that. We already talked about this anyway. I've talked it to death, actually, and I keep arriving at the same conclusion.

So here I am, married.

I'm Mrs. Bradley now, technically—even if I keep Barker. I'm just…not the Mrs. Bradley I always assumed I'd be.

We share in our first meal as husband and wife. We cut our honey and fig cake. We toast with champagne and chase it with peppermint schnapps.

Ms. Winston is gone, but we're carrying on all the traditions, which tells me that this all wasn't just for her benefit. It was for us, too.

Ford is ever the gentleman as he feeds me a piece of cake, and I do the same in a ladylike manner. I've seen enough brides in tears because their new husbands thought it would be funny to smash cake in their faces.

Spoiler alert: it's never funny.

We dance to a collection of songs I chose and put onto a playlist on my phone. Our first dance is to "Never Stop" by SafetySuit. I heard it once during a wedding, and it became the song I aspired to. As the singer talks about his heart racing, it feels like I've found that with Ford.

We dance until dusk gives way to night, and we say goodbye to the family members and friends who joined us here. The small staff I hired to help serve the food has finished cleaning and has left as well.

"It's just us in here, Mrs. Bradley," Ford says softly. He loops his arm around my waist and hauls me to him, and I giggle as I fall against his chest.

"What are you going to do about it?" I tease.

"Well, we have several options."

"Lay them out for me," I suggest.

"Option one, I take you in the same spot where I married you and make love to you."

"Mm," I murmur, closing my eyes as he nips a kiss to my neck.

"Option two, I take you upstairs to the owner's suite and have my way with you."

My eyes flip open. "I'm listening."

"Option three, I bend you over the kitchen counter."

I raise a brow. "Only if you perch me on top and put your mouth on me again."

He chuckles even as he shifts his hips against me to indicate what a swell idea he thinks that is.

"Option four, I take you outside and we make love under the stars."

"You weren't kidding when you said you had several options," I say, capturing his lips with mine.

"There's one more," he murmurs against my mouth.

I open my mouth to his, and our tongues dance a moment before I pull back. "Make it quick."

"Hotel," he pants. "We have sex there, then head down to the New Year's party with my cum dripping from your cunt."

I gasp. Literally. I've never heard him talk like that before, and it's like an inferno rises within me as the anticipation builds. I catch his lips with mine once more, and then I say, "That one."

I don't even have to think twice about it.

We'll have sex here someday, surely. But I want the first time to be exactly what he just said.

Snap DECISION

He kisses me again, the fervor rising as an intoxicating undercurrent of need and hunger pulses between us, and then he grabs my hand. I collect the envelopes left on the gift table, and Ford turns off the lights. We meet near the front door, and the car that's been waiting for us all day is out front.

We're taken to one of the most luxurious hotels in all of Tampa, and our driver hands Ford the key to the honeymoon suite. The driver already deposited our bags in our room, so Ford and I head inside and toward the elevator, his hand planted firmly in mine.

This is it. This is the moment I've been waiting far too many days for.

The anticipation has been building since he first uttered the words "New Year's Eve." It felt like this day would never get here just as much as the days have rushed by us, and now we're here. Waiting. Ready.

Wet. So, so wet.

We take the elevator up to the top floor, and we head down the hall. Ford opens the door, and he steps in first.

And then he sweeps me up into his arms as if I weigh nothing, and he carries me through the doorway.

I only catch a quick glimpse of the gorgeous room. Someone was just in here because candles are lit, soft music plays, and the entire scene is straight from a movie. It's perfection.

But it's only a glance because his lips are on mine again. He kisses me softly at first, but it escalates to urgency as the chemistry I tried for so long to deny takes over. Our tongues battle together in a war we're both winning as the need spreads inside me, heating me all over. It's reminiscent of our first kiss—not the one at the bakery when we ate that honey and fig cake, but our *real* first kiss, the one all those years ago in front of a keg. There's need and want and curiosity in this kiss, all things I felt twelve years ago that Ford still manages to make pulse within me.

Eventually I pull back, and he carries me to the bedroom. He sets me down on my feet still clad in my white heels, and he spins me around to start working the buttons on the back of my dress.

There are a lot of them. Twenty-eight, in fact.

He threads each one through the loops with patient but slightly trembling fingers while the anticipation continues to build. An ache throbs between my legs, in my breasts, in my chest.

I wonder if his fingers are trembling from nerves or from excitement. Both emotions plow into me as the need becomes overwhelming.

Clearly wedding dress designers only think about how gorgeous the dress looks on, not all the work it takes to get it off.

Once he finally gets it open, his fingers graze a soft caress down my spine before he leans forward and trails kisses there.

I shiver at the feel of him, and I spin around to force his jacket off his shoulders. It flutters to the ground in a pool, and I yank his tie off as my trembling fingers move to the buttons lining the front of his shirt. I try to be patient, but I'm needy. I'm aching. I'm so goddamn horny for him that one swipe of his finger through me will be enough to set me on fire.

He helps me by unbuttoning from the bottom up, and we meet in the middle. I push his shirt off, and he works the cufflinks and cuffs as I reach down and rub his cock over his slacks.

He's hard. So hard. Incredibly hard.

My brain short-circuits much like it did the day I first sat on his lap and realized that maybe he wasn't faking his feelings for me.

Snap DECISION

He reaches for the shoulders of my dress and slowly peels it forward, carefully helping me out of it to reveal the lacy white bra and panty set I wore beneath it. It's all I'm wearing, in fact, except for my matching white heels.

He backs up to check out the lingerie. "Jesus Christ, Tatum," he breathes, his voice thick with desire. "You're fucking perfect. I can't believe you're my wife."

I look demurely up at him, and I think back to his words about what he's going to do here to me now. "It's time to fuck your wife."

His tongue darts out to wet his bottom lip as his eyes dilate with need, and I reach for his belt buckle. I get it undone, pop the button of his slacks, and push them down. He steps out of them and kicks off his shoes at the same time, and then he's standing in just a pair of black boxer briefs with an enormous bulge tenting the front.

He pulls me into his arms to kiss me some more. I'd love to stay here and kiss him all night, but I'm so needy, so aroused, that I can't. I need him inside me. I need him. Now.

It's all my brain can focus on.

I pull back from his mouth and whimper, "I need you."

His eyes move to mine with concern, but he sees what he needs there.

"I'm on the pill," I say before he can ask, before we have that awkward conversation of whether we need to use a condom. I want his cum inside me just like he said would happen.

God, do I want it. All of him.

"Good, because I want to feel all of you." He reaches down into my panties, and he hisses as he roughly pushes a finger into me. "My wife is soaked for me," he rasps.

My wife.

The words plow into me with a force that nearly makes me come on the spot.

"It's all for you. And now I need my husband to fuck me."

He nods. "I'll make good on my promise. I'm not stopping until my cum is dripping out of you."

"My God, Ford. Get to it already."

He chuckles and starts peeling his boxer briefs off as I pull my bra off. We toss them on top of the rest of the clothes we've left on the floor, and he hooks his fingers into my panties and drags them down my legs.

I finally kick off the heels, and he takes my hand and leads me to the bed. He nods for me to go first, and I lie on my back, expecting him to hover over me. Instead, he grabs my legs and pulls my hips down toward the edge of the bed, and when his eyes meet mine, they're glazed with lust.

He moves down until he's resting on his knees, and he breaks our eye contact to gaze at my pussy for a few beats. And then he dives in. He licks his way through me, moaning and hissing as if this is the greatest thing he's ever tasted.

"Oh my God, Ford, yes," I moan. I can't believe this is my life. This is my husband. This is my future, this vault of pure pleasure only meant for him and me.

I want to return the favor, but I can't. I can't move, and not because he's got me pinned down or anything like that, but because the pleasure is so fast and hot and intense that I physically can't make myself move.

He stops, rocking back onto his feet, and my eyes fly open with a question as I wonder why he's stopping. He rises to his feet and sits on the bed. He helps me shift until I'm on his lap and pulls me down on top of him. I straddle him, and he fists his cock as I line up and sit down on top of him.

Our eyes are on each other as I lower myself and he pushes into me. Our bodies connect for the first time, and I gasp. He grunts as his massive cock impales me.

"Christ, you feel so good," he mutters. "Better than I imagined."

Snap DECISION

He imagined it. He imagined this moment, our bodies connecting intimately.

The thought warms me all over.

"You imagined it?" I ask tenderly.

"Every goddamn second of every goddamn day since I kissed you in the kitchen in front of the keg."

Tears well in my eyes. He never admitted that he remembered that kiss, too.

We'll talk more about that later. Feeling him as he moves inside me is causing everything in my brain to go haywire. My only focus is the need to move, to feel his friction as he pumps into me.

I grab onto his shoulders for support with shaking hands. He slides his palms under my ass, where he can control our rhythm from beneath me. He lifts me up, grunting as we start to find our pace. I ride him, my tits bouncing near his face, our eyes still on each other in what I can only describe as the most intimate, erotic moment of my life.

The only sounds in the room are our breathy gasps, our moans of need, and the sound of him moving in and out of me. He peels his eyes from mine long enough to catch one of my nipples in his mouth, and I arch back to give him the space to work my nipple as I continue rising and falling over him at the pace he sets by moving me up and down. It's glorious, the long, slow, forceful drives as he pushes us both toward the edge of bliss.

His fingers edge in closer to my anus, and I let out a moan as the anticipation of whether or not he's going to touch me there crashes into me. It only amplifies the need between us, and the first rush of release plows into me. I tighten over him, and he growls my name.

"Tatum, fuck. Your pussy feels so good. So tight. So perfect. And you're already falling apart." His voice is this low, sexy rasp, and it pushes me closer to the brink.

"Ford!" I yell, tossing my head back as I let the pleasure in. I claw at his shoulders now, his back, wherever I can get a grip on him as I travel up toward the peak.

"Yes, baby, just like that," he rasps around my nipple. "Ride my cock like you never want to stop."

"I never want to stop," I cry.

"Fuck yes," he hisses, and he pumps up harder into me and arches his neck back. He moves his palms from my ass to grip onto my hips as I leap over that wall of pleasure.

"More! Harder!" I yell, and he hammers harder into me, pushing me into the sort of bliss I've never known before.

It hits me all at once and goes on and on, my body contracting over his cock, and the feel of it all seems to push him into his own climax as I hear him yell between grunts and groans. "Fuck, Tatum—ahh, yes! I'm with you, baby. Fuck! Take it all!"

Cries of pleasure fall from us both as we seal the commitment we just made with this moment that was far too long in the making.

My mouth slams to his as I ride out the end of my orgasm, and as he continues to pump into me, leaving his cum behind just as he said he would.

We kiss our way through the end, and my body flushes with heat as he thrusts up one final time. He stays inside me even after we both finish, and I feel his cock twitching as I'm sure he can feel my pussy continuing to pulse over him.

I'm so drained after that exertion that I can barely hold my head up. I let go of his mouth, my head falling onto his shoulder, and I press a soft kiss to his neck. "I love you," I whisper.

"I love you, too," he whispers back, and then he gently pulls out of me. That's when I feel it…the promise he made me as his cum drips out of me.

Snap DECISION

He moves us so I'm lying on the bed for a few quiet moments of recovery where he lies beside me, and just like that, it feels like nothing will ever be the same again.

CHAPTER 38

FORD BRADLEY

Only an Hour Left

There are moments in life that we anticipate with excitement. Half the fun of anticipation is the wait. The thoughts about what lies on the other side of the event we're anticipating. The hope of how incredible it will be.

Rarely does the actual event meet expectations.

But tonight with Tatum? This night exceeded those expectations. In every possible way.

I have a *wife*, and she's the woman I pined for but never thought would possibly be mine. And yes, she agreed to this marriage out of convenience, but when she was faced with the choice, *she chose me*.

And that means everything.

It's not just for the sake of the money anymore. Not after the way we just connected on such a base, visceral level. It advanced my feelings for her in ways I didn't think possible. It wasn't just sex. It was the start of a connection that will bond us together for the rest of our lives.

Snap DECISION

We lie together in silence for a while, but I know she's not ready for this night to be over. I glance at the clock and see we're starting to run short on time. Eventually I ask, "You want to go get drunk and ring in the new year downstairs?"

She leans up on her elbow, and her eyes are twinkling when she says, "I think I'm drunk on you."

I nip a kiss to her lips. "You're welcome to continue drinking from this well anytime."

She wastes no time in taking that innuendo seriously. She starts to crawl down the bed, and she grabs my still half-hard cock in her fist.

She's about to take me in her mouth to get me hard when I chuckle and place a hand on her shoulder.

"I need a little more time to recover. Your pussy took it all out of me."

Her cheeks flush, and goddamn, she's beautiful. "You tell me when you're ready because I haven't had the pleasure of this cock in my mouth yet, and I feel like that needs to happen *this* year."

Jesus Christ. Did I hit the fucking jackpot or what?

"There's only an hour left of this year," I point out.

"Then you better get to recovering."

I chuckle. "And you better put some clothes on before we head downstairs. That cunt and those tits are mine now."

"Don't you forget it. Oh, and one more thing," she says, and she shifts back up to press a kiss to my lips.

"Hm?" I ask.

"The kiss in front of the keg?"

I smile sheepishly as I wrinkle my nose. "I didn't mean for that to slip out. I'm sure you forgot about it, but—"

She holds up a hand. "I never forgot," she whispers. "I think about that kiss all the time."

"So do I," I admit.

Our mouths collide just like they did that night all those years ago. Who knew there would be a twelve-year gap between kisses but that we'd end up *here*?

"Don't you ever forget that, either." She rolls off the bed and points a finger at me before she moves to sashay toward the bathroom, but she trips on the wedding attire tossed haphazardly all over the floor.

I leap to help steady her, but she's already standing upright by the time I get there. I just chuckle and shake my head. Tripping over her own wedding dress is *so* Tatum Barker...uh, Tatum *Bradley*.

She slips into a black cocktail dress, and I pull my tux back on for the party downstairs. She changes from the white heels to black, and the heels on these are so pointy that I ask her if she can actually walk in them.

"Of course I can," she says, rolling her eyes in exasperation.

"I mean, you *did* just trip on your own clothes."

"I blame that on the sex stupor. I'm fine now." She says the words, but as we leave our room and approach the elevator, she grabs onto my arm.

I guess if she can't walk in those shoes and chooses instead to hold onto my arm for the remainder of the evening, that's not really a bad thing for me.

We're alone on the elevator, and the heat between us is palpable.

"Are you recovered yet?" she asks quietly.

My eyes flick to hers, and I can't help it. I nod.

She's down on her knees in a second, reaching into my slacks without undoing the button. We only have fourteen more floors to go, and the elevator is pretty quick.

I tip my head back and close my eyes at the feel of her mouth on me, warm and wet as she sucks me in. I thrust my fingers into her hair, still done up for the wedding.

Snap DECISION

Fuck, it's good. So good. *Too* good. I want to come in her mouth. I want to shoot it to the back of her throat, to mark her mouth the way I just marked her cunt.

But the elevator is slowing. She holds me in, and the crown of my cock hits the back of her throat. I grunt at the feel of it, and I turn down to watch her.

She's looking up at me, need and desire clear in her eyes. She fists me at the base as she pulls me out of her mouth, sucking hard the entire way, and then she lifts to a stand just as the elevator skids to a stop. I push myself back into my pants, my glistening cock hard and ready and aching for more.

"This isn't over," I mutter.

"Not by a long shot," she agrees, shooting me a wide smile as the doors pull open and we find a group of people waiting to board.

We exit and head to the party in full swing. We find a server carrying a tray of champagne glasses, and we each take one and toss it back before we find the same guy and take another.

We head to the dance floor, and this party feels like it's sort of serving as a second reception—only just for the two of us instead of with family and friends.

My cock is still aching, though. She got me all worked up and ready to blow my load into her mouth, and then the fucking elevator had to stop moving.

Sometimes life's not fair.

I chug the rest of my champagne, and the deejay lets partygoers know that there's only a half hour left before it's a brand-new year.

We dance, we drink, we grind, we get hornier and hornier for each other. Eventually, Tatum grabs onto my arm and leads me toward a door. I don't even know how she saw this particular door, but it looks like it's a hallway leading back to the kitchens, only this particular hallway isn't being used tonight. It's dark, lit only by a small window at the top of a door on the other end of the hallway that must lead into the kitchen area.

Nobody's back here, and she drops back down to her knees.

"Fuck, Ford, your cock is so beautiful," she hums as she takes me back into her mouth. She moans as if she's getting off just by sucking *me* off, and it's a beautiful sight to witness. It's somehow the sexiest moment I've witnessed in my entire twenty-nine years. I've had blow jobs before, sure—but never this intimate. Never this sexy. Never from a woman I was in love with. Never from my wife.

She sucks on my cock, and she lets go of me to fist me and stroke up and down a few times. "You know," she says softly, and she sucks on the crown of my cock again before she continues talking. "I feel your cum in my pussy still. Now I want it in my mouth." She sucks me back in, and she bobs her head up and down as her fist moves along in time with her mouth.

Goddamn, she's good at this.

"You're about to get it," I grunt, and my fingers thread into her hair as I fuck her mouth, my hips delivering punishing thrusts in and out as she follows me, drive for aching drive.

I can't stop this freight train. It feels too good, too hot, too perfect. I burst inside her mouth with a growl as jet after jet of cum shoots to the back of her throat. She moans through it, and when I glance down at her as my climax comes to an end, she's got her free hand under her dress, and she's furiously rubbing her own clit.

She keeps rubbing, keeps sucking me even though I'm dry, and I reach under her armpits to haul her up. I bat her hand out of the way, and I slip my fingers down only to discover she's not wearing any panties.

Snap DECISION

Fuck. I could come again just at the mere thought.

I slip my finger into her, and I move slower than she was on herself. I slide my finger in, and I hold it there, curling it up before I pull it back out. I thrust a few times, and then I pull my finger out to use her own moisture to rub at her clit.

"Fuck, Ford! Fuck!" She clutches onto my shoulders as her sweet pleas are swallowed by the loud music just outside this door, where the party rages on and nobody is the wiser that we stole this intimate moment in this hallway.

Her legs tremble with the force of her second orgasm of the night, and she holds onto me like she'll fall over if she doesn't. I lean forward and kiss her lips, the salty taste of my semen still on her tongue as it dances with mine.

As the quakes subside, her legs continue to tremble, and she links her arms around my neck as I pull my fingers out of her and hold her tightly, turning something as simple as a blow job and a finger bang in a dark hallway into an emotional, meaningful moment for the two of us.

We take a moment for ourselves, breathing in each other deeply, and once she's straightened out her dress and I've tucked my cock back into my pants, we head back out to the party, no one any wiser as to what we just did in that hallway.

We grab more champagne, and when Tatum drops hers on the dance floor, the woman dancing beside her starts to slip. Tatum manages to catch her before she falls, but then her heels slip, too, and they both crash down to the floor.

And instead of rubbing the painful spot where they each fell on their asses, they laugh together from the floor.

That's Tatum. Chaos wherever she goes, but a shining light to make everyone around her happier at the same damn time.

I know she makes *me* happier.

The countdown begins. We kiss at midnight and toast with champagne.

Life feels pretty damn perfect as we dance the night away.

But if it *was* actually perfect, that would be our happy ending…right?

Instead, our story is just getting started.

CHAPTER 39

FORD BRADLEY

Spank Bank

The next ten days are a whirl of hot sex with my new wife and football…and a few headlines here and there about my new wife and football.

Once our wedding photos hit the media, her phone started ringing off the hook with couples wanting to book Winston Manor.

She's busy.

But she still makes time for me. For sex.

Sex in our bed. Sex bent over the terrace. Sex on the kitchen counter. The kitchen table. In the pantry—the site of the first place we ever had any sort of intimacy outside of a kiss.

It's a lot of sex as we make up for lost time, and each new experience we share feels better than the ones that came before it as we bond over this new transition in our relationship.

Snap DECISION

But as we slide into Wild Card Weekend, I know I need to take my foot off the gas just a little even though I don't want to.

I'm loving this new side to our relationship. But I need rest. I need focus. And I have neither when I'm staying up all hours of the night focusing on my wife's cunt instead of studying the film my coach gave me.

I need to be prepared, maybe especially because we're the underdogs. We're playing in Detroit this weekend, and it's going to be one of the toughest matchups of the season. But everyone loves a good underdog story, and the Beasts are ready to put up a fight.

If we lose this game, that means our season is over. If we win, we advance to the divisional round, where we'll face another tough opponent.

I don't want it to be over.

I want to fight.

But at the same time, I'm ready to have time to focus on Tatum. I've never really had this sort of conflict before.

"I hate to even say this, but I need to work tonight," Tatum says over dinner on Thursday night. "We're closing in on Lindsay and Devon's wedding date, and I have so much to do still."

"Can I help?" I ask before I really think it through. The truth is that I have a lot to do, too.

"I'm sure I can find stuff for you to do, but don't you have film to review?"

"I do," I say, shooting her a bit of a guilty look. "I have a lot to review, to be honest. I've been focusing on my wife instead of on football." I pull a face. "I'd rather focus on you, but we *have* to beat the Lions this weekend or we're out."

She reaches over and grabs my hand in hers. "I know. So go beat the hell out of them."

"I want you there."

She looks surprised. "Me?"

"Yeah. I can get you tickets, and I want you there. In my jersey."

"Won't it be cold?" she asks, wrinkling her nose at the thought of sitting at the game.

"It's a climate-controlled dome."

She laughs. "Oh! Great. Then I'm totally in."

I chuckle as I text our player engagement staff member that I need a single ticket in the best seat possible for Sunday.

Seeing her there in the stands cheering me on will give me everything I need.

I fly with the team the day before our game, and she flies out later the same evening. I'm busy running through drills and plays, so we don't get much time to talk. But I did manage to find time to leave a gift in her hotel room just so she'll know I'm thinking of her.

I know the moment she finds it because I get a text.

Tatum: *FORD! This is so perfect.*
Me: *I'm glad you like it. Can't wait to see it on.*
Tatum: *Can I see you?*
Me: *It's curfew. I have to stay in my room.*
Tatum: *I can come to you...*
Me: *Don't tempt me. If I get caught, I'll get my ass handed to me.*
Tatum: *Does this tempt you?*

A photo comes through a moment later of her wearing the gift I left in her room—a women's jersey with the number 86 on it with my last name emblazoned on the back.

Her last name now, too.

And it appears to be *all* she's wearing.

My mouth waters as my cock hardens.

Me: *It's more than tempting.*
Tatum: *So what are you going to do about it?*

I debate what to do. I can't leave my room, and I can't invite her to mine.

Snap DECISION

But nobody is in my room with me. We could have a little fun...

I snap a picture and send it to her before I even think twice. It's a shot of my hand down my shorts. I'm not showing any skin, but it's a clear enough message that I'm holding my cock in my hand and I'm ready to start stroking it.

Tatum: *Wishing it was my hand.*

Me: *What are you doing with your hand?*

Tatum: *I wasn't doing anything, but seeing that image has me doing this now.*

She sends back a picture similar to mine, and my mind runs wild with the possibilities of what her fingers are doing down there.

Me: *Tease that cunt for me. Slide a finger inside, but don't touch your clit yet.*

Tatum: *Why not?*

Me: *Because I'll tell you when I'm getting close so we can come together.*

Tatum: *How am I supposed to text you while I'm coming?*

Me: *You'll figure it out if you want it bad enough. Now take a tit out and pinch your nipple for me.*

She sends me a picture.

A goddamn picture of her nipple held tight between her fingertips, which means her other hand isn't in her pussy anymore.

Her face isn't in it, but Christ, that image is going in the spank bank for the rest of time.

Me: *You stopped touching your cunt.*

Tatum: *Only to send you that pic. Sliding my finger back in...now.*

Me: *How does it feel?*

Tatum: *I like it better when it's your finger, but getting these directions over text message is kinda hot.*

Me: *Just kinda hot? Maybe I need to step it up.*

I pull my cock out of my shorts, grip it at the base, and take a picture. I send it to her.

Tatum: *Oh my God, Ford. That's hot as hell.*

Me: *That's more like it. I'm going to slide my hand up and down it and think of your sweet, hot cunt while I do it.*

Tatum: *I want to touch my clit.*

Me: *Not yet.*

Tatum: *Please?*

Me: *No.*

I stroke harder as her texts come faster.

Tatum: *Ford, please.*

Tatum: *I need to.*

Me: *Not yet, baby. Take your time. Pull your finger out and taste yourself.*

I picture her dragging her finger out of her cunt as her lips twist and her eyes flash with the agony of needing a release. I hear her sweet, soft moans and her pleas to let her have it.

Tatum: *I wish it was you tasting me. I wish I had your cock in my mouth right now.*

Me: *That's my hot, dirty wife. I wish my cock was slipping into your ass right now.*

Tatum: *Oh, God, Ford. I want you to fuck me there.*

Me: *I will, baby.*

I think about fucking her in the ass, and it sends me to another level. My strokes get shorter and faster as the heat tears down my spine.

Me: *I'm getting close. Rub your clit.*

Instead of a text reply, she sends a voice clip. "Oh my God, oh my God, oh my God," she moans. "Ford, yes. I'm coming. Oh fuck, I'm coming so hard." She's whimpering by the end, and it's enough to send me into my own release.

I manage to hit the audio message button, and it's all ragged breathing and heavy grunts of her name as my release plows into me. "Fuck!" I roar as the surge bursts onto my hand.

Tatum: *saves audio file to add to spank bank*
Me: *Women have spank banks?*
Tatum: *Of course they do!*
Me: *That's hot as fuck, Tate.*
Tatum: *[laugh emoji]*
Me: *Saving your audio file as well.*

Instead of texting goodnight, I hit the call button.

"You know," she answers, "this would've been easier to do over an actual phone call versus a text from the start."

I chuckle. Leave it to her to put me in my place seconds after an orgasm. "Listen, then you wouldn't have that audio file for your spank bank."

"Neither would you."

"Good point. I just wanted to say goodnight, and I love you."

"Goodnight, and I love you, too. Go get 'em tomorrow, okay?" she says.

"Absolutely." I disconnect the call, and I head to bed with a warm feeling in my chest.

I sleep well, and I feel ready for game day when I wake.

I stretch a little to get my muscles warm with my pregame list blasting in my ears, and I head to the team breakfast. I eat light, allowing myself one piece of bacon along with an omelet, and I sit with Cole and a few of the wide receivers as we run through game scenarios together.

Coach Matthews gathers the tight ends to review our game plan, give us his extensive list of final reminders, and discuss our matchups.

Kickoff isn't until four thirty, so we hold a walkthrough in one of the hotel's ballrooms before we're released for a team lunch while we each hydrate with our electrolyte drink of preference, mine being Gatorade, and then some guys meet with trainers for treatment while others move onto their own pregame routines.

I listen to my playlist as I pace my hotel room.

I try to block everything out and focus.

But I keep coming back to that picture of Tatum's tits sitting on my phone. It's distracting me.

I let myself look anyway.

I blow out a breath. We're leaving for the stadium in twenty minutes. Now isn't the time for an erection.

I force it away and head down to meet my teammates, and we board a bus to the stadium. As the team bus pulls away, I spot Tatum standing near the hotel entrance. She's waving, and I wonder how I missed her as I walked through the lobby to get to the bus.

I wave, but the windows are tinted. There's no way she can see me.

But she looks fine as hell wearing my number.

We arrive at the stadium, and I strategically lay out my gear the same way I always do. It's a superstition for me, I guess. We head to the field for warm-ups, and I glance around at the crowd starting to gather.

This is it. I'm ready. We've practiced this hundreds of times. We're as ready as we'll ever be.

We get dressed. We gather in a circle around Coach Wilder, and he's fired up. "We're here to win. Let's show these Lions what kind of Beasts we are!"

He turns it over to the captains, who give similar sentiments and lead us in prayer, and then Coach Wilder has a few more words for us.

"This is it, team. This is everything we've worked for this whole season. We got here because of hard work, so let's show them what we're made of. Let's focus on today, this game, this win. Next week doesn't matter. Next year doesn't matter. All that matters is what's in front of us today. Right now. We have sixty minutes to leave it all out there on the field. Get out there and execute. Do the job you've trained for. You're prepared, you're ready, and now it's time to fight." He holds his hand out, and we gather around in a team huddle. "Beasts on three. One, two, three—"

"BEASTS!" The roar is solid and loud, a unified team ready to take on this opponent.

We race out to the field as our team is announced, and I bounce up and down on the balls of my feet to keep my muscles warm as the pre-game events take place. I glance through the crowd for Tatum, and my eyes zero in on her about a third of the way up directly behind our sideline. I tap the side of my helmet twice, and she grins down at me and goes wild as she waves at me.

She's beautiful there, her blonde hair somehow swaying despite the fact that we're indoors and there's no breeze in here. She's watching me, waiting for some signal from me, and she's thrilled that I gave her one. I find myself wanting to play to impress her. There's an added fire to my reasons for wanting to win. It's no longer just for me. It's so we have something else we can celebrate together.

She showed up for me, and somehow, it means more to me than I ever realized it would.

She's not just my friend anymore. She's my wife, and I want to do whatever I can to make her as happy as she makes me.

We sing the national anthem.

Our captains head out for the coin flip, which we lose, and the Lions defer the first play to us.

We take the field.

We're fucking ready.

It's the first snap of the game, and our center hikes it to Reggie. It's a little high for him, and he misses.

He fucking misses, and the ball drops to the field. He scrambles for it, but the Lions' defenders are all over that fucking ball. Reggie's too late. We all are.

The Lions recover the ball, and the stadium goes absolutely wild. It's deafeningly loud in here, and Coach Wilder tells Reggie to shake it off.

Reggie does not, in fact, take that advice.

He's nervous, and it shows—especially after the Lions score on that first turnover.

It gets worse from there.

The best we can do is a few field goals, and our season is over with a shitty final score of thirty-four to nine.

I showed up. I did my job.

But it wasn't enough.

Disappointment lances through me. If we just would've had Grant Landry here today instead of injured on the sidelines, we might've had a chance.

I can't blame the loss entirely on Reggie. It's a team effort.

But we sure could've used Grant's quick thinking today instead of Reggie's butterfingers.

Coach Wilder tried our third-string quarterback in the second half, and he's the one that got us close enough to try for field goals. He's the reason we weren't shut out.

It was too little, too late.

The locker room is quiet.

I imagine Coach will be taking a harder look at the quarterbacks coming up in this year's draft since our backup turned out to be a dud.

He gives us some platitudes about how we came together as a team, about how we can start looking forward to next season, about how we should be proud of the effort we gave in the face of so many obstacles. It's all a bunch of bullshit. The truth is that our season is over now.

The bus ride to the airport is quiet.

Snap DECISION

The flight home is even quieter.

We head our separate ways. Tomorrow will be for cleaning out lockers and saying goodbyes and tackling the exit process, including interviews with Coach Matthews, Coach Wilder, and our general manager, Richard Ellery.

And that'll be it. I'll have a longer break than I did last year when we made it to the conference championship. That was one game away from the big one, and we lost it.

It felt like more of a heartbreak to lose that one than today's game, which we were expected to lose.

Or maybe it's the fact that this year, I have someone waiting at home. I'm not going home to an empty condo to stare out over the view for the next six months.

And right now, I can't wait to get home to my wife.

CHAPTER 40

Tatum Barker

Branding

The Beasts take off on their team plane shortly after the game, and I'm waiting at the airport for my flight that keeps getting delayed due to inclement weather.

I'm exhausted. I just want to be home, but I still have a three-hour flight once we finally board.

I sit near an outlet so I can plug my phone in since I'm draining the battery doing my best to level up in Subway Surfers. I should download a movie or something, but I didn't think I'd be sitting at the airport this long.

A text comes through a little after ten.

Ford: *Just landed.*
Me: *Haven't even boarded yet.*
Ford: *You haven't?*
Me: *Right after your plane left, they delayed mine due to weather.*
Ford: *Shit. I'm sorry. Where are you?*
Me: *At the airport. Bored out of my mind.*
Ford: *We can sext again.*

Snap DECISION

Me: *LOL. In the middle of an airport?*

Ford: *Put your earbuds in.*

Me: *Maybe later. How are you doing?*

Ford: *Need you.*

Me: *Sorry about the game.*

Ford: *It wasn't the ending we were hoping for, but we never stood a chance.*

Me: *Of course you did. You wouldn't have been there if you didn't.*

Ford: *Season's over now. Not sure what I'll do with all this newfound time on my hands.*

Me: *Your wife?*

Ford: *Good call.*

Me: *I can use some help, to be honest. Ever since I released our wedding photos, my phone has been ringing nonstop to book Winston Manor. I've pushed out the first one to March so I can work on planning and get Devon and Lindsay under my belt, but I'm feeling a bit like I'm in over my head here.*

Ford: *Do you still have plans in Vegas?*

Me: *I do, but Kenzie is pretty self-sufficient. She calls me for the big stuff, but she can pretty much run things there.*

Ford: *Then we find you an assistant so you can run things here.*

Me: *Are you volunteering?*

Ford: *I could help with certain tasks, sure. But I'm only free for the next six months, give or take.*

Me: *Do you think Everleigh would be willing to help me with some branding stuff?*

Ford: *I can ask her.*

Me: *I talked to Madden a bit, and he's on board to help with reno work whenever I need him.*

Ford: *Good.*

Me: *Is that okay?*

Ford: *Yeah, sure.*

I'm trying to figure out what to say next when I hear a voice over the loudspeaker. "Flight twelve twenty-nine with service to Tampa Bay is now boarding at gate C-eleven."

Thank goodness.

I stand and stretch, and I unplug my phone, which should have enough battery to get me home.

I text Ford.

Me: *Hate to cut this short, but we're FINALLY boarding.*

Ford: *Safe flight. See you when you get here.*

When I finally do get home nearly four hours later, he's sleeping. He shifts when I climb into bed, and he kisses my neck as he wraps his arms around me.

I sleep in the next morning, and he's already gone when I wake up. I find a note from him on the kitchen counter.

Glad you're home safe. I need to head to the training facility for exit interviews. There's a breakfast order in the fridge for you from the restaurant downstairs if you want to heat it up.

I find the food and pour myself a cup of coffee, and then I grab my laptop and start to triage my poor, poor inbox.

I give up on that pretty quickly as I think about how Ford is absolutely right. I need an assistant.

I didn't find Kenzie until I rented an office space, and maybe it's time for me to get out and explore this city a bit more.

Though truth be told, I'm perfectly fine working out of the penthouse, and the offices at Winston Manor would be an ideal place if I needed to get away. But with either of those options, I don't have the luxury of meeting people.

I decide to take it to Starbucks for the day in hopes of meeting people and making a place for myself here.

Except when I arrive, I realize I left my laptop on the kitchen counter at the penthouse.

I grab myself a coffee, let out a heavy sigh, and head back home.

Snap DECISION

My phone rings as I'm in transit back home, and it's a Chicago number I don't recognize. I pick up.

"Tatum Barker," I answer.

"I thought it was Bradley now," the female voice on the other end says, and my brows dip as I wonder who the hell it is. "I'm teasing. This is Everleigh, by the way. Ford said you wanted to chat about branding?"

Wow. He made quick work of that one.

"Yeah," I mumble. "I do. I have one venue, and I'm planning to expand into more, but I'm overwhelmed with the one, and I have no idea how to build a brand. My entire business in Vegas has been word of mouth, and word's getting out here, and I need an assistant and someone who can make decisions and help me figure out my life but—"

"Tate," she interrupts, and I stop talking.

"I think this could be mutually beneficial. I'm just getting my branding business going, so I'd love to add you to my portfolio. This would be a full brand build for multiple venues, am I correct?"

"I guess that's what I'm looking for, yes," I say.

"Market value on that runs right around twenty thousand and would take me about a month to turn around to you."

"Twenty thousand?" I repeat. I mean, yeah, we just got that five million back from Ms. Winston when we opened her wedding envelope to us, but twenty thousand sounds steep when I'm trying to pinch pennies to invest in another venue and save a bit for any reno work we need to do at Winston.

"Oh, sorry—that's market value. I'd do yours free of charge, of course, as long as you agree to tell anyone and everyone that I'm your brand strategist and help me with my wedding to Maverick. And I'll agree to share your venues with everyone I know, too. As I said, I think we can help each other."

"Free of charge?" I echo. "For services you'd charge other people twenty thousand dollars for?"

"Well, yeah," she murmurs. "You're making me second-guess myself."

"No take backs! I agree! Send me the contract, okay bye!"

She laughs. "Don't hang up! Just to be clear, a full brand build would include new logos, color patterns, press kits, a growth campaign strategy, styled photoshoots, social media campaigns, advertising strategies, brand books…the works. Is that what you're looking for?"

"Yes. All of it." My voice is adamant. I'm ready for this.

"Then I'll send over the contract plus the paperwork that details everything I'll need from you to build your brand. Think mission, vision, brand pillars, even favorite colors for the palettes. And your company name, of course. Then I'll come up with a logo, a slogan, and everything else we talked about," she says.

"A company name?" I echo. "You mean…I can't just use Tatum Barker?"

She chuckles. "No. Not Tatum Barker. *You* are not the brand. Your company is. File the necessary paperwork to become an LLC. Something like Effortless Luxury, LLC. The Bradley Collective. Forever Estates Group. Something that sounds high-end. Use a buzzword like timeless, private, or prestigious. Barker Reserve Limited. Tatum Signature Collection."

Wow. She's good.

"Okay," I say meekly.

It appears I might have even more work cut out for me than I thought.

CHAPTER 41

FORD BRADLEY

Headliners

I was sort of glad we weren't able to talk last night.
I'm not quite sure what to do about the headlines. I hadn't even seen them myself—it was Cole who mentioned it to me as we sat together on the plane on the way home.

He had an article pulled up on his phone, and it was about Tatum and me and what the media decided to do with our *love* story.

The headline read *NFL Star Ford Bradley Marries MLB's Archer Bradley's Ex as Bride Plans Wedding for Teammate.*

The headline is gross enough, but the article insinuates that she wouldn't have gotten Devon and Lindsay's wedding if she wasn't involved with me, as if she couldn't get by on her own merits but instead is riding the Bradley family's coattails as she bed-hopped from one brother right to the next.

But then she asked me if Everleigh would lend her services to her. She chatted with Madden. That's four out of the seven of us she's been connected to in some way—four of us who

Snap DECISION

have helped or are planning to help her build her business in one way or another.

And it pulses a horrible thought in my mind. Is this article *really* all that far-fetched?

Would she have gotten Devon's wedding if I hadn't mentioned it to her and set up their meeting?

What if I went with love over logic for the first time in my life only to be burned by someone using me for my name and connections?

Tatum wouldn't do that...but the hard truth is that her business has been booming since she married me.

Yes, it's in part because of Winston Manor. That place sells itself, and we just happened to be in the right place at the right time for it to fall onto our laps the way it did. It felt like kismet, but what if it was some darker force at play?

My biggest fear has always been falling in love with someone who's only using me for what I can do for them, and it's not the first time since she came to stay with me that I've had that fear pulsing inside.

But this is Tatum. I've known her since high school. She's not like that. We were friends before I had the money and connections I have now. I don't have to worry about that sort of thing when it comes to her.

So why am I?

I push it all out of my mind as I head to my exit interview. I find my position coach, the head coach, and the general manager in there waiting for me.

Coach Wilder runs the meeting with an evaluation of my season that includes my stats, where I excelled, and what work I can do over the summer to prep for next season.

Coach Matthews says, "You're a steady, strong presence in the locker room."

Mr. Ellery adds, "And that's why we want you to consider being the offensive captain next season."

"Wow," I say softly. "What an honor. I'll think about it."

We review a strength and conditioning plan for the offseason, and they ask me if I have any feedback, which I do.

"We all worked hard, but we had too many penalties, and we lost a lot of morale when Landry went down. We need a reliable backup who can use his offense to get down the field, not one that'll buckle under pressure."

Coach Wilder nods. "Agreed." He glances through my contract. "You have two years left on this. What are your plans?"

"I'd love to stay here for the duration of my career. This is home. It's the only team I've ever played for, and I don't want to play anywhere else. I turn thirty on Friday, and I don't see an end at thirty-two."

Both coaches nod, and Mr. Ellery says, "That's the answer we were looking to hear."

I head down to the training room to get my medical clearance, clean out my locker, and say my goodbyes.

I'm on my way home before lunchtime, and my heart thunders as I try to figure out what the hell to say to my wife when I get home.

As it turns out, I don't have to say anything.

She's in her room, sitting at her desk and buried in some document on her laptop. She glances up when I walk in and has the kind of look on her face that tells me she could use some help. Stat.

I sit on the end of her bed. "What's wrong?"

"I have no idea what the hell I'm doing. But before we talk about me, tell me about your day."

I shrug. "It's the end of a season, and it ended in a way different from what we were hoping for, but the meeting went better than I expected."

"Well, that's good. Isn't it?" she asks. She narrows her eyes at me. "Why do you look like it isn't?"

"They told me they want me to consider being a team captain next year."

"Ford! That's freaking amazing! Right?" She seems confused, and I chuckle a little.

"Yeah, it's great. It's an honor. But I can't help but think I'm taking that position from someone else," I admit. It's the first time I've really even thought it, and the words slip out. I'm not sure why I felt a little melancholy when they asked me. Truly, it's an honor.

But Tatum manages to pull it out of me.

"Who's the captain now?"

"One of our wide receivers," I say. I stare out the window.

"Is he staying on the team next year?"

I shake my head. "He's retiring, so no. I guess it just feels like there are guys on the team more deserving than me."

"Why wouldn't you deserve it?"

"I don't know." I sigh. I don't really know what I'm getting at here. "It's just…I've been here playing with this team for a long time, and I guess somewhere deep down I feel like I should've been asked years ago. Why now? Because I'm one of the most senior members on offense? Because I don't have as many years left as some of these younger guys? I don't know. It just feels like…" I trail off, not sure of the words.

"Too little, too late?" she guesses.

"Yeah. Kinda."

That's the thing about Tatum. She just gets me. I don't have to say a word about the things that are bothering me because she can somehow easily assess them and put them into words, even if I can't.

"Ford. They wouldn't have asked you if they didn't think you deserved it. Now or back then. It's your turn. Your time. If you want it, take it."

She makes a good point.

"So what's all this?" I ask.

She sighs heavily. "Everleigh sent me a questionnaire so we can get the branding stuff underway, and it's, like, freaking *daunting*. She said it's okay if I don't have answers to everything right now, and once I fill out the majority, we can schedule a Zoom to chat about the rest. It's just like a million little decisions I have to make about this business. I'm going from a contractor in Vegas who plans weddings for fun to, like, this *business*. You know? With an *asset*. With *more assets* down the pike. It's a lot, and I haven't the first clue how to pull it all together into a brand."

Her phone starts to ring as she finishes her explanation, and she glances at it. "It's an eight-one-three number," she says. "Probably another couple who wants to book Winston Manor. I need to take this."

She answers the call, and I watch and listen as my mind runs wild with the things I can try to do to help her.

Sit with her while she fills out this form, for one—or figure out the way she might work best.

"Stand up," I demand once she ends the call.

She lifts to her feet and bounces on her toes a little bit. I stand up with her, and I take her hands in mine as I stand across from her.

"I'm happy to help in whatever way I can, Tate. My schedule is fairly open for the next six months, and today that means helping you complete this branding kit. Where are you most comfortable when you're thinking through something?"

Her eyes soften as she tilts her head. "You're really the best. Do you know that?"

I lift a modest shoulder.

"Either lying on the bed or sitting in one of the lounge chairs on your patio, looking out over the bay," she says, answering my question.

"Okay." I nod. "Your choice."

She glances at the bed and then back at me. She shakes her head a little. "Too dangerous."

I chuckle as I follow her out to the terrace after I unplug her laptop and carry it with me. She settles onto one of the lounge chairs, and once I'm beside her, I read the first question to her.

"What words do you want your brand to evoke in a potential client?"

She stares out over the bay as she thinks for a second, and then she fires off a few words. "Luxury, exclusive, forever."

I type the words as she says them. "What colors do you associate with those words?"

"Black and pale pink," she says, without missing a beat.

I wonder why not white—a color typically associated with weddings—but I don't question her. I just type.

I ask the next question and the next and the next. And while it's absolutely a lot, it's allowing her to start shaping the vision that she sees for her own company without the little blank boxes staring back at her.

We finish shortly before dinner, and I fire it off to Everleigh before Tatum can second-guess a single answer.

"That was incredible," she says. "I sat staring at that screen all morning, trying to come up with a single answer, and you managed to help me plow through it in a few hours."

"I told you, Tate. I'm here to help however I can, whether it's helping you figure out the answers that you're looking for or just helping you find a spot where you're comfortable enough to think."

"If only you could work some magic on my inbox," she says, with a bit of regret in her voice. "It's a freaking zoo right now. I open it up and get completely overwhelmed, so I shut down and don't do anything."

"Allow me to be the first to point out that not doing anything is probably costing you business. It may take some time to get you the kind of assistant you're looking for, but until that time comes, consider me here at your service."

"And allow me to thank you for your services by giving you a little service of my own." She wiggles her eyebrows even as her eyes heat over. She gets down on her knees and looks up at me with the salacious look in her eyes that I am an absolute sucker for.

She reaches into the waistband of my shorts and pulls my cock out. She sucks it into her mouth with a voracity that has shudders running down my back.

I slide my hand down to cup around her neck. "Jesus," I grunt. "You're so fucking gorgeous when you're down on your knees for me."

Her mouth moves up and down my shaft before she lets go of me to lick around the crown of my cock. A bead of precum leaks out, and she greedily laps it up with her tongue.

This. Her. Her on her knees like this.

Her beside me, walking through life with me.

This is all I've ever wanted, and somehow, some way…it's mine.

Until a text comes through from my Chicago realtor the next morning.

I'm sitting on the terrace with a cup of coffee by myself.

I glance at my phone purely to check the time, but I see a text from Sonny, my realtor back in Chicago.

Sonny: *Got an offer on the mansion. Full asking price, cash offer. I just need your green light.*

I stare at the text, my chest tightening as I think about what this could mean.

The end of an era, for one thing.

But also, in some ways, anyway, the end of the legacy my father always talks about. And maybe that's what this family needs. We need to let go of the place that once held us all together. We made our final memories there when we said goodbye to our mother. Now it's time to say goodbye to the place, too.

I blow out a breath.

Me: *Take it.*

It feels like a relief as I hit the send button.

I slide my phone into my pocket as Tatum walks out with her own steaming cup to join me, and it's such a nice morning out here that I decide to keep that news to myself.

CHAPTER 42

Tatum Barker

Turning Thirty

What do you get for your husband when he turns thirty?

That is my current dilemma.

It's particularly difficult since Ford has the option to buy pretty much anything he could possibly want…and that giant bottle of McGillicuddy's from Christmas is still three-quarters full.

The week passes quickly. Ford has been an incredible assistant to me, sorting through the inbox that I've been desperately ignoring and creating new systems for me to keep me organized and prevent continued overwhelm. Where I'm all chaos, he's all strategy.

He's even started organizing my *downloads* folder. If he thought the number of notifications I had was bad, well, those have nothing on the extreme number of files that clog my downloads folder on my laptop at any given time. We're talking in the tens of thousands.

Snap DECISION

So I need something great to celebrate this man, but the gifts I keep coming across seem ridiculously cliché. This birthday is a big deal, too. It's not every day that someone turns thirty.

With that in mind, I send Everleigh a covert text.

Me: *Can you help me out with a birthday present for Ford?*

She replies that she can, and I send her the details of my plan.

It's a lot to pull together with my already full plate, but it'll absolutely be worth it—and it'll mean so much more than a watch or another framed jersey.

Friday is the big day, and when we awake, we start the day with slow and sensual morning sex, where I ride on top of Ford's cock as I wish him a happy birthday between moans and grunts of pleasure.

I make him breakfast—or, rather, I order up from the restaurant downstairs, and I make sure to ask twice for extra bacon. We sit on the terrace and enjoy our food, and we take a long walk along the bay, hand-in-hand, as our bond somehow seems to strengthen.

I work for a few hours before my dinner plans, and just before I need to hop in the shower to start getting ready, I click on that old familiar listing for the mansion as I try to piece together how I can afford to put time into another venue even if it is my dream venue.

But something's different this time.

There's a red dot at the top of the page accompanied by the words *Accepting Backups*.

Accepting backups?

That means someone put in an offer.

That means Ford *accepted* an offer.

He didn't tell me.

He *knows* how much I love that mansion—how much we *all* love it, how much it means to all of us.

He also knows I can't afford it. Maybe he was just trying to save me from more heartache where the mansion is concerned, but an awful feeling that he kept it from me on purpose pulses up my spine.

I can't bring it up tonight. It's his birthday, and there's only one way that conversation will end: in a fight

I'm overreacting. I get that.

But I want that place with my whole entire soul, and somehow when there wasn't an offer on it, it still felt like I had a chance.

Seeing *accepting backups* means there is no chance.

My dreams of the perfect venue in the city I love with my whole heart go up in smoke.

I'll find another place. But he didn't *have* to sell. In fact, once upon a time, he made a promise he wouldn't sell without exploring all the options. He explored nothing with me or, to my knowledge anyway, with his siblings. He told me once that Liam didn't want him to sell. Everleigh wants to get married there.

And he still accepted that offer. I wonder if any of his siblings know.

He could've kept it in the family. It's his legacy. It's *their* legacy.

And he's choosing to pawn it off to the highest bidder, or something like that.

The only reason he'd accept a backup offer is if the first one fell through, and on a mansion like this, it'll be all cash. Whoever made a cash offer for fifteen million dollars wants that place, and the chances of them backing out of it now are exactly zero.

I can't help but feel like this is a crack. Keeping secrets was what led to the end of things with Archer, and now I'm at a point where I've let myself fall for Ford. I can't be pushed aside with the claim that it's for my protection from the

Bradley name. Not again. Not when he made a promise to me. Not when I think about the history we share.

I force the window closed and get in the shower as I debate how to handle this.

I guess not at all. It's his birthday, and I don't want to ruin it with a fight.

It was his right to sell that house. What doesn't sit right with me is the fact that he hasn't bothered to tell me that it sold. It hurts.

I shake it off. Tonight's for celebrating.

We head to the restaurant, and we're seated in an intimate corner booth. I order a double vodka soda, and he looks at me in surprise. I guess I'm hitting it a little harder than usual, but I play it off. "What? It's a celebration. It's not every day your husband turns thirty."

After we order, he glances at me. "Is everything all right?"

"Fine," I say tightly.

He lets it go.

"Do you want your gift?"

"Now?" he asks, raising an eyebrow.

I roll my eyes. "Not *that*. You already got that once today."

"I know. I've been wondering why it's been *only* once." He wiggles his eyebrows.

"Because I'm not a cum dumpster."

"That's a lovely image," he says, wrinkling his nose. "What's gotten into you?"

I clear my throat, ready to come out with the words, but something stops me. "Just work stuff. Devon and Lindsay's wedding is in three days, and it's my Tampa debut. There's a lot riding on it."

"I get that. It'll be perfect, Tate."

I press my lips together, and then I pull out my phone and pull up the video I spent countless hours working on. I shove it over to him and turn up the volume.

The first person in the video is me. "Happy thirtieth, husband. Here's to thirty more years of love, laughs, adventures, and memories." In the video, I hold up a glass, and when the glass pulls away, magically it's Everleigh.

"Happy birthday, little bro! Remember, thirty is just a number. Some of us age gracefully, and then there's—" She cuts off, and Dex is up next.

"Bro! Happy birthday from your older, better-looking big brother. Remember to always keep it dirty at thirty. Cheers!" He holds up a glass, and when that one moves away, it's Liam.

"Happy birthday to my old-as-fuck brother." He holds up a glass, and Ivy is pulling hers back.

"Happy birthday, Ford! Love you!"

She blows a kiss at the screen, and then she puts her hand over it. When the hand pulls away, it's Madden.

"Thirty is the new twenty, except when it comes to hangovers. Make it a great one, bro."

The video transitions from his siblings—minus Archer—to his teammates. I got Cole's number during our own wedding, and I put it to good use. Several of his teammates sent in videos, and when they're all done wishing him a happy birthday and the video ends, his eyes move up to meet mine.

"This is incredible, Tatum. Thank you. It means everything to me."

That's exactly what I was trying to go for up until a few hours ago.

I have got to get over this. It's only going to drive a wedge between us.

I'm just not sure how to move forward.

CHAPTER 43

FORD BRADLEY
Riding the Bradley Coattails

S omething's going on with her, but since I've never been around her during one of her weddings, I'm trying to chalk it up to that. She's stressed and wants this to be amazing. She told me so, and I'm choosing to believe that's why she's been a little quiet with me lately.

I also had football to focus on before. I was gone a good chunk of time each day. Maybe this is too much Ford for her.

I'm doing my best to strike a balance where she's getting the independence she needs while implementing systems to help automate some of her business.

And I've been actively looking for an assistant for her. As it turns out, the woman about to become Devon's wife has experience as an assistant, and I think depending how today's wedding goes, she may be interested in learning more about working for Tatum.

I peek into her room to see if she needs anything, but she's in the shower. While she's moved into my bed physically each night, she still works in here, and she hasn't yet made the transition to my closet and my bathroom. We've been a little busy, I guess.

An article is pulled up on her computer, and I glance at the headline.

How the Bradley Connection Landed an NFL Star's Wedding.

She has seventeen tabs open—not unusual for her—but as I scan the tabs, it looks like at least half of them are articles with a similar headline from the few words I can see of each.

Zillow is open, too. Nothing unusual about that. She's always looking at houses that could become potential venues.

I don't click on anything but instead slip out of her room as I hear the shower turn off.

I wonder why she's looking at those headlines. Is it true? Is she just using me for my name? Was she using Archer all those years for that same name? She built a thriving business in Vegas—a business that's still thriving and largely being run by her assistant there. Did she build it off Archer's back, though? Off his connections? Are we both so blinded by how we feel about her that we completely missed that?

Or is it just a lucky byproduct of being with professional athletes? She's damn good at what she does. She could've built this business without us. Easily. And it must be devastating to continually see accusations that she couldn't have.

Maybe that's why she's been quiet with me lately.

But something tells me that's not it.

It's neither the time nor the place, but when she joins me in the kitchen for a fresh cup of coffee before she finishes getting ready, I can't help but bring it up.

"Is everything okay?" I ask.

"I wish you'd stop asking me that," she snaps. "Everything's fine."

"For what it's worth, I think you are incredible, Tatum. Today is going to be amazing."

She presses her lips together and nods as she moves to walk out of the room.

"Those articles…they don't know what they're talking about."

She spins around to look at me. "What articles?"

"The ones pulled up on your computer."

She narrows her eyes at me. "Are you snooping on me?"

I reel back a little, my body physically reacting to the accusation. "Of course not. I came in to check if you needed anything, and I saw the headline on your screen. They got it wrong, Tate."

"You don't think I'm riding the Bradley coattails all the way to the bank?" she asks.

"Are you?"

She looks insulted I'd ask, and part of me feels relieved by that.

"Not intentionally, but none of these articles are giving me any credit at all for the work I've done. I don't know if they ever will, and that kind of hurts."

"It's not personal," I say, trying to make her feel better.

"Isn't it? They did the same damn thing with Archer back in Vegas." She shakes her head. "I'll never be recognized for my attributes as a woman. Only for my connections to the men in my life."

"I'm sorry."

"That's not the thing I wish you were sorry for," she mutters.

My brows dip as cluelessness claws its way in. "Excuse me?"

She presses her lips together and sets both hands on her hips, and then she lets me have it. "The mansion," she says flatly. "You sold it and didn't tell me."

I stare dumbly at her. "That's why you're mad?"

Snap DECISION

"Of course that's why I'm mad. You kept it from me. The fact that I wanted to figure out a way to buy it aside, your siblings didn't want you to sell it, either."

"We all *want* things. Little girls want unicorns. Lotto players want the jackpot," I point out. "Just because you want something doesn't mean you get to have it."

"Don't minimize what this is. That's not what it's about."

"Then what's it about?" I ask, truly dumbfounded, which only seems to make her angrier.

"It belongs to the Bradley family. It's your history. We can preserve it so you can all come home again."

"You just said you wanted me to figure out how to help *you* buy it," I point out.

"Exactly. And I thought marriage meant we'd make these decisions together. As a team." She purses her lips as she draws in a breath. "You made a promise to me that you wouldn't sell it without exploring all the options first. But you didn't. We could've gone in together with the money we got back from Winston and financed the rest."

"You know financing ten million dollars would cost you, what…sixty, seventy grand a month? How long are you making those payments before cash runs dry? This destination wedding brand is a great concept. But it's not a guaranteed cash cow, and you're already stretching yourself too thin."

She huffs out a frustrated breath that's paired with an *argh* sort of garbled sound. "It's not about the goddamn house. It's about the fact that you didn't tell me you took an offer. You kept it from me. It's trust, pure and simple. Why didn't you just treat me like a partner?"

"This! This right here," I say. "So we wouldn't fight about it. Everything always comes back to my family, and every time it comes back to them, it turns into a fight."

"Don't project your insecurities on me," she warns.

"I'm not. If I was, I'd be standing here asking you if you're really over my brother or if attaching yourself to me is some elaborate ploy to win him back."

"Is that what you think?" Her voice is eerily quiet as she practically hisses at me.

She stares across the space separating us as I wish I could take those words back.

"Of course not," I say a little weakly. It's not what I *think*. It's my biggest *fear* when it comes to her, and suddenly it feels like now that the words are out there floating between us…maybe it's not so far-fetched.

She spins on her heel and heads back to her room to finish getting ready as I stand in the kitchen wallowing in the fact that I really fucked that one up.

"You look beautiful," I say once she emerges from her room.

"Thanks," she mutters.

I walk over to her. "I'm sorry. I'm sorry we had a fight. Let's just put it behind us."

"I can't," she says thickly, and it's the first alarm bell ringing in my mind that tells me that maybe, just maybe…we won't make it past this.

"Why not?"

"Because you're sorry we had a fight. You're not sorry that you withheld information from me. I need to feel chosen, Ford. I need to feel like we're a team. Like we're making decisions together. Archer kept enough shit from me, and look at how that ended. I don't need it from you, too."

"You're right," I say. "And I'm sorry about all of it. I've spent my entire adult life waiting for the opportunity to choose you. Trust me. It's you."

"You said my business isn't a cash cow, though. It feels like you don't take me seriously as a businesswoman, and that hurts."

Snap DECISION

"How can you say that?" I practically roar. "I've spent the last week helping you with your business. I've automated systems and created strategies. I cleared out your inbox. I believe in you. In us."

She presses her lips together and brushes some hair off her forehead. "Maybe I'm too much of a dreamer and you're too practical. The things I want may feel unrealistic to you, but it's who I am."

My breath catches in my throat as she heads toward the door. It's not like this conversation is over if she walks out. We're driving to the manor together.

She jabs at the elevator call button as I join her in the hallway.

"You don't really believe that, do you?" I ask.

She folds her arms across her chest. "I don't know. Today doesn't much feel like love is enough." Her words are soft and broken as she whispers them.

"Can you really say that as you leave home to take care of every last detail for a wedding you've spent the last two months planning?" I ask.

"We're *married* now. We can't keep secrets from each other. And your secret makes me feel like you're not willing to take a risk on me, my business…or us."

It's not true—at least to me, it isn't. But the way she delivers those harsh words feels an awful lot like she's already made up her mind.

In my head, I just wanted to get rid of the mansion. To get my money back. To be done with it.

To her, it was an act of betrayal.

And no matter how much I love her, or how much she loves me, I'm not sure how we overcome that.

CHAPTER 44

Tatum Barker

More Venues

I've spent the day fighting back tears.

This isn't how I wanted to feel on the day of the first wedding I planned here in Tampa, but here we are. And I don't even know what to do about it. Where to go.

Ford has always been the person I'd run to, but I can't this time.

And that breaks my heart.

I need some space.

I walk away when things get hard. It's why Archer and I broke up as many times as we did. He wanted to stay and fight it out, and I wanted to shut down.

And *that* is the real reason why it felt so permanent this last time.

Because he's the one who ended it. He's the one who walked away. It was always *me* before. I'd get mad, and I'd run. I'd take a few days to cool down—or two months, that one time—but I'd come back.

Snap DECISION

It's different with Ford, though. I've never *had* to escape him. We've never had a fight about anything before.

"It's time," I say to Lindsay when I walk into the bridal suite. "You are stunning." I pull her veil into place, and she tears up as she smiles at me.

"It's been so much fun planning with you. I'll miss our check-in calls," she says, pulling me into a hug, and I feel a bit of surprise at that.

I guess somewhere along the way as we planned her wedding, we sort of became friends in all of this.

"I will, too," I admit. I think about asking her if she wants to come work with me, but it doesn't feel like the right time as she gets ready to walk down the aisle. Besides, she's pregnant, a fact she still hasn't told her parents. But either way, she'll have a newborn to tend to soon. She may not want to come work with me.

Everything's falling into place for her. Another bride whose dreams I helped facilitate while my own dreams continue to crash and burn.

God, what the hell is wrong with me?

It's me. I'm the problem.

I brush a tear away and pretend like it has something to do with the beautiful bride, and her bridesmaids gather, and we head downstairs so the bridal party can make their grand entrance.

I peek outside, and I spot Ford in the yard. He's in a suit, and if I weren't so mad, just catching his eye across the space separating us would be enough to pulse a hot ache between my legs.

But I *am* mad. The ache shows up anyway. It's always there with Ford, a fact I never realized until I started to fall for him. The intimacy with him is something fierce and out of this world, something completely unexpected.

Even that wouldn't be enough to fix things between us, though. Not this time.

I pull my gaze away and move back toward the bridal party sans the groom, who's waiting inside for his bride out in the yard just as Lindsay wanted. She holds onto her dad's arm, and the bridesmaids are all lined up with their groomsmen. I hear the music change and give the first couple the *go* signal.

Once the party enters, including the ring bearer and the flower girl, I close the door. I wait for the change in song, and as the guests stand for the bride, I throw the door open again for her dramatic entrance.

And that's it. Half an hour later, they're married. Photos are taken. Cocktails and hors d'oeuvres are served outside as the inside is ready for dinner and dancing.

Ford helps where he can without me even having to ask, as if he can read the room and the situation and execute what needs to be done instinctively—another painful reminder of how simpatico we are.

I head upstairs after the food is served, and I pull my phone out to take a look at my calendar.

The next event I need to be here in Tampa for is a meeting with a bride and groom toward the end of next month. It would be helpful to have someone here at the manor if I leave town to give tours for potential couples, but right now, I just need a few days to myself. Everything has happened so quickly that my head is spinning.

When I focus on work is when I make things happen. I was recovering from the end of my relationship with Archer when I fell into Winston Manor.

The thought that the next venue I purchase will be as I'm dealing with whatever this is with my *husband* has tears heating behind my eyes.

I'll focus on work. I have to.

Snap DECISION

I want more venues to add to my luxury collection. This isn't me wanting a unicorn. It's me building a business. If I can get a wedding booked at Winston Manor every weekend, this *could* be a cash cow.

I just need the right person who can help me manage all of that since I absolutely cannot do it alone.

I need to be making the highest-level decisions, and I'll need several employees in each city where I own a venue. Someone who knows each market, someone who can actually plan the events, a general manager responsible for the business side of things. Not to mention employing the event staff. We're looking at maybe five or ten employees per location plus event staff.

Even here, starting with my very first venue, I need help. That much is obvious after running through my first event here at the manor. It can't be Ford—even if we weren't fighting. He still has a job that keeps him pretty busy a good majority of the time.

But this is me. I'll find someone.

I must live under some lucky star when it comes to these types of things.

Kenzie fell onto my lap, and now she's not just one of my best friends, she's essentially running my entire business in Vegas with the occasional call into me for approvals. She's getting overwhelmed, though, too. She needs help. An assistant. A team behind her.

Winston Manor fell onto my lap when I threw myself into work last time, as did the money back from it so I could invest still more into my business.

So, while I throw myself into work once again, I think I'll add a little more to my already very full plate by finding the right venue in my old hometown. It's Chicago. My favorite city in the world. That city deserves a luxe venue that's part of the Tatum Signature Collection even if it isn't the Bradley Mansion.

And I intend to find it.

CHAPTER 45

Tatum Barker

Sold My Dream

"Where are you going?" Ford asks as I wheel my suitcase by him toward the front door after the wedding.

He rises to a stand from the couch where he's watching basketball highlights.

"Chicago."

"Tonight? We just got home. You're exhausted. Take a night, get some rest, and we'll regroup in the morning."

I shake my head. "I'm going tonight."

"Okay. I'll go with you."

I shake my head again. "I'm going alone."

"Oh. Can I ask why?"

I blow out a breath. "I'm angry, and when I'm angry, I just need some space. In the past, I've run to you, as you well know, but I can't do that this time. I just need a few days."

"Is this…are you…um—are *we*—" he stutters.

I hold up a hand. "I just need a break, Ford. I need to figure some things out for myself."

Snap DECISION

"What things?" he asks quietly.

"Us. If I'm always going to wonder if you're keeping things from me. And not just us, but me. The direction I want to take my business."

"I can help you figure those things out," he offers.

I shake my head. "I need to do this alone. We jumped into this so quickly, and I just need some time. Okay?"

He presses his lips together as he reluctantly nods. "For what it's worth, I'm willing to fight."

My gaze turns down to the floor. "I will keep that in mind."

He closes the gap between us and slides his arm around my waist. He hauls me to him, and he holds me. He's trembling a little, and his voice is filled with emotion as he says, "We're better off together, Tate. Please give me another chance to prove to you how much I believe in you."

"I'll take it all into consideration," I say briskly, not trusting myself to sink into his arms the way I really want to.

His lips move to my neck, and I close my eyes for a beat as I fight the urge to give in.

I force myself to back away. "I need to go. I have a flight to catch."

"Of course," he says quietly, and he lets me go until he doesn't. "Wait," he says. "Don't go. Let's work this out. Fight with me, Tate." He's begging.

I twist my lips. "You believe that you're right, and I believe that I am. To you, there's no emotional connection. To me, there was. You're too logical to see that. Neither of us is willing to bend on what we believe. If we do, we're betraying ourselves. So I just need a bit of time away. Okay? I'm hoping this time away might give us both enough perspective to pick up where we left off."

He sighs as I walk out the front door without another word. Moments later, I slip into the Uber I ordered to take me to the airport.

I check my inbox on my phone on the way. It's all organized now, and the only things I *have* to read are some new client inquiries about touring Winston Manor. I reply with calendar invitations a few weeks from now. I'll be back by then, at least for these meetings, or maybe by then I will have hired someone who can help me out with these sorts of things.

A little before midnight, I check into my hotel. I lie down since it's been a long day, but I feel restless.

I pull up the website for commercial-based properties on my phone and start looking for potential venues. I find one in the West Loop, an old church that looks to have been converted into an event center with six separate event spaces.

Damn. Six spaces. The idea of holding not one, or even two…but *six* events all at the same time is a tad overwhelming.

But with the right people in place, I can make anything happen.

While I'm here, I might as well tour the place. I click the *message* button to get in touch with the realtor and put in my request for tomorrow. It's worth a shot.

Against my better judgment, I pull up the Bradley Mansion again, too, and I look through the pictures. The listing still says it's accepting backups.

I should've been more insistent. I should've given Ford a plan before it was too late. I just got caught up with Winston Manor and our own wedding and Lindsay and Devon…all of it. It was my continual chaos that landed me right here, I'm afraid. I couldn't get my own shit together enough to present a valid plan to Ford to save that place for me.

Snap DECISION

I blow out a breath, and then, since I'm up, I look through some venues available in Vegas, too…because why the hell not? It doesn't hurt to look.

I spend the next few days burying myself in work. Ford is giving me the space I asked for, checking in via text message a few times a day but not calling me. In some ways, that makes it feel like an actual adult relationship. He's giving me what I requested, no matter how hard that is for him. Or he's making up for keeping something else from me. That's still something I'll just have to get over.

I have dinner with my brother, Layla, and Maddox one night, and I book a flight out to Vegas to check on things there and see if I can find any event spaces. I've searched online a bit, but everything I've found is either too industrial or it's an old hotel. I don't want to own a hotel.

But I know people in Vegas. It's where I built my business. I'll find someone who can help me find a place, and things will magically fall into place. They always do.

Right?

But Vegas…it's a tougher market. It's a travel destination, sure, but how do I make my venue stand out among all the other venues in town? The hotels, the chapels—the quickie weddings Vegas is *known* for. From extravagant and luxurious to cheap and cheesy, they already exist there.

Maybe I shouldn't pick Vegas as one of my cornerstones.

Man, these Bradley boys have really done a number on me if I'm sitting here doubting myself. It's not like me.

I blow out a breath as I board the plane to Vegas.

It was home for the last five years, and even though I've already let Archer go, I'm not quite ready to let this city go.

Ford texts just after I buckle into my seat.

Ford: *Checking in. How are you today?*
Me: *I'm okay. On my way to Vegas.*

He doesn't reply, and I don't either.

I miss him. I miss Tampa. I miss what we built there. I miss being his partner and his teammate.

I miss his *friendship*.

I want to go back in time to when he got the offer. I want him to discuss it with me like two married adults should do.

Yes, it was his mansion to do with what he wished, but his siblings didn't want him to sell. I didn't want him to sell. After he started helping me out with my business…I guess I got overly excited. I really thought we were going to find some way to team up on it like we did with Winston Manor.

I sweep those thoughts behind me. No sense in dwelling on it now.

Instead, I stare out the little airplane window as day turns to night and contemplate whether I can move past all that so we can get back to where we were.

CHAPTER 46

FORD BRADLEY

Well and Truly Alone

Vegas?

She's going to fucking *Vegas*?

Maybe she's there for work. But I keep coming back to another reason. Maybe she chose to go back there right now because she decided to choose Archer after all.

Friends becoming more is something people read about in books. It doesn't happen in real life just because one person has pined for the other for years.

What the fuck was I thinking? Allowing myself to get to this place was pure fucking stupidity on my part.

I should've listened to my brain. Instead, I went with my heart, and now I'm married to someone who's ditching me for Chicago and Vegas and thinks I don't believe in her.

Of course I believe in her.

I go to bed alone. I wake up alone. This is just like how it used to be, except back then, I held onto this streak of hope that someday I'd admit my real feelings to her.

Snap DECISION

Well, I did. And now...it's over. I think. Maybe. We're paused, anyway, and I don't like how it feels.

I realize that in many ways, I did this to myself. I should have told her when I got the offer on the mansion. I get that now. I should have given her a chance to plead her case before I accepted that offer. I guess there are a lot of things I should have done differently. Not give into temptation, for one. Not listen to my heart—for another.

It's just a painful reminder that emotions wreck everything. Back when we were just friends, I wished we could be more. And now that I've had more, I wish we could get back to what we had before.

Perhaps I should have listened to my siblings, too. Liam was pretty insistent that I shouldn't sell, but I went with my gut. My gut puts logic over emotions, and financial responsibility won over whatever ties we have to that place. Besides, would letting Tatum gut the place to turn it into her dream venue really be any better than selling it to strangers who are going to live there?

I know the answer even as the question forms in my head. No. She'd preserve it and respect it, and it's why she wanted to work with Madden. It would stay in the family for generations to come, mirroring Winston Manor in so many ways. Just because we can't all live there doesn't mean we can't all find a purpose for the place. Everleigh's wedding. Maybe eventually Liam's and Ivy's, too, if that's what they want.

Our family may be falling apart between losing our mother and our father going on trial for some pretty serious crimes, but maybe the mansion was the one thing that could've bonded us together.

But I sold it.

And now she's going back to Vegas, maybe going back to Archer, going back to how life was before. She'll get there only to realize she never should have left, just like she's done *so many times* before, and I'll be stuck here all alone, walking into the room that was once hers and staring at the three cups left behind on her desk with regret.

It feels like I'm well and truly alone.

I suppose I could join in on one of the invitations that I've gotten for workouts or to join my buddies for a night out, but in the last couple of weeks, I *haven't* accepted any of them. All that means is that fewer of them are coming through to my inbox. And all that means is that I'm sitting by myself on a Friday night.

It's not like I'd go pick up a regret, as Cole would put it. Hell, I barely did that in my pre-husband days, but now there's a hell of a lot more to lose…even if I've already lost it.

I finally decide to text Cole anyway.

Me: *When's the next workout?*

He doesn't respond until the next morning.

Cole: *Monday at eight. Kellan's place.*

Me: *Count me in.*

Cole: *Too bad you missed out on last night. Found myself not one but *two* regrets.*

Me: *Living life in the fast lane.*

Cole: *Something like that. On my way home from their place now. At least I'm not inventing reasons to get them to leave.*

I don't really know what to say to that, but another text comes through from him before I say anything at all.

Cole: *What's up with you?*

Me: *What do you mean?*

Cole: *Where you been lately? Busy with the wife?*

Me: *Something like that.*

Cole: *Everything okay?*

Me: *We'll talk Monday.*

Cole: *See you then.*

Snap DECISION

I should've taken him up on his line of questioning. Maybe it would've helped to get some of this load off my chest. I'm not sure Cole Andrews, the biggest playboy on the Tampa Bay Beasts, would have much advice to give, but I guess I've been wrong about these things before. Still, I put him off. And that's why I'm surprised when the front desk calls up to me fifteen minutes later.

"I have a Cole Andrews here to see you."

"Send him up," I say.

A minute later, he's knocking on my door, and I open it.

"You look like shit," he says to me, surveying me from head to toe.

I tilt my head and study him for a second. He doesn't *look* like he just came from a wild night with two ladies at the same time, but I guess that's not something you can see on a person.

Heartbreak, however, must be a more visual type of thing.

"Warn a guy when you're stopping by so I can clean up a little," I say.

"Not for me, man." He chuckles as he steps past me into my place. "What's going on?"

"She left."

"You? Town? Left clothes on the floor? I'm gonna need you to be a little more specific." He plops himself down on my couch, and I walk over and sit across from him.

"I don't know. She needed some space, and now she's in Vegas, probably getting back together with Archer because she *always* gets back together with him. I think I might've fucked up my one chance with her."

"She's married to you, man. She's not getting back together with your brother. Pull yourself together and think rationally. It's like the *one* thing I can count on with you."

I shoot him a glare.

"What the hell did you do?" he asks as he sticks his feet up on my coffee table. "I thought you had this all worked out."

"I sold my parents' mansion." I throw both hands up in one of those *I don't know* kinds of gestures.

He wrinkles his nose. "And that somehow fucked your relationship with her?"

"She wanted it. She wanted to acquire it for her brand, gut it, reno it, and turn it into a wedding venue."

"Ahh," he says, nodding as he moves his feet back to the floor and leans forward with his elbows on his knees. "Why didn't she buy it first if she wanted it?"

"Finances, for one thing."

"So you sold it to someone who had the money, thus killing that conversation," he guesses.

"Yeah. A cash offer that killed her dream, apparently. I guess I didn't know I needed her permission to sell my own parents' house."

"Fucking women," he commiserates.

"Yeah…except truth be told, it's not all that simple. She has a point. It should've been a decision we made together. A partnership. She feels betrayed that I sold it without telling her. She found out from Zillow."

He holds a hand to his chest in mock surprise. "From Zillow?" he repeats.

I chuckle. "Yeah. She should've heard it from me. I knew she wanted it, but I wanted to distance myself from it. I put up money to get my dad out of prison, and when the sale closes, I'll get my money back. But it's not just that. She feels like I don't believe in her vision, in her dream."

"Because of one house?" He looks confused.

"One house that holds a lot of history for us. She saw it as a fallen kingdom she wanted to rebuild. I saw it as a tie to my family I wanted to sever."

"Sounds to me like she's throwing a tantrum because she didn't get what she wanted." He sinks back into the couch and crosses his leg over his other knee.

I blow out a breath. "She isn't. She's hurt that I never gave her the chance. And honestly...I think she might be right. For a while, I started to wonder if the only reason she ran to me after she left Archer was because he wouldn't give her what she wanted. She turned to me thinking I would. But then I didn't."

"This isn't a very convincing argument that she's not throwing a tantrum," he points out. "You got any coffee, by the way? It was a late night, and my head's pounding."

"Yeah." I get up and walk over toward the coffee pot, and I pour him a cup as I talk. "We were a little busy planning our own wedding, making a playoff run, and working on Devon and Lindsay's wedding. Her phone's been blowing up with new clients, and she's been overwhelmed, so it just didn't come up again until it was too late. Her needing space is less about a tantrum and more about her setting a boundary that she's not going to stay with someone who doesn't fully believe in her and support her vision for the future of her brand." I hand him the coffee mug.

"Thanks. Do you?"

"Do I what?" I ask.

"Believe in her. Support her vision."

"Of course I do," I say, my voice full of passion. "I think she's fucking brilliant and will succeed at anything she puts her mind to."

"Yeah, you're definitely a man in love." He presses his lips together and sighs. "So what are you going to do?"

I shrug. "What *can* I do?"

"You said you'll get the money back when the sale goes through. Are you saying it hasn't actually sold yet?" he asks quietly.

It's not like it's the first time I've had the thought, but I suppose it *is* the first time someone has voiced that thought aloud.

"No. The sale isn't final," I admit.

He raises his brows. "Then I think you know what you need to do."

CHAPTER 47

Tatum Barker

Trash Pile

I could probably stop paying for this office space since I'm never here, but I haven't. If I stopped paying, I'd have to clean it out, and I haven't exactly been around to do that.

"Tater!" Kenzie says when she walks by the office. I'm on the floor, surrounded by paperwork in the usual chaos that's my style.

"Morning," I say absently. I pick up a folder and read the name on the tab. Do I really need to keep a file for clients who were married three years ago and have already gotten a divorce?

Their centerpieces were lovely, though. I set the folder in the *keep* pile.

"When did you get in?" she asks. She walks in and leans on the doorframe. She knew I was here since I texted her I was coming and would be picking up my car from where it's been parked on the street across from her house.

"Last night."

"Where are you staying?"

"I booked a room at the Venetian for a few nights." I pick up another folder and set it in the *trash* pile as I think about that term. Trash pile. Sort of like my life at the moment.

"Our casita is still open. Come stay with me," she says.

"I'm okay." I set another folder in *keep*. Another one in *trash*. I take a sip of my coffee and set it back on the floor beside me, and I glance up at the doorway. Kenzie's hand is on her hip, and she's staring at me.

"You are *so* clearly *not* okay. What's going on, Tate?"

I blow out a breath, and then it all comes tumbling out.

All of it.

I end with a shaky voice as tears tumble down my cheeks. "It just feels like he doesn't believe in me."

She walks in and kneels down on the floor in front of me. "Oh, babe. I'm so sorry."

I sniffle. "This isn't how I thought things would go between us. I'm happy with him, you know? This is our first fight. I have to set boundaries, but he does, too. And that's the thing. Our boundaries, our goals…they clash. How do we make it work when we're fighting for opposite ideals?" I swipe at the tears that are coming faster now.

She rocks back so she's sitting on her own heels. "It comes down to a single question, Tate."

"What?" I'm desperate for an answer.

"If you can't have both, what's more important to you: the mansion or the man?"

"Ford," I answer without reservation.

"Then you have to let the mansion thing go. If Ford is your forever and he had his own reasons, you have to find a way to move on."

"What if I can't?" I ask, fear very apparent in my tone.

"Then you lose Ford, and you *still* don't get the mansion."

"Yeah." I blow out a breath. This hasn't helped even though she's right. "Fill me in on what I've missed," I say, changing the subject.

She launches into the upcoming weddings we have, and I answer the millions of questions she's been holding for me. We work until five, and I tell her to go home to her family.

"Come with me," she begs.

I shake my head. "I'm fine at the hotel. I just need a little alone time, that's all. I need to figure out how to make this work."

She gives me a long hug, which feels good, and I fight off more tears.

She leaves, and I finish up what I'm working on. And then I get into my car and drive toward my old house.

I don't text first, and I'm not sure why. Maybe because if he doesn't open the door, then I can pretend I never came in the first place.

I ring the bell, and to my surprise, he *does* answer the door.

"Tatum," Archer says softly. "What are you doing here?"

I burst into tears.

Fuck. This isn't how I wanted this conversation to go.

"What did he do to you?" he asks darkly.

"Nothing," I mutter, and he pulls me into the house.

It feels comfortable here. It even *smells* comfortable, like home.

He pulls me into a hug, and I sink into his arms the way I did so goddamn many times over the last decade.

"I miss you," he says, and he runs a soothing hand up and down my back.

I'm about to reply that I miss him, too. It's an automatic reply. But even as I think the words, I'm able to pinpoint exactly what it is I miss. I miss his friendship. I miss his warmth. I miss the way he opened up to me, even when it was *only* to me. I miss *knowing* the mysterious Bradley baseball player. I miss the ease we had with each other. But all that was over a long, long time ago. Much longer than a few months ago when we broke it off for the last time, and I flew to Florida to stay with Ford while I figured things out. But a year or two ago, back when things were good and we still had fun together.

As we embrace, though, I realize for the very first time that what I miss isn't the intimacy. It isn't the love. It's the friendship.

But when I'm away from Ford, I feel like a piece of myself is still with him.

He finally pulls back from our hug. "Come on in." His voice is a little weary, but I follow him into the home I shared with him for the last five years.

And then I tell him everything.

CHAPTER 48

FORD BRADLEY

What the Fuck Did You Do to Her?

She's been gone a week now, and each day that passes pushes me a little further down into a hole I'm not sure I'll be able to climb out of.

It's dark down here. It's lonely. I hate it.

I miss her. My chest aches for her. My stomach feels like it's constantly in knots, and the pain doesn't ease up day after day. If anything, it just gets worse.

It's like a piece of me is missing, an essential piece that she took with her, and I want it back. I want *her* back.

I text her daily, mainly to check in, but also to wish her a good morning and a good night.

She doesn't always reply, and I'm trying to adhere to the boundaries she's setting even though my heart is telling me to fight harder. I don't know where the line of her boundary exists. I want to give her space, but I also don't. I want her right back here by my side.

She said she needed time, and I'm trying to give her that even though I don't want to.

Snap DECISION

She'll be back. I keep telling myself that. She *has* to come back. She has appointments lined up, though they're still two weeks away.

How do I continue through this storm for another two weeks?

I'm not sure how to answer that.

I just want to figure out how to get her back, and I feel like I know the answer, but I've been too scared to make the call.

Scared of what...I'm not quite sure. Maybe admitting I made a mistake. Maybe showing a weakness. Maybe taking on the Bradley curse. Maybe finding out it's too late. Then what?

But there are also the other effects I'm putting in jeopardy—burning bridges with my realtor and the buyer, for one thing. Not to mention the financial impacts of trying to halt wheels already in motion.

And not only all that, but there's the fact that I'm willing to back down on all this to give her what she wants—what she needs—but that doesn't automatically mean she's going to come running back. What if I do this, execute this senseless plan, and end up right back where I am? What if it's not really what she wants at all and I'm completely mishandling the entire situation?

For someone who lives by practicality and responsibility, well...doing what *feels* like the right choice isn't either of those. And in bending who I am as a man, what if I'm giving Tatum a version of myself that isn't what she wants?

What if all of this backfires and I end up worse off than I am now?

This is what I've been pondering for days now, and sitting around my condo isn't giving me the answers I'm looking for.

It's why working out with friends yesterday morning felt good. Great, even. It gave me the chance to blow off some steam, and at the same time, it helped take my mind off the things I'm not sure how to fix right now.

I needed it. I needed to get out, to think about something different for a while.

It gave me a little perspective, I think. That paired with my conversation with Cole has me questioning the way I've handled everything…and the way to get it all back before it's too late.

I call Liam and tell him what Cole suggested.

"You think there's a way to back out of the sale?" he asks.

"I think until the ink is dry, there's always a way. Right? But I don't know what to do."

"I didn't want you to sell in the first place," he reminds me. "So I'm not exactly sure what you want me to say here."

"But you'd be okay with me hanging onto it and letting Tatum reno the place?" I ask.

"It's not like any of us are ever going to live there again. Even Ivy already moved out. I just wanted it to stay in the family. You know? The legacy Dad always talks about, the same one we always roll our eyes over. I guess we all just have so many core memories there that I don't want to let it go if we don't have to. And Tatum is family. She wants to work with Madden on the reno. Also family. He would preserve it. You know that. Ev could have her wedding there. We could bring our kids there to run around the backyard between events. Nerf wars in an even bigger space."

"There you go talking about kids again," I mutter. "What about your bail money?"

He blows out a breath. "A million bucks is a lot. Would I like it back? Yes. Of course. I could invest it, make more money off of it, whatever. But am I going to be okay if it's tied up in court for a while? Also yes."

His words give me something to think about.

As I sit at dinner on Tuesday evening by myself at my kitchen table, I'm halfway between bewildered and shocked when my phone starts to ring and I see who's calling.

Snap DECISION

I pick up, fully expecting my brother to gloat that he got her back and I'm left in the dust.

"Hello?"

He shocks me further by saying, "What the fuck did you do to her, man?"

"I didn't do anything," I protest.

"Bullshit. She left Vegas with a light in her eyes, and you put it out in just over two months."

Guilt racks me at his words. "I didn't mean to, but trust when I say that she put mine out, too."

"Then figure your shit out so I don't have to step in and figure it out for you," he mutters. "Do you have any idea how awkward it is to comfort your ex when she's crying over her new husband who happens to be your older brother?"

I blow out a breath. "I thought I was doing the right thing."

"By hurting her?"

"By protecting myself. One of my biggest fears in any relationship is that I'm only being used for my money and my connections. Did she tell you the reason she walked away?"

"Do you really think she'd do that?" he asks, not answering my question.

When it really comes down to it, the answer is clear. She wouldn't *use* me for those things, but that doesn't mean she can't reap the benefits of being with someone with connections anyway—the same way I could reap benefits with various investments of my own connected to her business. "No."

"Then get her the fuck back, you idiot."

"I thought you were calling to brag that she came running to you."

"She did come running to me, but not for whatever leap you might be making. It was very clear that what she and I had is in the past. But you? You're her future, Ford. Well, you know—if you can figure out some way to show her that you believe in her. Because I have to be honest with you. I've never seen her like this. She's lost, and she needs you to find her."

I blow out a breath as the pain of his words slices into my chest. I hate that she's feeling that way, but I also know that a few days away for perspective is in line with her personality.

It used to be me she ran to. I've never given her a reason to run the other way.

Until now.

And I need to fucking fix this.

CHAPTER 49

Tatum Barker

Dancing

I'm not cleaning out my office.

I'm *not*.

That's what I keep telling myself. The cups are multiplying, and there are six on my desk right now. See? Not cleaning it out. Making a bigger mess, maybe.

I'm organizing, that's all. This had to be done.

It didn't have to be done *right now*, I suppose, but here we are. I'm in town, and really, I don't need to pay for both my office *and* Kenzie's. If I'm hardly ever here, we could share one space, and I've made the executive decision that I won't displace her in all of this.

So maybe I am cleaning it out, after all.

Truth be told, I have no clue what I'm doing.

She's offered to help me, but she has plenty of work to do herself, which I gently remind her of any time she stands in my doorway asking me what's wrong.

I've talked it to death. I don't want to talk about it anymore.

Snap DECISION

Besides, being here, looking through files and folders and five years' worth of work, is taking my mind off my indecision, and that's exactly what I need right now.

Archer seems to think Ford cares about me and would never intentionally hurt me.

I know we can find our way out of this. He could help me be a bit more practical. As I scan the mess I've made of my office, Lord knows I could use another dose or two of his sensibility.

And maybe it wouldn't hurt him to dream a little more. To have an unrealistic side. Dream big or go home. What's the point of a dream if it's not big and bold? Anything can happen. Even big and bold.

I need a break. I head out to the break room and pour myself another cup of coffee in one of the paper cups sitting on the counter, and I head back toward my office. I put on some music, shut the door, and have a little dance party all by myself to get my muscles moving a little. I'm stiff from sitting on the floor for yet another day. I think this makes four or five in a row, and I'm definitely making progress in here. Instead of keeping an entire file folder on a particular couple purely because I like the centerpieces, I'm organizing. A rather large order from Amazon arrived yesterday, and so far, I've created binders for centerpieces, cakes, bridal party attire, rings, ceremony ideas, and reception ideas. There's more to organize, but it's a good start.

I shake my booty through Taylor Swift's "Shake it Off," and I feel a rush of adrenaline to keep moving, so I keep dancing as "Cruel Summer" comes on next. It may be winter, but it feels like a lot of cruel twists have hit me these last few months.

I'm breathless when I hear a knock on the door. I'm still shaking my ass as I move to open it, assuming it's Kenzie, and I'm singing at the top of my lungs when I toss open the door in the middle of the chorus only to find Ford standing on the other side of the door.

I stop mid-lyric, and I'm pretty sure a little squeaking sound escapes me as my eyes widen and my jaw drops.

I blink a few times, and then I grab my phone and pause the song as I clear my throat and shake my head to make sure it's not some vision I'm seeing standing in front of me.

An amused smile lifts the corners of his lips as I turn to look at him again.

"Ford," I finally manage.

"Tatum," he says softly.

"What are you doing here?" I ask.

He fills my doorway with his big, athletic body, and his dark eyes are glowing at me. His hair is perfectly styled as usual, and he's got a little more scruff on his jaw than he usually wears. His eyes are fixed on me, and God, he's hot.

And he's here.

He's *here*.

"I'm so sorry," he says quietly. "I'm sorry you ever thought I doubted you. I'm sorry you felt the need to run. I'm sorry I didn't tell you about the sale. I'm sorry I didn't come running for you sooner. I'm sorry about all of it. I've been alone for so long now that I've never really had to consider someone else's place in my life, but I know exactly where I want you to be, and it's not nearly the entire way across the country."

"Where is it?" I ask.

"Right next to me. By my side. Always. I've been torn between respecting your need for distance through these boundaries you've set and my need to fight for you and hold you in my arms again."

I rush toward him as the realization of exactly how much I've missed him over this last week plows into me.

This right here. This feeling. This warmth, this safety, this cocoon of love...that's what I want.

Snap DECISION

"I'm sorry, too," I sob. "I'm sorry I needed space. Now that you're here, I don't want space. I don't want to be away from you. I just wanted your belief in me. I wanted you to be honest with me, and I need you to promise I'll have those two things from you. Always."

"You're my wife, and you deserve my honesty and support. Always." He lowers his head until our lips meet, sealing the promise as he bands his arms tightly around me, but he pulls back and loosens his grip as he blows out a breath. "I brought you something." He holds out a manila envelope, and my brows dip as I glance at the envelope and back at his eyes.

"What is it?" I reach out and take it.

He nods as if to say *go ahead*, so I undo the clasp and open the top. I pull out some papers, and I read the top page.

Warranty Deed

For the consideration of One Million Dollars ($1,000,000), in hand paid, Ford Bradley, Grantor, of Cook County, Illinois, conveys and warrants to Ford Bradley and Tatum Barker, of Clark County, Nevada, Joint Grantees, as tenants in common, each owning an undivided fifty percent interest of the following described real estate: The Bradley Mansion, situated in the County of Cook, State of Illinois.

My voice is low and trembling when I murmur, "Ford, what is this?"

"It's the mansion. It's yours. Well, ours. For the bargain price of one million dollars so I can pay Liam back his portion of the bail money."

"Oh my God," I murmur, my eyes wide as my heart pounds.

"I'd like to direct your attention to the part where the paperwork says we'll be joint grantees splitting the property fifty-fifty," he says.

"Yeah?"

"That's my belief in you, Tatum." His voice is low and raspy. Sexy. "I'm covering the rest of the sale and splitting the proceeds evenly between my siblings. Not my father. Seven of us split fourteen million pretty easily. Then together you and I will own the mansion without my father's money hanging over us, and it's another joint venture. I don't know how you deduced from our fight that I don't believe in you. I went in on Winston Manor with you because of my belief in you, and I want to keep investing in properties with you because I know you have the tools to bring your vision to life. I want you to be a part of this family in more than just name and convenience, but in every way that matters. I want you to use VanBrad for construction. I want you to use Everleigh for branding. And I want to be the man standing beside you, helping you leap forward toward each and every risky, daring, huge dream your beautiful mind can possibly dare to dream."

My breath catches in my throat as his words settle over me. "Is this for real?" I ask cautiously.

"It's for real," he murmurs.

I stare at him another moment, and then I rush into his arms again. I slam into him hard enough to force a little *oof* out of him, but he's so solid that he doesn't move from where his feet are planted as he laces his arms around me.

I move to my tiptoes, and our mouths collide in a sweet and sentimental kiss that's about to turn indecent right here in this office building.

He drops his head down and brushes his lips against my neck as he buries his face there, and I draw in a deep breath, one deeper than I've drawn in days, as if a part of me couldn't physically breathe without him by my side.

"I'm sorry," he says again.

"So am I. I love you so much," I say, and I tighten my hold around his torso as I hope that we're over the worst of it and I'll never have to let go again.

CHAPTER 50

FORD BRADLEY

Feels Like Forever

"I love you, too," I murmur, and my mouth finds hers again. Our kiss turns urgent in a matter of mere seconds, my tongue delving into her mouth and claiming what's mine, what's been missing for far too long even though it's only been a week since we were last together.

I need her. I crave her. I want her right here, right now.

Her office is a disaster. Folders are all over the floor. I counted six cups on her desk.

But there's a door, and it has a lock, and we're going to make up right now. I walk her backward into her office, and we're both standing on something. A pile of papers, maybe. She doesn't seem overly concerned, and she doesn't stop kissing me as she reaches around me to push the door shut.

She pulls back. "Sorry about the mess. I'm cleaning out my office."

"I see that. Can I help?" I'm trying to be gentlemanly here. Cleaning out an office at this moment in time is about the lowest priority on my list. Getting Tatum naked and filling her cunt with my cock ranks somewhere around priority one.

"Later," she says, and she pulls out her desk chair, pushes me down onto it, and straddles my lap. "I need you to fuck me now."

Fuck.

"I'd love nothing more than to fuck you now."

We're both in jeans. There are too many clothes in the way, but she just asked for it.

I want to kiss her, too. I want to revel in the feel of her soft skin as she cups my jaw in her hands and kisses me in that soft, sweet way she does that's still somehow lined with this carnal need that we both ignored for far too long because it wasn't our time.

But it's our time now.

I shift my hips up, and she moans as she gyrates over me.

She must feel how hard I am for her because she moves all the way off me. She grabs her phone and hits play on her playlist, and she flips the lock on her door. She looks across the small space at me, and I think for a split second she might give me the sort of dance that will live on in my dreams.

Instead, she reaches for the hem of her shirt, pulls it over her head, unhooks her bra, and tosses it to the floor. She shimmies out of her jeans and panties, kicking her shoes off as she slides her clothes down her legs, and then she's back in front of me, but this time completely naked.

"You're so goddamn gorgeous," I say, my mouth watering as my eyes flick to her tits.

My cock pulses painfully in my jeans, hot and hard as I wait for her next move.

"You're not so bad yourself," she says, and she moves toward me. She straddles me again, and she starts to shift her hips over mine. She's moaning, and I think she's catching a rough spot on my jeans with her clit because she tosses her head back in ecstasy. It only serves to shove her tits closer to my face, and I suck one of her nipples into my mouth.

My cheeks hollow as I suck hard on the already tight bud, and I run my tongue back and forth across the tip. She moans louder at the feel, her hips moving wildly, and I let go of my hold on her tit and reach down between us to slide a finger inside her cunt.

"You're so wet," I murmur, my eyes flicking up to watch the show in front of me.

Her moan turns to a cry, and I feel her pussy as it clenches onto me, greedy and wanting.

"Fuck, I need to be inside you," I mutter.

"Yes," she cries breathlessly. "Fuck me, Ford. Fuck me now."

I pull my finger out, quickly work my jeans button and zipper, pull my cock out, and aim it up at her. She seats herself down on me, sliding right over my cock as I enter her perfect cunt.

She stills, our eyes meeting erotically for a beat before she starts to move in earnest. Up and down, with our eyes connected, and the intimacy from it is un-fucking-real as we form this connection unlike any I've had before.

It feels like forever.

I rest my hands under her ass, and I inch a finger over until I push into the tight hole back there. She gasps, and her eyes darken as I pump my finger in and out of her ass in time with the way her body moves over mine.

"Oh my God," she screams. "Yes, oh God, I love it when you're touching my ass."

"I'm going to fuck this ass next," I growl.

"Please," she whimpers. "It's yours to fuck."

Jesus Christ. Her words set me on fire, and my body responds as fire bursts from my veins and into my blood. I start to come inside her, my body betraying me without

Snap DECISION

warning. I growl her name through it as I erupt, pushing her into her own climax.

She cries out a string of incoherent words as I shove my finger further into her ass, and her body explodes into convulsions just as I start to come down from my own high. I keep pumping into her, and I reach in front to rub her clit as I take her tit back in my mouth, sparking every erogenous zone I possibly can as her orgasm carries on and on and on.

Eventually she collapses against my shoulder, worn and spent, and she's panting as she tries to catch her breath.

"Welcome to Vegas," she teases.

"Good to be here," I tease back, and I press a soft kiss to the side of her neck.

It doesn't matter where in the world she is. Vegas, Chicago, Tampa, hell, the fucking middle of nowhere. I'll be there.

No matter what.

It may have been a snap decision that landed us here, but it doesn't matter. It was the start of our forever.

EPILOGUE

Tatum Barker

Snap Decision

Nearly every moment of every day is riddled with decisions to make. Some are made in the blink of an eye, and some require a lot more effort. Some are easy, and some are hard.

It may have been a snap decision to marry Ford Bradley, but even if it hadn't been, it would have been an easy choice. And now that I'm standing at the front door to the Bradley Mansion a week after we figured our shit out in Vegas, I have this sense that I'm home again.

Chicago has always been home, and because I had such a crush on Archer Bradley, I probably spent more time at the Bradley Mansion than I did at my own home back when I was in high school. It laid the groundwork for the foundation of friendship for Ford and me even though I had no idea that's what I was doing. I thought I was just being friendly with the older brother of the guy I was destined to be with. I had no clue at the time that *he* was the one I was *actually* going to end up with.

Snap DECISION

I look over at him, and his eyes are on me. He's always looking at me with adoration in his eyes, something I never noticed before.

It makes me feel safe and loved.

In the last week, I paid one million dollars for this mansion, and he transferred that cash to Liam. We cleaned out my office, looked at venues in Vegas, and also shopped for homes in Vegas. We agreed that Tampa Bay is home for now while he continues to play for the Beasts, but that doesn't mean we can't have a home base in each city that feels like home.

We didn't buy anything in Vegas yet, but we have some stuff on our radar. I cleaned out my belongings from Kenzie's casita, too, and all my stuff is in storage…for now. We'll be back, and maybe once Ford retires, that's where we'll land.

Or maybe it'll be here in Chicago, the hometown we both hail from.

Maybe it'll be somewhere in the Caribbean. Ford confessed that he's been looking at investment properties for destination weddings, and he's found a few located directly on the beach with plenty of rental properties nearby—and he even mentioned acquiring a handful of those, too, so all the profits for these destination weddings go directly into our pockets.

We've agreed that it doesn't really matter where our home base is as long as we're together.

And then there was this morning when we met with the title company to officially close on the transfer of ownership. Who would've thought one snap decision would land us here on the doorstep of the Bradley Mansion?

"You go first," he says softly.

"Will your father be here?"

He shakes his head. "I told him I sold it. I didn't say it was to us. But it's not like I left him homeless. Madden's letting him stay at his condo for now. We'll reevaluate in a few months when the trial starts."

"Madden's okay with that?" I ask, sort of surprised given what I know of their relationship.

"Not really. Our father has managed to hurt all of his kids in one form or another, but he's still our father, and for as much as he's hurt us, there have also been times when he hasn't." He lifts a shoulder.

"I get that. Family's important, and if not for him, you wouldn't be here. Or Madden or the rest of your crew."

He presses his lips together and nods. "I think all that's what gave me so many reservations about keeping this place."

I tilt my head as a stab of guilt lances through me. "I'm sorry. I was so caught up in my own shit that I didn't give you a chance to unload any of that."

He lifts a shoulder. "It's okay. You had a right to be upset with me. I never should've kept any of it from you. Regardless, now it's ours, and I can't wait to see what you're going to do with it." He holds the key out in his hand.

I grin at him, and I lift onto my tiptoes to press a kiss to his lips.

And then I take that key and unlock our destiny.

Before I know what he's doing, Ford lifts me up into his arms and carries me over the threshold to my laughter.

"I'm not tempting fate," he declares as we walk in that way.

My breath catches in my throat as I survey the foyer, and he sets me down. We walk around as ideas form in my mind about what we can do in here. We've only been here for maybe five minutes or so when the doorbell rings.

My brows dip as I glance over at Ford, and he just shrugs as we walk together to open the door to see who's there.

I'm shocked when I come face-to-face with Madden Bradley.

Snap DECISION

"I heard you're looking for a construction crew to gut and reno this place to turn it into Chicago's best new event venue, and I'm here to bid on the job," he says.

"Oh my God!" I say, and I flap my hands up and down as I try to be cool, which is definitely impossible in this situation. "You're hired!"

"Now, wait a second, Tate," Ford warns. "We should really take a look at some other companies—"

"You shush!" I say to him, and I turn back to Madden. "As I was saying, you're hired. Come on in."

The brothers both laugh, and the three of us walk through the house as we exchange ideas. Madden takes some notes, assures me he'll work with the city to rezone this place from residential, and even comes up with a plan for guest parking.

He leaves to meet his wife for lunch, promising that he'll have plans to me by the end of the week, and then it's just Ford and me in here.

I can't help it. I lift myself up onto the kitchen counter and sit there swinging my heels for a beat, and then I stand. Ford just laughs at me. Instead of yelling at me to get down this time, though, he pulls his phone out of his pocket and turns on the first song we danced to at our wedding.

He hops up onto the counter more gracefully than I did, takes me in his arms, and we dance right there on the counter.

He kisses me, and then he dips me down low as I laugh.

It's the laughter and the joy I feel with this man that tell me this one's going to last. Sometimes we think we're in the right situation, the right place, the right time, but it turns out we're really not.

And when it comes down to it, sometimes those snap decisions that come from trusting our gut even when there are risks involved turn out to be better than we ever could have imagined.

And that's what life with Ford Bradley is to me. Better than I ever could have imagined.

The End

Want more Ford & Tatum?
Scan this QR code to download a bonus epilogue!

Scan this code to join Lisa on Facebook at Team LS: Lisa Suzanne's Reader Group!

Acknowledgments

Big thanks first as always to my family. Thank you to Matt for the love and support and to our kids who all this is for.

Thank you to Valentine PR for your incredible work on the launch of this book.

Thank you to Valentine Grinstead, Christine Yates, Billie DeSchalit, Serena Cracchiolo, Patricia Rohrs, Diane Holtry, Alaine McDaniel, and Nicole Hernandez for beta reading/listening and proofreading. I value your insight and comments so much.

Big thanks to my ride or die bestie, Julie Saman. We'll always push each other to hit those deadlines no matter how impossible they may seem!

Thank you to my ARC Team for loving this sports world that is so real to us. Thank you to the members of the Vegas Aces and Vegas Heat Recovery Room and Team LS, and all the influencers and bloggers for reading, reviewing, posting, and sharing.

And finally, thank YOU for reading. I can't wait to bring you more sports romances where swoony superstar heroes ride emotional roller coasters to their happily ever afters.

Cheers until next season!

xoxo,
Lisa Suzanne

About the Author

Lisa Suzanne is an Amazon Top Ten Bestselling author of swoon-worthy superstar heroes, emotional roller coasters, and all the angst. She resides in Arizona with her husband and two kids. When she's not chasing her kids, she can be found working on her latest romance book or watching reruns of *Friends*.

Also by Lisa Suzanne

Grayson & Ava   Spencer & Grace   Asher & Desi

Tanner & Cassie   Miller & Sophie

FIND MORE AT
AUTHORLISASUZANNE.COM/BOOKS

www.ingramcontent.com/pod-product-compliance
Lightning Source LLC
LaVergne TN
LVHW040038080526
838202LV00045B/3386